Praise for The Vanishers

by *Heidi Julavits*

"Sharply original. . . . Stylish and fiercely funny. . . . A wild, fun ride that doesn't let up until the last sentence. . . . Julavits is a fearlessly inventive writer."
                                                                                    —*Elle*

"Julavits is an evocative writer she conjures up the supernatural in a way that feels plausible. . . . Haunting."   —*The Economist*

"The protagonist . . . could join the ranks of literature's most unreliable narrators, alongside Humbert Humbert and Huck Finn."
                                                                —*The Wall Street Journal*

"Themes of loss, reinvention and the ways women build each other up and tear each other down . . . run through *The Vanishers*. But Julavits balances the emotional vertigo with sharp wit. . . . Like a dream, it's never anything but intriguing."   —*The Seattle Times*

"Julavits has a questing, eclectic intellect. . . . She creates a sophisticated symmetry in the final surprising moments of Julia's story, and, as if in an encore, adds an adroit comic flip at the end."
                                                                        —*The Boston Globe*

"Thrilling, subversive insights. . . . Powerful in many ways. . . . On the subject of loss in particular, Julavits is an expert, writing with eloquence and poetry."   —*The Philadelphia Inquirer*

"A fascinating inquiry into matriarchal structures: their power struggles, the projections, distortions and anxieties that result, and, above all, the creative—and destructive—energies that they unleash. A real achievement."   —Tom McCarthy,
                                          author of *Remainder* and *C*

"Bristling with wicked humor and sharp-edged irony, *The Vanishers* explores the ways in which the dead can haunt the living and the often painful persistence of memory."   —*The Huffington Post*

"A blistering read. . . . If you're lucky, you have one brazen friend who can mesmerize the room with a wild story. If you're not, *The Vanishers* will provide a similar jolt of transgressive, feminine thrill."
                                                —*The Plain Dealer*

"Julavits is no ordinary writer, and the meta-heavy brilliance of her fourth novel is something akin to a Sylvia Plath poem transferred telepathically to a psychic who happens to be solving a missing-person's case while being film-followed by artist Sophie Calle."
                                                          —*Interview*

"One of the best novels I've ever read, delivering all the immediate pleasures of mystery, horror, and satire while exploring grief in language that is as shocking for its originality as its precision. Julavits takes readers on a wild ride that hops continents and decades, but the real setting of *The Vanishers* is the gray territory between sickness and health, sanity and delusion, love and hatred, life and death."   —Karen Russell, author of *Swamplandia!* and
                                St. Lucy's Home for Girls Raised by Wolves

Heidi Julavits

The Vanishers

⸺⸺⸺

A founding editor of *The Believer* magazine and the
recipient of a Guggenheim Fellowship, Heidi Julavits is
also the author of three critically acclaimed novels: *The
Uses of Enchantment, The Effect of Living Backwards,*
and *The Mineral Palace.*

The Vanishers

Also by Heidi Julavits

NOVELS
The Uses of Enchantment
The Effect of Living Backwards
The Mineral Palace

IN COLLABORATION
Hotel Andromeda (*with Jenny Gage*)

AS EDITOR
Read Hard: Five Years of Great Writing
 from *The Believer*

The Vanishers

Heidi Julavits

ANCHOR BOOKS

A Division of Random House, Inc.

New York

FIRST ANCHOR BOOKS EDITION, JANUARY 2013

Copyright © 2012 by Heidi Julavits

All rights reserved. Published in the United States by
Anchor Books, a division of Random House, Inc., New York,
and in Canada by Random House of Canada Limited, Toronto.
Originally published in hardcover in the United States by Doubleday,
a division of Random House, Inc., New York, in 2012.

Anchor Books and colophon are registered
trademarks of Random House, Inc.

The Library of Congress has cataloged the Doubleday edition as follows:
Julavits, Heidi.
The vanishers / by Heidi Julavits.—1st ed.
p. cm.
1. Women psychics—Fiction.
2. Children of suicide victims—Fiction.
3. Missing persons—Fiction.
4. Mothers and daughters—Fiction.
5. Psychological fiction. I. Title.
PS3560.U522V36 2012
813'.54— dc23
2011019130

Anchor ISBN: 978-0-307-38736-3

Book design by Maria Carella

www.anchorbooks.com

Printed in the United States of America
10 9 8 7 6 5 4 3 2 1

For Ben

A talent is not a weapon in every culture.

—ADAM PHILLIPS

The Vanishers

The story I'm about to tell could be judged preposterous. Fine. Judge how you must. Protect yourself by scare-quoting me as the so-called psychic, the so-called victim of a psychic attack. Quarantine this account however you must so that you can safely hear it. What happened to me could never happen to you.

Tell yourself that. Even though what happened to me happens to people like you all the time.

In the beginning, an attack can look just like regular life. You wake to discover eyelashes on your pillow, bruises on your skin where you've never been touched. You smell a stranger on your bedsheets and that stranger is you.

As the weeks pass, you notice other humiliations. An unceasing bout of acid reflux and an irritable bowel. Gums that bleed when you sip hot tea. Fingernails that snap when you push your hands through the sleeves of a sweater. The ghostly withdrawal of pigmentation from your cheeks. A rash on your torso. A rash on your hands. A rash on your scalp.

And so it goes, your body's hurtle along a failure trajectory that no doctor can explain. There is only the numb leg, the searing esophagus, the face—its frostbit complexion, its vinegar stare—you no longer recognize as your own.

I'm overworked and need to take more vitamins, you'll tell yourself. Maybe I'm allergic to wheat or my new car. Maybe I'm depressed, or not enough in love anymore with my life, my spouse, my self. You'll schedule beach vacations or more time at the gym, but no matter how many times you dunk yourself in oceans or flush the liquid content of your body through your pores, you can't escape the suspicion that a cancer drifts through your anatomy, that it will soon metastasize to your personality, that it is only a matter of time before it breaches the cellular firewall encircling your soul.

When this happened to me, I did what people do: I saw my doctor. She sent me to another doctor. And he to another. I saw so many, many doctors. I was pricked and I was bled, I was leashed to computers, scanners, drips, I was MRI-ed, EEG-ed, and CT-scanned, my body subjected to a battery of lie detector tests that, because the claims it spouted were deemed inconclusive, it apparently did not pass. I acquired a medical file so thick it practically required its own gurney to be moved. I was greeted by each new specialist with a weary smile. I was patronizingly quoted Donne. ("There is no health. We, at best, enjoy but a neutrality.") Because the doctors could not cure me, they decided I could not be sick.

They told me it was all in my head. Namely, I was to blame. I was the sickness.

Which I don't deny. I brought this on myself. I failed to take the proper cares and cautions, I failed to live invisibly or wisely. Besides, don't the healthy always suspect the afflicted? *She drove herself to exhaustion. She was so stressed out. She never dealt properly with the death of her mother.*

All of this is true. However. I cannot take all the credit. I say this humbly, not reproachfully. Someone else made me sick.

Let me explain this in terms you can understand. People make people sick, it is not a stretch to claim this. What remains up for debate is the degree of malice involved when a person makes another person sick. Did your sister, for example, intend to give you her head cold? In most cases, not. We do not blame head colds on other people's heads, we blame them on their bodies.

But what if your sister or girlfriend or roommate or coworker intended to give you a cold? What if, while you were in the bathroom, he or she coughed on purpose into your water glass?

And what if we're not referring to people as carriers of disease but people as diseases? The self is a source of contagion, oftentimes an unwitting one. *He makes me sick*, you've said of your ex-boyfriend. *She's toxic*, you've said of your boss.

And maybe he did, maybe she is. After you become afflicted, after the doctors finger you as the cause, it's instinctual to blame others for your physical misfortune. But blame is lonely, and your loneliness is compounded by the fact that you're scared to go outside. To be near others is to risk further exposure and, worse, humiliation. Even your best friend can't help staring at the sores on your mouth.

In retaliation, to preserve whatever small amount of pride you still possess, you become the secret curator of the suffering of others. Homebound now, you do online searches for people from your past. You're pleased to discover that your college roommate's looks have been lost, that a former coworker's start-up went bankrupt, that an ex-girlfriend's Broadway dreams did not pan out. You spend your days monitoring demises. You become, over time, the connoisseur of downfall, a covert expertise that distracts you from your own decline.

You might realize, as I realized, that there exists one individual whose downfall over which you fixate, even obsess. For me that individual was a woman named Dominique Varga. She was a mother to me when no one else wanted the job. My own mother killed herself a long time ago. But your obsession might be a basketball coach, a softball coach, a graduate TA, a personal accountant, or a special, unlucky stranger you choose at random, as though from a police lineup, and falsely accuse. Why be fair? Nobody's been fair to you. Monitoring this person's disappointments functions as a course of steroids might, each new failure for her registering as an improvement for you. Her marriage implodes, your rash subsides. The economics of revenge. Your stock rises as hers declines. Perhaps you befriend her, and send the occasional e-mail. Otherwise you watch and harmlessly wait for your fortunes to reverse.

But what if you are not the only victim here? What if your daily online visits to this person whose ruin you've charted are not so benign? What if you are not a spectator to her demise? What if you're to blame for her shitty life?

What if you are her disease?

In other words, this is not just a story about how you can become sick by knowing other people. This is a story about how other people can become sick by knowing you.

part One

The attack, we later agreed, occurred at Madame Ackermann's forty-third birthday party.

The evening was typical for late October—icebox air, onyx sky, White Mountains humped darkly in the distance, and peripherally visible as a more opaque variety of night. Because I knew that Madame Ackermann's A-frame would be underheated, I wore a wool jumper and wool tights and a pair of silver riding boots purchased from the Nepalese import store, run by an aging WASP hippie. Hers was one of seven businesses in the town of East Warwick, New Hampshire (there was also a vegan pizza parlor, a hardware store, a purveyor of Fair Isle knitwear, a bank, a pub, and a real estate agent), a town that existed in the minds of some to provide basic material support to the faculty and students at the Institute of Integrated Parapsychology—referred to locally, and by those in the field, as the Workshop.

That I—Julia Severn, a second-year initiate and Madame Ackermann's stenographer—had been invited to her forty-third birthday party was an anomaly that I failed to probe. When I let slip to my stenographic predecessor, Miranda, that I had been asked to Madame Ackermann's for a social occasion, Miranda tried to hide her wounded incredulity by playing with the pearl choker she habitually wore and, in apprehensive moments such as these, rolled into her mouth, allowing the pearls to yank on the corners of her lips like a horse's bit.

Madame Ackermann observed a firm boundary between her academic and personal lives, Miranda said, removing her pearls halfway, wedging them now into the recession above her chin.

She was not the kind of professor, Miranda cautioned, straining her necklace's string with her lower jaw until it threatened to snap, to invite an initiate to her house for a social occasion, not even as a volunteer passer of hors d'oeuvres.

Miranda's jealousy was understandable. Madame Ackermann's attentions were the prize over which we initiates competed, the reason we'd come to the Workshop—to study with her, hopefully, yes, but in more pitiable terms to partake of her forbidding, imperial aura by walking behind her on the many footpaths that vivisectioned the campus quad into slivers of mud or grass or snow.

Thus, I reassured Miranda (who, despite the year she'd spent as her stenographer, clearly did not know Madame Ackermann), one of the many admirable qualities Madame Ackermann possessed was that, even as a relentless investigator of past lives, she could permit bygones to be bygones. Yes, she'd selected me, from a pool of thirty-five initiates, to be her stenographer, and yes we'd both immediately come to regret this choice of hers. But after weeks of misunderstandings, deceptions, and hostilities between us, Madame Ackermann was not above extending an olive branch.

And so on the night of October 25 I donned my silver boots and, awash in optimism and specialness, drove to Madame Ackermann's A-frame. As I passed the custodian-lit Workshop buildings, their windows flickering behind the spruces, I allowed myself to view the scene from the future perspective of an older self, wrought by nostalgia for this place I'd yet to leave or miss. In order to prolong my anticipation of what was sure to be a momentous evening, I took the scenic way along the Connecticut River; in the moonlight, the water, whisked to a sharp chop by the wind, appeared seized into a treacherous hoar of ice. I spied a hunter emerging from an old barn whom I mistook, for the shadowy half second before my car beams illuminated him, to be wearing the decapitated head of a deer. A bat died against my windshield. And yet despite these dark portents I somehow failed to divine, as I turned off the river road and began the slow ascent to Madame Ackermann's A-frame, that I would never drive along this river again. Or that I would drive along this river again, yes, but I would no longer be the sort of person who wore silver boots to parties and believed that bygones could be bygones.

⸻

Madame Ackermann greeted me at the door, eyes starfished by mascara, hair a slab of polished obsidian against the puffball white of her sweater, and dropped my birthday present—a warm bottle of Tokay—on a credenza beside the pile of regifted chutneys and spice rubs from her colleagues. Then she led me to her great room, an inverted-V-shaped atrium lined with bookshelves (the books secured by a series of crisscrossing bungee cords), packed with her friends and coworkers, the majority of them men.

In retrospect: I should have found it odd, given she'd presumably forgiven me, that she should refuse to meet my gaze, that she should take the first available opportunity to slough me onto the other guests.

"You know Julia," she said, shoving me into a trio of professors, all of whom, though I'd studied with each at one point or another, regarded me blankly. "She's my archivist."

The trio (Professors Blake, Janklow, and Penry) resumed their discussion of the death of a Workshop professor named Gerald, their eyebrow hairs antenna-like as they derisively extolled Gerald's virtues.

"Archivist," Professor Blake said to me. He pronounced archivist with a judgmental inflection.

"Stenographer," I clarified, "is the original service she hired me to perform."

I did not mention the word demotion. I'd been hired as her stenographer, true, but I'd recently been demoted to the position of archivist.

I glanced at Madame Ackermann to see if she'd heard me; I didn't want to appear to be contradicting her in public, especially now that our relationship was presumably on the mend. She was preoccupied, fortunately, by the sight of Professor Elkin huddling with Professor Yuen behind a kentia palm. Professor Yuen wore her hair in two long braids that narrowed to tips like floppy knives; she spoke to Professor Elkin about a topic that required her to bullet-point the air with an index finger, no doubt something to do with the recent dissolving of the Princeton Engineering Anomalies Research laboratory, and whether its failure sounded a death knell for the Workshop's future prospects as well.

"Ah," said Professor Janklow. "Stenographer." He held between his thumb and forefinger a half-eaten shrimp. He eyed the goblet of cocktail sauce on the table beside him, clearly wondering if he could dip his shrimp a second time without being spotted, or calculating the amount of time one must wait to ensure that the same-shrimp dips are no longer seen as consecutive acts, but as two unique events.

"Samuel Beckett was James Joyce's stenographer," I said.

"Secretary," said Professor Janklow.

"Did you ever study with Gerald?" asked Professor Blake. "Before he died, I mean?"

"In fact that's a myth about Beckett," said Professor Penry.

"Couldn't make a martini to save his life," said Professor Janklow. "Gerald wasn't a fellow who could grasp the subtler requests such as *whisper of vermouth.*"

"Poor Gerald," said Madame Ackermann, returning to our fold. I suspected it from her insincere tone: she had slept with the man.

"You, however," said Professor Janklow, presenting his empty martini glass to Madame Ackermann, "are all subtlety and whispers."

Madame Ackermann twisted downward on her sweater's cowl neck to reveal a turquoise filament of bra and a décolletage dotted by pale moles. This gesture was meant to suggest that she was embarrassed by the compliment, while also suggesting that she was not remotely embarrassed by it. No one, least of all me, would deny that Madame Ackermann, even at the dawn of forty-three, was a bewitching, pixie creature, *girlish* the term most often used to describe her mixture of naïveté and wiliness, her middle-parted night hair and Eva Hesse Bavarian élan, her habit, during class, of placing one foot on her chair and resting her chin atop a corduroyed knee. She'd preserved her body, or so it seemed, through sheer force of mind. The suppleness of her gray matter—I'm ashamed to admit that I'd imagined how it would feel to the touch—was reflected in the pearly suppleness of her eyes, her hair, her skin.

We were all of us—the female initiates more than the male ones—in some form of love with her. (The fact that Madame Ackermann so closely resembled my dead mother did not render my obsession with the woman any less complicated.)

And thus we tried, as girls in confused love with women will do, in every superficial way to mimic her. We were rapt apprentices of the twisted cowl neck, the peevish cuticle nibble, the messy, pencil-stabbed chignon. We purchased cardigans in yellowed greens and tarry mascaras, we blended our own teas and sewed them into tiny muslin bags that we steeped in chunky mugs and carried with us to class, our socked feet sliding, like hers, atop the wooden platforms of our Dr. Scholl's sandals. We also slept around. We slept with everyone, but only once. We were, we told ourselves in moments when we felt most pathetic and unmoored, not just imitating Madame Ackermann, we were embracing the culture of the Workshop—the disloyalty, the distrust, the refusal to be known for fear of what people might actually come to know about you.

It was a lonely time.

Anna, Madame Ackermann's housekeeper, struggled to light a fire in the fireplace and was finally assisted by Professor Janklow, who propped his shrimp in a dirty ashtray in order to show Anna the proper tepee-like way to arrange the kindling, the exact pressure to apply to a newspaper ball to achieve the optimal degree of oxygenated scrunch.

Once the fire was lit, Madame Ackermann dimmed the horn chandelier and announced that it was time to tell a story.

"Gosh," sniped Professor Yuen. "I wonder which story it will be."

The story—about Madame Ackermann's seminal psychic experience, and with which we were all familiar—was this.

Madame Ackermann, freshly graduated from the Workshop (summa cum laude, she made sure to mention), decided to decompress via a backpacking trip through southeast Asia with her tragic boyfriend, a rising third-year initiate of no academic distinction whatsoever who abandoned her, without warning or explanation, in a beach hut on the coast of Thailand. She'd told herself, upon discovering him gone, that she'd long ago fallen out of love with this boyfriend, and to prove it slept that afternoon with a local fisherman, drank half a bottle of Mekong whiskey, and stumbled into bed alone, only to awake two hours later to see, at the foot of her bed, a milky shimmer. But then this specter grew bones before her eyes. Its skeleton rulered the air with wet, gray notches; it thickened with muscle and then bound itself in an opalescent casing from which sprouted a steely fur. Two eyeballs emerged above a snout that cracked apart to display a prehistoric maw of teeth, row upon row of enamel sawblades to which it appeared the pinking shears of a vicious evolution had been applied.

Fenrir. Madame Ackermann identified the specter immediately: her boyfriend had forgotten his beach read, a book of Norse mythology called the *Poetic Edda*, and Madame Ackermann had, before falling asleep, finished the stanza in which an old woman living in a forest had *bred there broods of Fenrir. There will come from them all one of that number to be a moon-snatcher in troll's skin.*

At first, Madame Ackermann said, she believed this mythical Norse wolf monster had been sent to attack her by her boyfriend, a man prone to territorial jealousy even toward women he'd discarded, a man who would "ultimately prove not untalented in the psychic arts," this assessment based on the fact that he would, by his late twenties, become a successful real estate speculator on the Iberian peninsula.

But then Madame Ackermann saw, connecting her to Fenrir, a kinked, reptilian umbilical, a viscous mirage through which she could slice her hands but which she could not, no matter how she thrashed, sever. Despite her Mekong whiskey fugue, she understood: this monster had not been sent by the boyfriend. It had initiated from her. It was, she claimed, the literal embodiment of her humiliated, heartsick rage.

Then the wolf—her wolf—attacked her.

I tried to kill myself, she was known to claim. *I was the victim of my own worst self, loosed upon the world.*

As Fenrir closed its giant jaws around her chest—she would show, as proof of this attempt to puncture her heart, the moles flecking her chest, each of them, she claimed, an indelible astral tooth mark—she lost consciousness. When she awoke she discovered a pile of pitted black rocks on her hut's threshold, byproducts of her psychic eruption. (These she employed as bookends on her office shelf. I had held them in my hands; they were weightless, as though made of malt.)

And so. While I had never before attended one of Madame Ackermann's birthday parties, I had nonetheless heard the Fenrir story numerous times since I'd matriculated at the Workshop the previous fall. I'd first heard it during the opening lecture of Madame Ackermann's Basics seminar, the details of which we'd slavishly recorded in our notebooks; she'd repeated the Fenrir story during my one-on-one student conference, presenting it as a secret she'd chosen to share only with me. She'd told it to me last April, when she interviewed me for the stenographer position, again in May when she called to officially offer me the position, and most recently when we were sorting through storage boxes in her A-frame's crawlspace. One couldn't study with Madame Ackermann, and become her protégée, and then her stenographer, and then her archivist, without coming to know the Fenrir story as familiarly as one's own personal memory of a vindictive family pet.

I was not alone. As Madame Ackermann described the rat droppings she'd found on her beach-hut pillowcase before falling into her drunken slumber, the party guests, Professor Yuen in particular, projected an air of jealous boredom.

I was bored but not jealous; rather than listening to Madame Ackermann, I leafed through the new paperback edition of her latest book, *E-mails from the Dead*. Because while the Fenrir story was told to emphasize to us, her students, and to these birthday guests, her colleagues, her potency as a master of the paranormal— few people, it was true, had the ability to create "visible thought forms"—I had come, over the unsettled course of my relationship with Madame Ackermann, to understand its meaning differently. As much as it destroyed me to admit it, the Fenrir story was not about the dawning of her powers; rather, it represented the youthful apex of her career, to which she now, in her gloaming hours, desperately clung.

As her stenographer, I'd gained unwanted firsthand knowledge of Madame Ackermann's troubles. My job, as Madame Ackermann had described it when she'd hired me, was thus: beginning the first week of August, I would join her in her home office and sit in a chair across from the Biedermeier sofa where she reclined, eyes blinded beneath a silk pillow. Since she'd inherited a *not insignificant* collection of mid-century modern furniture from her father, she informed me, I'd have the honor of sitting in his favorite Barcelona chair.

At the time—sitting in a Workshop-issue molded bucket chair in her office, one that reminded me, in its shape and its color, of an institutional bed pan—her father's Barcelona chair sounded really delightful, its name inspiring visions of Picasso trailing a parasol-wielding Dora Maar along the sand, of salt-stained canvas awnings, of bottles of lukewarm cava and abandoned espadrilles.

Then, on my first official day as Madame Ackermann's stenographer, I saw the actual chair. Despite its beachy rock-skip of a name, my first thought was, *Oh, that chair.* I'd seen it in movies and on TV, usually in thuggish pairs, usually in the offices of slickly evil corporations or the living rooms of loveless career couples.

While Madame Ackermann brewed tea, I took wary stock of my Barcelona chair. Its frame looked like two swords locked in a fencing parry, the inside edges made safe for human repose by a pair of quilted black leather slabs. When I later mentioned my guarded impression to Miranda, she laughingly referred to the chair as the "Blowjob Chair," because her older brother, a screenwriter in Los Angeles, kept one in *his* office for the following reason—given the angle of recline, the shortened legs, the offered-to-the-sky cant of the seat, it was engineered perfectly for someone to give, for someone to receive.

In my capacity as stenographer, I sat in the Barcelona chair five mornings a week—knees splayed, a mug of tea on the floor—while Madame Ackermann projected her consciousness at will, to any human, alive or dead, occupying any space or time, while I recorded, on a notepad, every word that she said.

Unfortunately, Madame Ackermann did not tend to do much more than plain sleep in my presence.

She was, in a word, blocked.

This alarmed me more than it alarmed Madame Ackermann, who chalked up her troubles to our mutual adjustment period. Miranda, when I discreetly inquired about her first weeks working with Madame Ackermann, claimed that Madame Ackermann had been at the height of her powers when she, Miranda, sat in the Barcelona chair, scribbling on pads of ghost-grid paper with a special automatic writing pen made in Düsseldorf. Miranda was happy enough to corroborate my worry that I was the problem, that I was the equivalent of an electrical short, impeding the crucial energy flow required between regressor and stenographer.

Following one month of failed regressions, however, Madame Ackermann turned her frustration on me. What did you eat this morning? Nothing containing garlic, I hope? Did you dream about buzzards or poppies? Are there stones in your pocket that might contain traces of quartz?

Prior to our meetings, Madame Ackermann began sealing herself inside her Faraday cage, a copper cubicle in her basement that blocked all electromagnetic waves, radio frequencies, and wireless signals and was, for psychics, like being forced into a coma. She'd eat her steel-cut oats and read the morning paper in her Faraday, hoping to rest her mind before our sessions.

This ritual made no difference.

Soon she began grousing about innocuous behaviors of mine. I made too much noise in the Barcelona chair, which had a tendency to creak in that fleshy high-pitched way peculiar to Barcelona chairs. My breathing was erratic, distracting. My ecological laundry detergent smelled of rhubarb. I switched detergents, I sat with perfect stillness in the Barcelona chair, I counted each inhale and exhale (five counts in, eight counts out), to achieve absolute breathing regularity. Still Madame Ackermann could not regress. Instead she fell asleep. She'd wake up an hour later and ask me to read back to her, in its entirety, the nothing that she'd reported from her journey.

Compounding her frustration was this: Madame Ackermann had been hired, while on a summer vacation to the Hebrides, by a French film studies academic who'd been staying at her hotel, a man named Colophon Martin, to perform a freelance regression.

Colophon needed her help to find the missing second reel of a propaganda film commissioned by fascist politician and founder of the French *Front National* Jean-Marie Le Pen. This film had been shot by an artist Madame Ackermann referred to as the Leni Riefenstahl of France (I was not, at this point, aware that she possessed any other name), a woman who'd disappeared in 1984 and was presumed dead. Colophon asked Madame Ackermann if she might, during one of her regressions, find her way to the Leni Riefenstahl of France's office at the Paris Institute of Geophysics and take note of the serial number stamped on the underside of her film safe. The missing reel, his research had led him to conclude (he was writing a book about this Leni Riefenstahl of France), remained inside that film safe, and that film safe belonged to one of five possible collectors of old film safes, none of whom would cop to possessing the missing reel, because they hoped to sell it to a private collector for a great deal of money. However, if he could get the precise number of the film safe he could check it against the auction house records and file for government repossession under some French law that protected treasures of national cultural significance.

So Madame Ackermann had agreed to regress herself to Paris between the years of 1983 and 1984, when the Leni Riefenstahl of France was employed by this geophysics institute, and e-mail Colophon with the number of the film safe.

But by the middle of September, no successful regressions to Paris had been achieved. Also by the middle of September, Madame Ackermann's attitude toward me, as witness to or cause of her troubles, had brittled considerably.

What choice did I have? I knew what happened to the students Madame Ackermann disliked, and I was becoming one of those students. That I should have been selected as her protégée, the ultimate Initiate of Promise, came as a surprise to no one in the Workshop more than me; even though I'd started school as one of the most heralded Initiates of Promise (my entrance exam scores placed me at the top of my class), my mind had responded poorly to training. I'd proven slow to grasp even the most basic concepts in her Basics seminar (constructive triangulation, for example; wavelike vs. particle-like operations of consciousness, for example), and I'd failed to be regressed during her office hours. And yet, over Franz, who had been regressed ten times (once without Madame Ackermann's assistance), over Maurice, who was descended from the famous Moriarty, over Rebecca, whose automatic writing samples were, according to Madame Ackermann, *stained-glass windows unto the astral abyss*, I had been chosen. By my idol, one of parapsychological scholarship's most renowned stars, a woman who'd been awarded, at the age of twenty-eight, the occult equivalent of a Mac-Arthur and who heart-scramblingly resembled—with her black veil of hair and winking, shards-of-mica eyes that suggested a smile was forthcoming even when it never was—an enigmatic photograph I'd cherished of my mother. I had been chosen. And I could not, I decided, be unchosen.

<hr />

Scattered claps from the birthday guests.

"Speech!" yelled Professor Blake, holding an upturned martini glass on his head.

I overheard Professor Yuen complain to Professor Penry that Madame Ackermann's Fenrir story didn't benefit from retellings; over the years, it had come to sound like the plot of an inane children's book.

Madame Ackermann fanned away the applause, already concluded. Then she proposed they play a few rounds of Spooky Action at a Distance, a mental telepathy parlor game during which the "thrower" mentally projects the image of an object and the "catchers" compete over who can identify the object first.

Because it was her birthday party, Madame Ackermann designated herself the SAD thrower.

"Not fair," yelled Professor Yuen. She accused Madame Ackermann of throwing torques, wherein the image that's telepathically communicated shape-shifts mid-journey. Professor Yuen deemed such practices *dirty playing*.

"Torques are not dirty," said Madame Ackermann, implying, by her intonation, that Professor Yuen was sexually unadventurous. "But in deference to your blunter powers of perception, Karen, I promise to throw no torques."

A handful of guests chuckled. It was no secret that Madame Ackermann and Professor Yuen had been squabbling for months over the Workshop's financial woes. Madame Ackermann, who liked to remind people that "esoteric means 'intended for an initiated few,'" wanted to introduce a reverse scholarship system, in which students would be charged for getting poor grades and monopolizing professors whose energies might be more worthily expended on Initiates of Promise. Professor Yuen believed this violated some discrimination clause in the school's bylaws, to which Madame Ackermann replied, "talentless people need to learn more, thus they should pay more. It would be discriminatory against the Initiates of Promise to have it otherwise."

("Greatness cannot be taught," Madame Ackermann was known to say. To which Professor Yuen habitually rejoined: "You mean *you* cannot teach it.")

Madame Ackermann shut her eyes and tucked her top knuckles into the front pockets of her jeans. She crooked her head forward, knocking from behind her ears two glossy plaits of hair that individuated into strands and bead-curtained her face from view. She clicked the wooden heels of her Dr. Scholl's three times and threw.

A telepathic novice, I had no intention of catching Madame Ackermann's throw. Two years of study were required before we initiates were permitted to attempt acts of mental telepathy, and no initiate was accepted into Madame Ackermann's advanced workshop until they'd first proven their psychic fitness by petrifying a piece of meat. Indeed. For two hours a day during August and leading up to the meeting of the first classes in September, all rising third-years dedicated their energies toward petrifying a one-pound chunk of pork, stashed out of sight on a high bookshelf in our rooms. Despite the rising third-years' familiarity with Bell's Theorem, the success rate for this exercise was pitifully low, and explained why the initiate dormitory, by the end of August, stank like an abattoir. Even so, each year one or two initiates managed to arrive for the first day of class with a blackened, odorless object in a book bag, one that resembled a mummified human head. (Madame Ackermann kept her own petrified meat samples, cracked in half, atop her desk. Hers were like geodes—fanged, crystallized, a display of gorgeous knives.)

Which is to say that I had no intention, given my lack of training and run of academic failures, of participating in the SAD game; I was happy enough to be the spectator to a sport with no balls and no visible signs of participation save a few bunched-up brows and jalandara-bandha-tucked chins. I did, however, create a contest for myself—I decided to test if I could read in a catcher's expression his or her clear reception of Madame Ackermann's throw.

In particular I concentrated on the boyishly moist Professor Penry, who, after Madame Ackermann, was the most sought professor, and who'd recently returned to the Workshop following a year's "reprieve," forced upon him by the administration because of an affair with a second-year initiate, now mother to his infant son.

So I was looking at Professor Penry when his face, sheenier now due to his enthusiastic martini consumption, receded into a haze of pink, tinted on the edges by a ring of blue. The pink moved counterclockwise and mutated into a funnel, at the far end of which I saw a black spider with silver legs.

"Spider," I heard Professor Yuen call out.

"Spider," confirmed Professor Penry.

"Spider," said Professor Blake.

But then something unexpected occurred. The spider continued to evolve. It caught a leg in the candy-cotton whirl (or so it appeared); the funnel dismembered the spider, its legs cycling about like the metal remnants of a shuttle drifting through deep space. As they approached me, the pieces reassembled into a very familiar shape.

"Spider," said an unidentifiable someone.

"I don't know what's wrong with me," said the emeritus and senile Professor Wibley. "I can see nothing but a piece of bacon."

"It's not a spider," I said.

Nobody heard me.

"It's not a spider," I repeated. "It's a Barcelona chair."

The moment I said "Barcelona chair" the vision evaporated, leaving me naked before a great room's worth of eyes, but none so penetratingly set upon me as Madame Ackermann's.

Glaring between her bead curtains of hair, her single visible eye appearing not unlike a funnel that could tear me limb from limb should I catch a toe in it, Madame Ackermann said, "I'm sorry, Julia. It was a spider."

I receded into the landing's shadow. I knew she was lying, and she knew I knew she was lying. This disturbed me, but not for the reasons it ought to have disturbed me. I felt humiliated, as I had when she'd insisted on telling the professors that I was her archivist, thereby more or less announcing that I had failed as her stenographer. She'd invited me to her party, I began to suspect, to embarrass me.

This was, I later learned, the mildest interpretation of her intentions.

The throwing continued. Keeping her promise to Professor Yuen, Madame Ackermann stuck to dull, unevolving objects: A hurricane lamp missing its shade. A tin trunk with an overbite. A chipped enamel skillet. A dust-jacket-less copy of The Joy of Cooking. It was like being at a metaphysical yard sale. That she should be throwing old and broken domestic items could, in the kindliest of scenarios, be seen as a form of housecleaning—Madame Ackermann, on her forty-third birthday, wanted to dispense with the deadweight of her mental storage space—but could also, and less charitably, be read as a direct insult to her birthday guests. Madame

Ackermann was known for her unsubtle throwing subtexts, especially when Professor Yuen was involved, and she'd been in such a foul mood since her regression troubles began that it seemed justifiable to her, perhaps, to pelt her schadenfreudy colleagues with telepathic junk.

But I was far more transfixed by this: not only could I receive everything Madame Ackermann threw, but I received her throws nearly a full second before anyone else. I didn't know how this could be; I'd yet to even attempt to petrify meat or earn beyond a B in any of my courses. And yet I proved to be unexpectedly good at SAD; I was, based on my observations, the best player of SAD in the room. Better than Professor Penry (who, granted, had had too much to drink), better even than Professor Yuen, who, despite Madame Ackermann's slight, was the furthest thing from a blunt perceiver.

This realization—that I, without the proper training, excelled at SAD—made me reconsider a few other happenings of the past few weeks. For example, the missing film reel sought by Colophon Martin. True, Madame Ackermann had failed to regress herself to the Paris Institute of Geophysics circa 1983–1984. But of this failure I'd made certain she was unaware.

In the second week of September I decided that unless Madame Ackermann awoke from her nap to some evidence that she'd regressed, my presence would be eradicated. I'd lose my position as her stenographer; I'd be demoted from Initiate of Promise to, as she termed the less adept students at the Workshop, a Mortgage Payment, i.e., a hopelessly untalented person whose only conceivable contribution to the world of psychic scholarship was to help pay, with their tuition money, the Workshop's bills. Starting around that second week of September, I guaranteed that Madame Ackermann awoke to find, curled on the floor between us, a pile of scrawled-upon ghost-grid paper, from which I would then read aloud.

In other words: I made shit up.

The risk was considerable; typically, per Miranda, Madame Ackermann emerged from her regressions with an accurate memory of what she'd reported. I thus worried that when Madame Ackermann awoke to be told, for example, that she'd spoken in the voice of an Argentinian-born psychotherapist living in London during the Falklands War, a woman who'd engaged in amatory adventures with her Cabinet patients in order to acquire strategic military information for her brother, a commander of the Argentine navy, she would be perplexed and then suspicious, recalling none of this.

So I did some research. Madame Ackermann, ironically, provided me my own best alibi. While completing her postdoc at the Koestler Parapsychology Unit at Edinburgh University, she'd written a paper called "Trance Qualities and the Ideal of Bodily Departure," which claimed the ideal trance state to be indistinguishable from what she called a *living death*. Such deep trances—identifiable by certain measurable physiological responses, such as heart rate—allowed a person to travel beyond the boundaries of consciousness, resulting in regressions of unusual detail. But most notable, for my purposes, was this: the living-dead regressor awoke from these trances with no memory of where she'd been. She relied, for proof of her journey, on her stenographer.

During the meeting prior to my first planned deception, I set the stage for her success. I woke her from her nap (she was snoring) in a false panic. She'd ceased breathing, I said. She'd turned gray, I said. I'd thought she was dead, I said.

Madame Ackermann ordered me to get the blood pressure cuff she kept in her desk drawer. She was so pleased with my reading (I divided her actual numbers in half) that she invited me to stay for coffee.

When we met the next day, I allowed Madame Ackermann to nap without interruption. I wandered around her house; I snooped. I discovered that she kept nothing in her refrigerator but olives, kefir, and an uncorked, half-drunk bottle of Vouvray. That her cupboards housed stacks of melamine dinner plates and a few foggy plastic bags of bulk nuts. That atop her bathroom toilet tank she kept a catalog that sold overpriced sheets in shades of whites named *qualia* and *bastille*.

I returned to her study, but instead of sitting in the Barcelona chair I sat in Madame Ackermann's Knoll desk chair, an original Charles Pollock design upholstered in royal blue wool and much more comfortable than the Barcelona chair. I flipped on her antique desktop computer that made hideous gear-grinding noises as it booted up. First I read the newspaper. Then I checked her search history. I was unsurprised to learn she'd been researching a procedure wherein a metal plate is inserted between the two lobes of the brain in order to prevent a condition called *bilateral contamination*. Typically recommended for psychics twice her age, the procedure was described on this particular site as a "facelift for the mind."

Then I unsheathed the Düsseldorf pen and began to write.

Madame Ackermann, when she gave me this pen, told me that its creator, before he turned his brilliance to writing utensils, was an unacknowledged pioneer in parabolic ski design. His pens were called "hypnosis tools for the hand." The mind, she said, is freer to wander if it's not attached to the mechanics of transcription.

I didn't have an exact story in mind for Madame Ackermann's regression, so I began by writing about a house by a lake that looked quite a bit like a lake house in the Northeast Kingdom of Vermont where I'd vacationed as a teenager with my father and then-new stepmother, Blanche. I described the path through the woods that led to the dock, though as I described this path I understood that it wasn't going to lead me to the dock. And it did not. I emerged from the woods at the end of the hallway of an apartment building to see a young woman knocking on a door. An older woman in a sailor-striped shirt, her face out of focus, let the young woman into the apartment. She unbuttoned the younger woman's coat, she positioned her against the bedroom window and handed her a video camera before closing the drapes around her, but not so tightly that the camera's lens could not film the room through the fabric gap. A key turned in the door and a young man entered. He stared at the older woman with a look of revulsion and intimidation as, without speaking to her, he undressed. The woman pushed him onto the bed with a veined hand and said, before she violently kissed him, *Who's pitiful now?*

The pen, as promised, had a seductive snaking motion that required little effort, forming words that were mine though I could claim no real attachment to them.

I was still writing when Madame Ackermann began to stir.

When I read the story back to her, it was as if I, too, were encountering it for the first time. I told her about the hallway, the young woman, the young man.

"And there was an older woman," I said. "But you couldn't see her face."

"Then how did I know she was older?" she asked.

"You said her hands looked as though they'd spent a lot of time squeezing other people's necks," I said, recalling how they'd appeared to me.

And so our meetings normalized. Madame Ackermann was thrilled by her living-dead trances. I was thrilled that Madame Ackermann had renewed faith in me, and thus dedicated very little thought as to why my deceptions were so easy. I had found a way to be enabled by Madame Ackermann's psychically powerful presence, or this is what I told myself, and thus our relationship proceeded as I'd always imagined it might—me the worshipful initiate, she the skilled mentor.

Except, of course, we were neither of these.

———◦∞∞◦———

Here was the day in early October when things began to go wrong.

I arrived at Madame Ackermann's house to find her in a manic frenzy. Her feet were bare, her hair plumed from a Pucci scarf knotted on the top of her head, her eyes raccooned by day-old mascara.

"Julia," she said, tumbling her hands as though she were plotting an underling's demise (she'd had a case of dry skin she couldn't eradicate; she was forever rubbing Vaseline into her palms), "we must get to work *instantly.*" She claimed that we needed *by that afternoon* to procure the serial number stamped on the bottom of the film safe formerly belonging to the Leni Riefenstahl of France.

I sat in the Barcelona chair. Outside I could hear the witchy baying of coyotes that I'd mistaken, when I first arrived in East Warwick, for wolves.

Madame Ackermann handed me a mug of lapsong. She blended her own and the result was, in my opinion, a fair approximation of septic effluent. She arranged herself on the Biedermeier and within five minutes was asleep, a filament of drool catching the gray New Hampshire light through her study windows, making her look as though she were seeping mercury from the mouth. She clutched in her hand a scrap of paper, like a boarding pass, with her intended destination: Paris Institute of Geophysics. Room 315 Tour Zamansky.

I switched from the Barcelona to the Pollock—not to write, but to google. I ascertained, via a crazed collector's website, that the best film safes were produced in France; I guessed the Leni Riefenstahl of France would be partial to French film safes, and, given her fascist leanings, she'd have chosen a safe produced by the best of the French film safe manufacturers, a company called Le Polinaire. Le Polinaire, I learned, marked their safes with a seven-digit serial number hyphenated and concluding with two letters—for example, 1234567-AA.

I'd never been gifted at probability calculations, but I estimated that my chances of guessing the correct safe number were in the vicinity of ten to the seventh power multiplied by thirty-six twice, or something equivalently shitty.

I returned to the Barcelona chair. I stared at Madame Ackermann, snoring. *Regress*, I urged her. *Paris Institute of Geophysics, Room 315 Tour Zamansky. Tell me the serial number on the bottom of the film safe.*

Madame Ackermann stirred. She mumbled.

"What did you say?" I asked her.

"Fifteen," she said.

Useless Madame Ackermann.

I retreated to her kitchen; I slugged kefir from the bottle. On her refrigerator she'd magneted the free calendar delivered by the local heating oil supplier, each page featuring a photograph of a month-appropriate New England scene. Madame Ackermann's calendar was correctly turned to the October page and its picturesque snapshot of a pond papered over by bright red leaves, an image that didn't make you think of lots and lots of blood only if you refused to stare at it for very long.

Returning to her study I sat in the Pollock chair and began to write—not words, but a series of tight wavy lines, a block of EKG squiggles. I continued to let the pen skate around the page, watch-

ing as Madame Ackermann slipped a hand under her blouse to
scratch her rib cage.

Time passed. I tried to imagine the Tour Zamansky, a building
I figured would be Gothic, constructed of bluestone and varicosed
by dead ivy. I climbed a staircase, I entered a door, I sat on a leather
couch, positioned across from a mirror that leaned against a wall of
bookshelves. And here's where I started to see things that surprised
me. For example, the couch on which I sat appeared in the mirror,
but I did not. Where I should have been I saw a hypnotically flickering bright spot, like a tear in an old film print. Numbers flashed
in that gap where my face should have been; so did a dismembered
hand.

In her laundry room, Madame Ackermann's drier alarm goose-
honked the end of its cycle, and the Tour Zamansky, such as it
dimly existed for me, disappeared. I checked my watch; I was surprised to note that an hour had passed.

Madame Ackermann slept on.

My calves ached. I lay on the floor and did some runner's
stretches. I returned to the desk.

I stared at my notepad.

During my visualization of the Tour Zamansky, I had somehow
drawn that heating oil calendar pond covered in leaves, each leaf a
puzzle piece interlocking with its neighbors. I squinted at the drawing, the outlines of the leaves blurring when I did so and almost
hieroglyphing into meaning.

But when I viewed the drawing peripherally—a trick we'd
studied first semester, peripheral vision forcing a bend in the optic
nerve, and explaining what the less scientifically minded referred to
as the power of the third eye—I saw that something extra, or that
something else, and I saw it as clearly as if I were staring at a license
plate: 3258432-TR.

On a clean piece of paper I wrote this down, and preceded it by a detailed and hopefully convincing description of Room 315 right down to an ashtray I hadn't seen overflowing with olive pits.

I stood over Madame Ackermann, still sleeping, still scratching herself. She'd pushed her blouse up to expose her stomach and the boundary lace of her bra. Her ribs jutted vulnerably upward, causing the skin to drop toward her bellybutton before rising again on either side to upholster the prows of her hipbones.

I hovered my hand over her bellybutton; I absorbed, through my palm, her ambient heat. Madame Ackermann had decided against having children, she'd told me, because she couldn't bear to part with her stomach. At the time this had struck me as an excessively vain preoccupation, even for her. But observing her stomach now, radiating a trapped solar glow like a desert dune, I had to agree that it was worth whatever human sacrifices she'd made to preserve it.

I noticed, too, what Madame Ackermann had been scratching— an angry patch of eczema the size of a quarter, high on her rib cage. Unlike rashes on the wane, this one bulged at its borders. Its rampaging had just begun.

The poor woman, I thought. Her psychic blockage had taken its toll. Her face was savaged by stress—the puppet folds straddling her mouth deeper, her eyelids the dark turquoise color of those just-beneath-the-skin wrist veins. She really did look kind of dead. I angled a cheek a millimeter from her mouth to test if she was breathing. Her tea exhalations condensed on my skin, hot, cold, hot, cold.

She was alive. Sort of. Maybe, I thought, I should put her out of her misery. Finish the drawn-out job that age, or mental weakness, had just begun. Nothing but more failure awaited her. I turned my head and put my mouth atop her mouth. To inhale her life force, I told myself. To thieve the last spark of vitality from her. I kissed her. Her mouth spasmed beneath mine—kissing me back? Or maybe struggling for air. Whatever she needed, whatever she possessed, I blocked it, I stole it. I pressed downward until I could feel, beneath her lips, her teeth, her skull.

Outside, the neighbor's schnauzer freaked at a passing car. I guiltily resumed my position in the Barcelona chair and hid the pond drawing in my pocket. Madame Ackermann opened her eyes and I said, *Congratulations*. I "read" to her the story of her trip to the Tour Zamansky as she palpated her bottom lip with a finger. Then I showed her the serial number.

She was relieved. I was relieved.

Madame Ackermann and I broke for coffee, she e-mailed the serial number to Colophon Martin, and that, for the time being, was that.

Then, a week or two later, I arrived at Madame Ackermann's A-frame to find Madame Ackermann in a very weird mood.

"Sit," she said, gesturing to the Wegman rope chair by her fireplace.

I sat.

I was in some kind of trouble; she'd possibly discovered that I had, while she was asleep, kissed her.

But instead Madame Ackermann asked me if I knew who she'd met for breakfast that morning. I said that I had no idea, a claim Madame Ackermann met with very apparent dubiousness.

Madame Ackermann informed me that Colophon Martin had flown over from France because he'd found the missing film reel in the film safe stamped with the serial number 3258432-TR and was so astonished that he wanted to interview her about her regression process.

"That's wonderful news," I said.

Madame Ackermann lit a cigarette. Her lower face crinkled meanly around the filter when she inhaled.

She explained the situation further.

The reason Colophon was so interested in her regression process was because the serial number, which *did* correspond to the film safe in which Colophon discovered the missing film reel, *did not* correspond to the film safe once owned by the Leni Riefenstahl of France.

The film safe in which the reel was located had belonged, Madame Ackermann continued, at least according to auction house records, to the estate of a man known as Cortez—an anti-fascist painter with whom, it had been rumored though never proven, the Leni Riefenstahl of France had had an affair.

"Colophon Martin believes that she met Cortez at a gallery opening, after which they fell in love and plotted a performance art piece," she said. "Which would mean that, when she accepted the commission from Jean-Marie Le Pen to direct a fascist propaganda film, she did so as an artistically subversive act."

In short, the discovery of the missing film reel paled beside the discovery that the Leni Riefenstahl of France had known, and possibly collaborated and/or slept with, the painter Cortez.

"Very intriguing," I said.

"*Very* intriguing," Madame Ackermann agreed, left leg viper-coiled around the right. Her eyes probed, with subdermal intensity, my face.

"But what I'm wondering, Julia," she said, "is how I found the correct serial number, as you claimed I did, on the bottom of a safe in Room 315 of the Tour Zamansky."

I saw, then, what this was about. She didn't care whether or not the Leni Riefenstahl of France had collaborated/slept with this Cortez person. She only cared to know how she'd found the correct film number on the bottom of a safe that was not the correct film safe, because the correct film safe belonged to somebody else.

"You described to me her office in the Tour Zamansky," Madame Ackermann said, reviewing the transcript I'd provided.

"You described it," I lied. "I just wrote it down."

Then I asked Madame Ackermann if it were possible that the Leni Riefenstahl of France kept two safes in her office.

Madame Ackermann did not concede this possibility. I blundered forth.

Madame Ackermann, I posited, when she'd regressed to the Tour Zamansky, hadn't noticed the two film safes, but luckily she'd reported to me the serial number from the correct film safe.

Again: no response from Madame Ackermann.

"Meaning," I said, "if the Leni Riefenstahl of France and this Cortez person became lovers and collaborators, isn't it likely that she eventually gave him her extra film safe, in which she'd left one of her film reels?"

Madame Ackermann telescoped her cigarette in an ashtray and stood over me. She smoothed the wrinkles on her black silk pants.

"There's a popular saying among non-occultists," said Madame Ackermann, dry palms hissing over the silk. "Anything is possible."

At our next meeting, we did not talk about the film safe incident. Madame Ackermann claimed to be too bothered by allergies to regress; she suggested my time might be better spent replacing the bungees in her built-ins. The following week, she handed me a three-ring binder and a glue stick, and directed me to a drawer of her review clippings. We settled into a "strictly professional work relationship," rife with all the tensions and incrementally building resentments that phrase implies. Madame Ackermann, without officially demoting me, employed me like any old intern, sending me to town to xerox recipes from a cookbook on loan from Professor Penry, or to deliver receipts to a tax accountant at her offices located on a literal mountaintop.

One day she tasked me to clean her family photos with an herbal disinfectant that she sprayed obsessively on light switches and doorknobs. Madame Ackermann stood behind me as I was wiping a photograph of her mother holding a baby, presumably her.

"Whatever could have possessed her," she said, staring at her own swaddled image, "to do such a thing?"

"Her?" I said. "What did she do?"

I scrutinized Madame Ackermann's mother (a sweet Viennese woman—I'd met her once) whose young face resembled a blurrier version of Madame Ackermann's. Even then she was no match for her own daughter, an ominous, night-haired squib equipped, at that negligible age, with an untamed laser glare seemingly capable of setting her own blankets ablaze.

"My mother used to say," Madame Ackermann continued, "that she'd rather die than miss a single day of my life."

I waited for her to laugh. She did not laugh. Perhaps, I thought, this was a famous Austrian saying that, translated word-for-word, became a cannabalistic koan.

Madame Ackermann flapped her starfish eyes at me. They gleamed with a liquid substance I would never mistake for tears.

I understood, then, what she was referring to. We'd never spoken about my mother's suicide, but she'd had access to the medical interviews I'd undergone prior to matriculation at the Workshop, the results of which claimed I suffered from a physiological and psychological syndrome called febrile disconnection or "pure motherlessness"—and described how, from nearly birth, I had compensated for this lack by developing alternate ways of linking my internal world with my outside one.

Madame Ackermann grasped my wrist. We were about to have the exchange I'd had with so many teachers and mothers of friends, the squirmy upshot of which was this: *you poor dear.*

Except, of course, we weren't.

"Poor Julia, you must believe that you're innately unlovable," Madame Ackermann said. "No wonder you need so much from me."

I pulled my wrist away.

"Also, you're handicapped by guilt," she said.

"Me?"

"You shouldn't be so ashamed," she persisted. "No one blames you for hating her because she abandoned you."

"I don't hate her," I said.

Madame Ackermann kinked a dubious brow.

"You can't hate a person you never knew," I said.

"Plenty of people hate complete strangers," she said.

"I guess I lack imagination," I said.

"And whose fault is that?" she retorted, possibly implying that my mother, by swallowing a bottle of sleeping pills when I was a month old, and dying alone in the middle of the day in her bedroom, had also lacked imagination. Suicide by pills was *such a cliché*, or so the whispering wives of my father's friends would claim, women whom I'd eavesdropped upon (really eavesdropped upon) at the barbecues and the picnics to which we were invited throughout my childhood. I'd wanted to ask them: What, to their minds, counted as a less clichéd way to kill oneself? Was hanging oneself also clichéd? Was it a cliché to fill one's pocket with stones and walk into a river? Was it a cliché to shoot oneself through the mouth, or hurl oneself into the path of an eighteen-wheeler, or take an overdose of hemlock, or douse oneself in gasoline and strike a match? Or was the act of suicide itself a cliché? Regardless, I had to wonder how much, when deciding to kill oneself, matters of originality came to bear.

"It can't help the situation," Madame Ackermann continued, "that I look so much like her."

Then Madame Ackermann drifted off to her study, as if we'd

been discussing nothing more fraught than her upcoming dermatologist appointment (the eczema on her rib cage had begun its march north).

I sprayed and wiped and sprayed and wiped. I emptied an entire bottle onto that picture frame, trying to disinfect it. To my knowledge, Madame Ackermann had never seen a photograph of my mother, thus how could she have known how much she resembled her? Which suggested that, perhaps while considering my stenographer application last spring, Madame Ackermann had done a psychic background check on me. Perhaps she'd been places I had never been. Perhaps she'd visited my mother. This made me feel betrayed, violated, spied upon, the expected reactions. But it also made me feel humiliated, as though I'd been beaten at a game at which I should have been uniquely positioned to excel. Because, despite my supposed gifts, I had never visited my own mother. She had never allowed it.

The first time I'd tried and failed I was nine; I'd taken a photograph of her to a carnival psychic, who ignored the photo and insisted instead on reading my tarot cards. Outside the psychic's tent a barometric vise squeezed the air, the pressure creating a tear in the atmosphere above us, from which issued a chilly black exhalation. The carnival psychic, her hand atop the tarot deck, began to perspire; though a fake, she was not numb to dark warnings. I think we both knew, before she flipped the card, that it would be the Fool, cautioning me not to take the imprudent path.

For a year or so, I had not taken the imprudent path. I decided that I would not force myself upon my mother. She would have to visit me first.

But she hadn't visited me. Not on my birthday, not on her birthday, not on her death day, not on Halloween or Easter or Christmas, not even on those plain old Tuesdays or Mondays when the hectopascals, which I measured religiously with a meteorologist's digital barometer, indicated an atmospheric pressure so low, so hospitable to astral invasions, that even we heavy cow humans, with a minimum of struggle, might hope to pierce the membrane that separated alive from dead and turn like clouds above the world. On the days when the pressure was unfriendly to her kind and maniacally high, I'd still been attuned, I'd still been open, I'd still been willing to see her—as I've heard even the least psychically inclined mourners can sometimes see their dead—in the wind or in the polygraph chittering of tree branches. I'd searched for her in the bottoms of teacups and under the bed in which she'd died, the only grave she'd been afforded because her body had been burned, her ashes scattered on a mountain that was always cold when we visited. I had looked into the backyard brush fires my father fed with things a husband should not burn. But I had never found her. She had not wanted to be found. And if I had gone to the Workshop to sharpen my finding abilities so that I could track this most reluctant woman—so what? Sillier reasons drive people to read the air.

That night I confided the Madame Ackermann situation to a Mortgage Payment named Stan. Stan had never understood why I had been chosen to rise from the bottom of the initiate heap; he was relieved to see order restored. I allowed him his moment of delight. Then I asked him what I should do.

"Break up with her," Stan said.

"I'm not *dating* her," I said.

"Quit," he said. "Whatever."

I told him I couldn't quit. No one had ever "quit" Madame Ackermann.

"Exactly," Stan said.

Thus I arrived at Madame Ackermann's house the next morning, my letter of resignation in my pocket, my thigh muscles shaky after a night of fucking Stan.

She greeted me with her old quasi-conspiratorial warmth. She'd intuited my intentions, I later came to think, hours before I arrived.

"Good morning, Julia," she said. "Something *exquisite* has come up."

We sat in her kitchen alcove. We drank septic tea.

Certain odd-yeared Octobers, she explained, wanding honey over my mug without asking if I took honey, were famously poor months to attempt regressions (something, she offered, having to do with di-annually recurring autumnal planetary configurations; I later googled the phrase "di-annually recurring autumnal planetary configurations" and got zero results), which explained why she'd had me doing such drab tasks; but now, she said, I could assist her with an exciting archiving project. The Koestler Parapsychology Unit at Edinburgh University had purchased her private papers; the curator of the university's museum needed an archival install-ment for an upcoming exhibition of the university's holdings called ParaPhernalia.

Madame Ackermann escorted me to her crawlspace, reached by pulling a metal ladder out of the ceiling of her guest room; I felt, each time I climbed it, as if I were stepping aboard a small com-muter plane. The crawlspace was windowless and lit by a thin fluo-rescent fixture with a seizure-inducing flicker. The walls—some sheetrocked and others not, revealing between the studs a cottony insulation the color of peed-on snow—were lined with cardboard boxes, badly stacked, heavy boxes riding atop lighter boxes that had become accordion-squashed over the years.

The air, overheated and dense with micro-particulates, had, when I inhaled, a felted quality.

In these boxes, Madame Ackermann announced, on that first odd-yeared poorly planetarily configured October day, in no par-ticular order, is my life.

I allowed myself, for about five minutes, to misinterpret this announcement as a promotion. Madame Ackermann was allowing me—me!—to read her private correspondence, in which there might be a letter from the famed lover who'd inspired the Fenrir appearance, or maybe early drafts of her many parapsychology game-changing books such as *E-mails from the Dead*, in which she detailed the recent rise in technological paranormal occurrences (ephemeral, frequency-based forms of communication being much easier for astral imprints to hijack than manual forms). Perhaps, too, there'd be old journals or a notebook that refuted (or confirmed) the rumors surrounding the source of Professor Yuen's dislike of Madame Ackermann, a scuffle dating back to their student days when Professor Yuen accused Madame Ackermann of stealing her dissertation idea.

Madame Ackermann, or so I optimistically concluded, kept these incendiary materials in her crawlspace, and I had, after passing an inscrutable series of tests, proved worthy of her confidence. Which furthermore meant she was no longer bent on punishing me for the transgression I'd committed regarding the film safe incident. She was communicating her forgiveness and respect by promoting me to an airless, mausoleum-like space, meant to aggravate my mild claustrophobia and promote future fiberglass-particle-inspired respiratory ailments.

Exactly.

It took me less time than I needed to finish my first capful of septic tea (Madame Ackermann supplied me with a full thermos) to realize that I had been really and truly demoted.

For starters, the boxes in her crawlspace did not contain letters, or photos, or journals, or anything of overt interest to anyone driven by nobly archival rather than creepily prurient aims. In these boxes were bills. Bank statements. Dry-cleaning tickets. Bottles of expired malaria pills and Benadryl blister packs. Unpaid parking tickets (twenty in one box, all from Provincetown, Massachusetts, all issued within a period of five days). Jury duty notices. Dog-eared linen catalogs. Grocery lists. Unfilled prescriptions. A note written on the back of a pristine scratch-off lottery ticket that said, *apologies I hit your car but I don't have insurance so instead I am giving you this lottery ticket good luck!*

She instructed me to organize the box contents into a kind of chronological life portrait collaged from this paper detritus. I was to match the credit card statement to the parking tickets received during that time period, the prescriptions written, and so forth (this per the request of the curator of ParaPhernalia).

"But what about undated items?" I asked. Meaning, for example, her grocery lists.

"One doesn't shop for leg of lamb in the summer months," Madame Ackermann replied.

She left me to my sorting. Did I learn anything unusual about Madame Ackermann during those hours I spent dry-sweating in her crawlspace? I learned that she had, according to her statements, an intense Norma Kamali bathing suit habit; that she rarely bought organic meat and was more familiar than I wished her to be with diet TV dinners; that she desired, but apparently never purchased, an Austrian featherbed; that she visited a general practitioner who prescribed her enemas and dandruff shampoo; that her preferred stationary vehicular violation was the double park; that she tended to drop thirty items simultaneously at the Bon French dry cleaner, located in a mini-mall on the outskirts of East Warwick, and was never required to produce a ticket in order to pick up her clothing.

For seven long afternoons, I puzzled these paper scraps into a chronologically accurate approximation of Madame Ackermann's existence. These scraps failed to suggest that Madame Ackermann was a woman of unusual psychic talents. They failed to suggest she was unusual in any way at all.

This experience made me question, as I sorted receipts into piles while drinking capful after venomous capful of septic tea, whether Madame Ackermann was anything more than the averagely constipated, irresponsible, dry-scalped, high-thread-count-sheet-desiring person. There was nothing special about this woman I'd idolized, mimicked, and, in my confused way, desired; it was even possible that practically anybody—maybe even I—was more gifted than she.

Which is to explain why, at her forty-third birthday party, I called out "Barcelona chair." Because I was more eager than ever to prove to the attendees of Madame Ackermann's party that they had underestimated me.

I was, in a word, stupider.

In the end, nobody in that A-frame save Madame Ackermann understood the import of my calling out "Barcelona chair," because no one else had caught her torque. When I called out "Barcelona chair" I received, from my professors (who'd all, save Wibley, seen a spider), disapproving glares. By calling out "Barcelona chair" I exposed myself to Madame Ackermann alone.

No, that's not true.

I also exposed myself to me.

When I called out "Barcelona chair," the personal toll exacted by my deception, like the image of the chair itself, spun into focus. I was psychically exhausted by the charade of the past months; I wanted Madame Ackermann to know that I had not, from the ten-to-the-seventh-power-multiplied-by-thirty-six-twice options, *accidentally* doodled my way to the correct film safe serial number. As she snored on the Biedermeier sofa beneath her silk eye pillow, she was not enabling me. If anything, I had succeeded despite her.

Even so, I wasn't prescient enough to avoid stepping into what we later came to understand as Madame Ackermann's trap. She'd stashed me in her crawlspace like a pound of meat—hidden from view, awaiting petrification. She'd invited me, her demoted, deceitful stenographer, to her forty-third birthday party, and I'd been foolish enough to interpret the overture as a peace offering, when in fact she was bringing me into the killing arena. This was blood sport for her. But first she wanted to be certain that I was the person she suspected me of being.

I was only too happy to oblige.

After catching Madame Ackermann's yard sale junk for nearly thirty minutes, the professors began to get bored. Professor Blake, unable to secure a martini refill, defaulted to sipping abandoned drinks. "Is it cake time?" whined Professor Hales. Professor Yuen, a recreational harpist, strummed a bookshelf bungee.

"One last throw," Madame Ackermann begged. "A torque for the road."

The professors, Yuen included, agreed to humor Madame Ackermann.

I stood on the landing of Madame Ackermann's staircase, hands gripping the banister, peering over the heads of my professors, ego inflamed by my superior conviction that I was, in so many literal ways, above them all.

Again Madame Ackermann hair-curtained her eyes, locked her chin. She leaned so far forward, shins hovering at a ninety-degree angle, it was as though she'd nail-gunned her Dr. Scholl's to the floorboards. For the last time that evening, she threw.

This was the throw for which she'd been reserving her energies, and explained why she'd spent the past half hour lobbing meaning-less trash; she'd been building to what was known as a psychic cas-cade, when a person's superior abilities have been utilized for silly tasks, thereby causing a surplus of energy to accumulate.

I did not intend to "catch" what Madame Ackermann threw, but to avoid doing so was like trying not to watch a car burn. What tumulted through the air was a wheel of horror (dismembered limbs, splatters of gray matter) that repeated its sequence as it rolled toward me. I clutched the banister. *Dizzy* did not begin to describe how I felt.

The wheel slowed as it came within inches of my face, the images condensing into a compact gory redness. *She threw a bloody egg,* I thought. But no. Spidery fault lines appeared in the egg's sur-face as Madame Ackermann's hairy-eared torque emerged from its chrysalis.

Fenrir.

His oversized wolf jaws parted and I saw, bobbing in the glottal gloom, my own disembodied head.

More distressing still: nobody else saw what I was seeing.

"Sorry, love," I heard Professor Penry say to Madame Acker-mann. "Botched that one."

"The risk of throwing torques when you're forty," said Professor Yuen. "The blank rate is one in three."

"Cake time," said Professor Wibley.

In my sensitized state, I could practically *hear* the gloating. My professors thought Madame Ackermann had thrown a blank (i.e., a torque that fails, from the outset, to coalescence into anything more precise than a blob of spinning fog). And she had thrown a blank. An intentional blank. But that wasn't all. Whereas her first throw of the night had been a straightforward torque—a single throw that appears to most as one thing, but to the skilled few as its evolved, "second-phase" form—her final throw was a double torque, wherein two unique throws occur in parallel, in this case a blank *and* a spiral (alone a highly advanced maneuver).

At that moment, however, I was too locked inside my own skull to see anything beyond its dome, upon whose surface strobe-lighted an explosion of over-exposed images.

Then my life went dark.

I awoke on Madame Ackermann's Biedermeier to the clipped sounds of Professor Yuen speaking on her cell phone to the school nurse. I felt as though someone had inserted a hacksaw at my hairline and removed the top of my skull. A foggy substance whisked over my brain, cooling it dangerously, cooling it to the point of hyperthermia; I *sensed* my brain shutting down, and yet in the midst of this psychic twilight I was beset by visions, the last ones I'd have for a while. I stared at the water-stained ceiling above the Biedermeier. *This is what she sees from here.* Madame Ackermann, poor dear, looked at her ceiling and saw only a ceiling. A hilarious idea intruded on my delusional state, one destabilized, still, by the peripheral darts of jaws and teeth—*someday I'll take her place.*

Then I heard a horrible noise, like someone mortar-and-pestling shards of glass. I turned my head. Madame Ackermann, I noticed and with some alarm—had I spoken my thoughts aloud?—sat next to me on the Barcelona chair, attention trained on Professor Yuen while one hand rested on my forehead, holding against it an icy dish rag.

She scratched an oval of eczema on her collarbone. The bottom of the oval disappeared into her shirt, presumably connected to the original patch now armoring her entire abdomen and making a play for her face. Her fingers provoked an irritated blush that yielded, as she clawed her way downward, to the sleepy burble of actual blood.

She appeared pursued, even trapped.

Madame Ackermann was scared.

This unnerved me more than the dizziness, more than the snouts and teeth that continued to buzz my optic nerve, more than the one-by-one extinguishing of my brain cells. What was she scared of? Who was going to help me now?

I groaned.

Madame Ackermann noticed that I was conscious and reset her facial expression, staring at me with what I still stupidly read as concern.

She leaned over me. I thought, for a deranged half second, that she was going to kiss me on the lips.

"You poor thing," Madame Ackermann whispered, mouth inches from mine, fingers raking her neck. "You look like you've seen a wolf."

The rumor that made the rounds claimed I'd had a seizure at Madame Ackermann's house, brought on by my attempts to catch as a novice. I'd strained something, or broken something, or disturbed some precious equilibrium by exhorting my brain to perform an activity it was not trained to perform.

I believed this, too.

I remained at the Workshop through the end of the semester even though I spent most of my waking hours in bed, too ill to attend class. Madame Ackermann released me from my stenographer/archivist duties and replaced me, "only until you feel well enough to resume your position," with an initiate named Pam. At the behest of Madame Ackermann, Pam became my unofficial nursemaid, appearing at my apartment with tin-pan strudels and liter containers of broth. Because I was too weak to drive, Pam took me to my appointments at the hospital in the next town. There I was administered blood tests, screened for Lyme disease, lymphoma, mono, lupus, and MS, prescribed antibiotics, anti-seizure meds, SSRIs. By winter break, I had been diagnosed with seven different diseases, fetal medical hunches that never survived the subsequent rounds of testing.

The very worst of my symptoms, however, was this: a chronic insomnia unhelped by the winking pricks of light I saw on the backsides of my eyelids. To close my eyes was akin to being flashed by a car's high beams.

Before the Workshop closed for winter break, I received a letter from Professor Yuen suggesting that I take a leave of absence. She followed her suggestion with a citation of policy, something to the effect that new semesters could not be embarked upon until the incompletes issued the previous semester had been resolved.

On December 12, I packed my suitcases and broke my lease. I e-mailed Madame Ackermann to thank her for all she'd done, and two days later got an auto-response from her that said, "This message has no content." Soon I began receiving regular spam from an online dating service whose e-mail handle was "aconcernedfriend"; their motto was "Anything Is Possible." When I clicked the video attachment, all I saw was a blob of clockwise-spinning fog, inside of which I could occasionally discern the shape of a woman lying motionless on a bed.

Madame Ackermann, at least via the usual channels, never contacted me again.

part Two

The first time I met Alwyn I mistook her for a Lydia.

It was just past lunchtime on a broody day in December, the sky issuing over Manhattan a slushy gruel. A girl hurried through the electronic glass doors of the Belgian Natural Fiber Flooring Company Showroom balancing, on one upturned palm, a molded takeout tray plugged with four coffee cups.

In the twelve months since I'd left the Workshop and assumed my position at the flooring company—literally, I'd been hired to *assume a position*, to sit for eight hours a day in a chair whose name, if it even had one, I never bothered to learn—I'd ascertained that the majority of our customers weren't customers at all, but tourists who mistook me for an art installation. Despite its name the showroom showed very little save a clear Lucite desk, a jute rug— a barbed and unkempt thing, woven of coconut shell fibers and resembling, because of its swirled weave, the hair that collects over a shower drain—a red dial telephone, and me; as pedestrians walked by the plate glass that faced Park Avenue, I'd been instructed to hold the phone against my ear and move my lips. Because wires would have been visible behind the clear desk, the phone wasn't connected; nonetheless, when a person entered the showroom I was to speak in prescripted Arabic to a pretend customer calling from a state within the United Arab Emirates. When I asked my boss, a beautiful Belgian-Iraqi woman, about the significance of the Emirates, she responded, arms outstretched to indicate the whole of our white, hypercooled space, "Because we call this concept The Emirates."

But this girl—I categorized her as an unusual customer. I noticed her sodden Mary Janes, her so-thin-it-was-pointless coat, the sticker adhered to her lapel; beneath the preprinted HELLO a person, presumably she, had written LYDIA in blue ink.

I experienced a twang of jealousy for these assistants and the interns of the city, robust young people running around in imprudent outerwear with no need for health insurance, people who were the same age as me but who'd proven immune to physical and psychological downturns lasting longer than a weekend matinee.

As this unusual customer beelined for my desk, however, she caught her toe on the corner of the jute rug and departed the floor, kraft tray outstretched and then released so that it collided with my chest as I'd been uttering in Arabic to no one, "I'll transfer you to the sales department."

The brown milk soaked my dress, but given that my late-morning round of pills had hummed into effect—blunting both my nerves and my reaction time—I felt neither the heat nor the shock.

The girl lay in a heap of coat, two fingers pressed above her eyebrow.

"Are you OK?" I asked.

She peered upward through the Lucite desk, the curve of which distorted her head into an encephalitic swoop. She had red hair and blond roots that were the photographic negative of most roots, white instead of dark. They made her middle part seem two inches wide, a firebreak shaved over her skull that traced the exact path of the longitudinal brain fissure located beneath the bone.

"Huh," I said, staring at that firebreak.

She palpated her left frontal lobe.

"Some people have an electrified steel plate inserted between their left and right brain hemispheres," I said, wondering if perhaps she'd had this operation.

"What?" she said.

"To prevent bilateral contamination," I said.

"I hardly think it's that serious," she said. "It was just a little graze."

She trained her eyes spacily on my feet.

"I like your boots," she said.

I was wearing my silver party boots, though I now considered them simply boots. The last party I'd attended I'd been felled by such a gutting attack of vertigo that I'd been forced to spend the night in the stairwell of the hostess's apartment building, the flights of steps throbbing above me like a stressed vascular system. The last date I'd been on I'd bled from the mouth when kissed. My last visit to a restaurant I'd spent voiding my intestines in the unisex bathroom. Whereas I'd once been able to infiltrate other people's lives and heads while I remained unknown to them, now the opposite was true. Everyone was an impenetrable stranger to me, while I proved a livid advertisement for myself. My symptoms were an ugly secret I couldn't help but share. Save to go to my job or the occasional doctor appointment or yoga class taught by the soothing adherents of a Canadian named John, I'd become a hermit. If I could not prevent the nausea, the insomnia-provoking pricks of light on the insides of my eyelids, the canker sores, the explosive bowel, the numb extremities, the swollen joints, the eczema-covered hands, I could at least limit the unattractive way that people came to know me when I was anything but alone.

"Thank you," I said of my boots.

"Your dress," she said. "I've ruined it."

"It's fine," I said, though it was not.

"And your rug," she said.

"Not my rug," I said.

"Do you have any stain remover?" she asked. "It's important to apply stain remover within the first two minutes of the stain event."

"I believe there's some in the break room," I said.

I started alone toward the break room, where there was a folding table and a charry old coffeemaker—we'd been told never to bring a customer to the break room—but it seemed lawsuit-worthy, not to mention very mean, to abandon a customer with a head injury.

"Come with me," I said. "We'll get you some ice."

The girl stood woozily, though it's possible she always stood that way—her body was a bad bit of engineering, her legs pick-thin and double-jointed, her large breasts seemingly transplanted from another girl.

"I don't need ice," said the girl. She held out her hand. "I'm Alwyn," she said.

I glanced at her HELLO LYDIA nametag.

She unbuttoned her coat to reveal a mussy cardigan underneath, to which was affixed a HELLO ALWYN sticker. While Lydia wrote her name in architecturally precise caps, Alwyn's script looped around like a piece of dropped string.

"I'm Julia," I said.

I located the stain remover in the cupboard above the coffeemaker.

"Dry cleaners will scold you for pretreating a stain," Alwyn said, "but thirty-five percent of stains can be positively impacted by pretreatment."

"You know a lot about stains," I observed as Alwyn, seated at the folding table, sprayed my dress.

"I'm the daughter of a textile magnate," she said. "When I was young I thought that meant he was a man to whom fabrics would gravitate and stick."

"Are you in town on textile business?" I asked. This, of course, would explain why she had entered the showroom.

"I'm here for a conference," she said.

The conference was being held at a hotel I hadn't heard of called the Regnor.

"There," she said, finishing with my dress. "Let's do the carpet."

She stood up. She sat back down.

"Dizzy," she said.

My cell phone rang. It was the Belgian-Iraqi woman.

She said she'd heard there'd been a mishap at the Emirates. I confirmed this to be the case. She ordered me to lock the doors.

"But I have a customer right now," I said.

"Get rid of the customer," she said. "Take the rest of the day off."

For what would prove to be the first but not the last time in our relationship, I wondered how to get rid of Alwyn.

"Why don't I walk you back to your hotel," I offered.

To replace the coffees she'd spilled, I took her to a Greek café that served hot beverages in Styrofoam cups, the kind with the rims you can't resist biting.

As I was waiting for her to pay, my cell phone rang again. The Belgian-Iraqi woman, I assumed, checking to make sure I'd locked the showroom doors. I dug around in my bag, trying to distinguish by touch the plastic of my many pill bottles from the plastic of my phone. The plastic of my phone pretended, to the eye, to be stainless steel, and to the touch it did feel slightly colder, though perhaps that was my imagination.

It was not the Belgian-Iraqi woman.

"Hi," said my father.

"Hi," I said.

While he said nothing I held the phone a safe few inches from my ear, his audible unease registering to me like a neglected tea-kettle's whistle. He and my stepmother Blanche had just arrived from Monmouth, New Hampshire, where I'd grown up, where they still lived. They'd come to Manhattan on the pretense of see-ing a ceramics exhibit of a onetime mistress of Duchamp, but their real reason, I knew, was to check on me.

Finally he spoke.

"I'm just making sure we're still on for dinner," he said.

"We're still on," I said. My poor father acted around me like a guy expecting to be dumped.

I asked him what else he and Blanche had planned during their visit.

"Tomorrow I'm having lunch with a former colleague from South America," he offered. "He's in town delivering a paper about the sinkholes in Guatemala City." My father also specialized in sinkholes, though his area of expertise was a man-made phenom-enon called "chemical weathering."

"The Guatemala City sinks," my father continued, "certainly have, I'm not denying it, an inexplicably perfect roundness."

He paused. He'd been headed somewhere with this informa-tion, but he'd temporarily forgotten where.

"Oh," he said, remembering. "The inexplicable perfect round-ness. Did you know there's such a thing as Paranormal Geology?"

"I didn't know that, no," I said. Of course I knew it, but it excited him to think he was telling me something I didn't.

"I thought you might get a kick out of that," he said, making it clear that he absolutely did not get a kick out of it—territorial incursions by soft science into hard he found distressing—but that he could, as a father, allow himself to get a kick out of my getting a kick out of it, and wasn't that something?

I had to agree that it was.

More ill-at-ease silence. I held the phone away from my head, the full length of my arm. I recognized, however, now as always, it wasn't his fault that he behaved toward me as he did. To be honest, I doubt I would have been able to receive his adoration in any less clumsy or oblique a manner. Our relationship was a sensitive co-production, no one person's brainchild, no one person's fault.

"And so how are you feeling?" he asked.

"Fine," I said.

"Good," he said. "Good, good. By any chance did you get the article Blanche sent about candida?"

"The opera?"

"The systemic yeast infection," he said. "A common affliction among unmarried women in their twenties. You should ask your doctors about it."

I promised I would. This prompted him to launch into a story about a colleague who'd contracted a rare variety of flesh-eating bacteria while hiking in New Hampshire, but none of the doctors could quite believe he'd contracted the flesh-eating bacteria where he claimed to have contracted it, because this particular flesh-eating bacteria had never been documented so far north of the equator.

I wasn't sure what to make of this anecdote. That doctors were immune to surprise? That his colleague was a hypochondriac, an amnesiac, or a liar?

The latter was the more likely interpretation, given my father and Blanche were effortlessly, incurably healthy people, and thus convinced that a variety of mental weakness must plague any person who wasn't equally vigorous. Though neither my father nor Blanche had ever said as much, I knew they both figured me for a hysteric, Blanche repeatedly plying me with copies of Charlotte Perkins Gilman's *The Yellow Wallpaper* and reminding me that "hysteria, in Greek, means 'traveling uterus.'" They were concerned but skeptical; they doubted the symptoms, if not the existence of a cause.

I did not take their concerned skepticism personally. Concerned skepticism, after all, had been my father's default mode toward me since the age of three, when I was diagnosed by a pediatric neurologist with electromagnetic hyperactivity, which explained why our household appliances—toasters, radios, computers—were perpetually blowing fuses or known to spontaneously, in my presence, fail. By the time I was eight I could darken streetlamps by walking beneath them, I could set off car and house alarms and inspire automatic garage doors to a state of rapid fibrillation. By the time I was twelve I realized that I could, on the random occasion, mindfully direct these electrons (if that's what they were) into spaces where my body had never been. I knew when I saw a woman crying on the street that she'd had her purse stolen on the train. I knew by the backs of a bank teller's hands that his wife had recently suffered a miscarriage.

My father and I did not speak about my predilections, and I honored his sense of decorum by keeping to innocuous practices, such as telling him that he should be very nice to his secretary because her husband had lost their nest egg at the track. We functioned as a family until I started menstruating and Blanche became necessary. When I left for boarding school, at fourteen, my father treasured me as much as anyone can humanly treasure a person who has come to resemble his dead first wife.

"And now he's lost his foot," my father said of his colleague.

"Insane," I said.

"Which could be good for him," my father said. "A disruption to the given system."

I indulged a mental eye roll. "A disruption to the given system" was a well-worn phrase of my father's, his way of cauterizing any conversation or situation that risked devolving into an emotionally messy bleed-out.

"At any rate, keep a lookout for that candida article. You should have received it last week."

"It could be a while," I said. "My mailman's an alcoholic."

This initiated a different sort of silence from my father, a disapproving silence. My internist had forbidden any type of psychic activity, and had gone so far as to prescribe an anti-seizure medication that cut all psychic radio signals, making it impossible to disobey his orders even if I'd wanted to.

"He stinks of gin and has a clown nose," I said. "Even you would know he was a drunk."

Alwyn, I noticed, was resting her head miserably on the pastry display case. I thought, *the weight of the world*. I thought, *the girl with two lonely, decontaminated brains*. Then I remembered: she was hurt.

"I've got to go," I said. "I'll see you at the restaurant."

"Good," he said.

"Good," I said.

"Very good," he said. "Good-bye."

Good-bye, I started to say.

Instead I said: "I can't wait to see you."

"We'll talk then," he said.

"Then we'll talk," I said.

I snapped our connection to a close, but an aftershock remained. From within my phone's fake metal shell I sensed the weakening pulse of the many words we never found we much needed, once confronted with each other's actual faces, to say.

The Regnor was located on the kind of generic Manhattan block that vanishes the moment you leave it. We passed a dry cleaner and a florist and a butcher with signs that read DRY CLEANER and FLORIST and BUTCHER. I paused to stare at the unpetrified roasts in the butcher's window, their wet surfaces appearing, in the mute December daylight, shellacked.

Once inside the Regnor's lobby, Alwyn dropped onto a velvet deco couch, its nap balded to the backing fabric in certain popular butt- and head-resting places. Overhead, the lobby was degloomed by a stained-glass skylight that might have portrayed an image of twining ivy, though the ivy might have been snakes. I positioned myself on an armchair so that I couldn't see my reflection in the giant mirror on the opposite wall. My face—meds-bloated and, due to the recent onset of Bell's palsy, afflicted by a droopy right eyelid—remained a surprise I could not avoid inspecting.

Alwyn set her coffees on the table, unbuttoned the HELLO LYDIA coat, and lay back, her head notching into one of the upholstery's denuded spaces.

"My skull's killing me," she said.

I reached into my bag's inner pocket and withdrew a handful of plastic pharmacy bottles.

I shook three painkillers into my palm.

"Pick one," I said.

Alwyn chose a pink Darvocet and washed it down with a swig of cappuccino. I followed with six different pills. These I swallowed dry. Caffeine was contraindicated for thirteen of my twenty-three medications; plus I was a practiced pill taker now, my esophagus an inflatable airplane slide. Nor did I mind that these medications caused my psychic abilities to disappear. Shorting out a streetlamp by walking beneath it seemed as impossible to me now as extinguishing, by walking beneath it, the sun.

"So this is where the textile conference is being held?" I said.

"What textile conference?" Alwyn said.

"Aren't you here for a textile conference?" I said.

"No," she said. "A film conference."

"Ah," I said, wondering where I had come up with the idea of the textile conference. This was not unusual for me these days, to fail to make proper inquiries of people, to stopper their blanks with my uninformed filler. In the past, I hadn't needed to ask. "What kind of film conference?"

"A lost film conference," she said.

"Ah," I said again. "The films were lost?"

" 'Lost' refers to the people in the films," she said. "Though it's slightly more complicated than that."

I nodded as if I understood. She dug into the pocket of the HELLO LYDIA coat and withdrew an enameled cigarette case that she, or more likely Lydia, used to store breath mints.

"So," she said, "what's up with all the medication?"

"I'm living the dream," I said. "Bewildered girl in her mid-twenties moves to the big city, works a crappy, unrewarding job, and dulls her existential disorientation with drugs."

"These are recreational," she said. "You're not sick anymore."

My eyelid spasmed.

"I heard you'd been sick for a long time," she said.

Behind her, the lobby elevator disgorged a trio of ashen people. One of them was crying.

"I'm sorry," I said. "Do we know each other?"

"Thirteen and a half months," she said.

"Since we've met?"

"Since you became sick."

I did some creaky arithmetic.

"That's more or less correct," I said.

"More or less since the twenty-fifth of October, two Octobers ago."

"More or less exactly," I said, getting nervous. Who the hell was this person?

Alwyn leaned closer.

"I say this as a friend," she said. "There's nothing you could tell me about yourself that we don't already know."

We, I thought. Then, *Ah*. Alwyn was a Workshop person; maybe, it occurred to me, and not without a little bit of envy and indignation, she was Madame Ackermann's new stenographer. Or maybe she'd been sent here by Professor Yuen to check on me, less because Professor Yuen cared, more because she needed, from an administrative perspective, to discover whether or not I "merited" another semester's medical leave. ("The student must prove," she'd written in an e-mail, roboticized by her trademark form-letter-speak, "by submitting a T-76 form, filled out by a physician, an ongoing medical condition, or take a leave of absence and pay $1,000 per semester to hold his or her spot until that future point when he or she is medically sanctioned to return.")

"But you're not my friend," I said.

Alwyn considered this.

"True," she conceded, flopping back against the couch. "But I will be."

I registered this as a threat.

OK, I thought, bored enough by my life to find her coyness intriguing. *I'll play your game.*

"Could I have a mint?" I asked.

I recognized her now, or at least I thought I did. She was Stan's cousin; she'd visited him a few falls ago as a Workshop prospective.

That Madame Ackermann or any of my old friends at the Workshop were gossiping about me struck me as the height of insensitivity, especially when not a single one of them (save Professor Yuen) had bothered to shoot me so much as an e-mail to see how I was doing. The only person who wrote to me was aconcernedfriend; the e-mails themselves had no content, but they always included the same video attachment of swirling fog, through which I could see a woman on a bed.

But my indignation ebbed, replaced by a far more pathetic response. People at the Workshop were talking about me, Madame Ackermann was talking about me, ergo—I still mattered.

Alwyn offered the cigarette case. I accepted a mint. I suctioned quick craters in the surface.

"So," I said. "You must be a first-year Initiate."

"I'm no longer at the Workshop," she said. "According to Madame Ackermann, I wasn't 'initiate material.'"

"You were never her stenographer?" I said.

"I was a Mortgage Payment," she said.

She appeared more bothered by this failure than she cared to let on.

She gestured to a porter.

"Could I get a sherry, please?" she asked.

The porter nodded. He peered at me.

"Nothing for me, thanks," I said.

"Nothing?" Alwyn asked.

"Maybe a seltzer," I said.

"We have a lot in common, more than just our rejection by Madame Ackermann," Alwyn said, and then proceeded to describe a life with which mine shared nothing in common (including "rejection by Madame Ackermann"—I didn't have the energy to parse the distinctions between her and me on this matter; I had never been a Mortgage Payment). She'd grown up in Scarsdale and gone to boarding school in Switzerland, her mother had once been a famous shampoo model known as "the Breck Girl," her father died when she was thirteen, after which her mother had a series of boyfriends before marrying a Jungian psychotherapist and moving to Berne.

Before her brief stint at the Workshop, Alwyn had been a Women's Studies major at Bryn Mawr, where she'd written her thesis on passivity as a form of feminist protest in the films of Dominique Varga.

She stared at me as though I were meant to glean some extra significance from this information.

"Dominique Varga," she repeated.

"Who's that?" I said.

"Dominique Varga is the Leni Riefenstahl of France," Alwyn said. "The woman whose office you visited when you were Madame Ackermann's stenographer."

My eyelid spasmed again and refused, this time, to stop. I associated the Leni Riefenstahl of France with my Autumn of Deception, which was, I believed at that point, to blame for my sickness. Chronic fraudulence, and endeavoring to do things beyond my abilities, had destroyed my immune system—in the words of one internist, I'd *zapped my motherboard.*

I put a finger over my eyelid; I pushed. I often had the sense that my symptoms were insects, and to eradicate them was to cause a mess of little deaths.

"You mean Madame Ackermann visited her office," I corrected her. "I wrote down what she told me."

Alwyn smirked.

"Right, well," she said. "I'm sure it's hard to tell who did what. I imagine you must have lost your sense of self while working for such a visionary. In an exciting way, I mean."

A waiter arrived with the sherry and the seltzer. Alwyn signed the check and held out her glass.

"To Dominique Varga," Alwyn said.

I clinked her glass warily. My seltzer was flat. As with all previously carbonated liquids, the departed air made the remaining liquid seem heavier than regular liquid, like a saline syrup.

"Varga's best known for her political propaganda," Alwyn said, "but I'm more interested in her porn films. As part of my college thesis, I remade a few of them."

"You made porn films?"

"And starred in them."

"Huh," I said. I suspected that I was being baited, but couldn't divine what with or for what purpose. "Did you lose your sense of self in an exciting way?"

She squinted at the skylight.

"You sound like Colophon," she said.

"Colophon?" I said.

"Even though we work together we've never seen eye to eye, ideologically speaking, on Varga's porn."

"Colophon Martin?" I said. I repeated his name in my head, though with far less composure.

"I'd call him to come meet us but the lobby's courtesy phone is busted," she said. "And there's no cell reception in here."

"No, really," I assured her. "That's fine."

The elevator dinged. Seven people emerged. Three of them were crying.

This encounter was now officially freaking me out.

"I'm sorry," I said to Alwyn. *"Who are you?"*

"I'm the person who's here to help you," she said.

She stared at my hands, oven-mitted by eczema. I slid them beneath my thighs.

"Contrary to how it might appear," I said, "I don't need your help."

"Trust me," Alwyn said. "You do. Colophon will explain everything. He's excited to collaborate with you on his Varga project."

"What Varga project?" I said.

"I should also tell you that I've slept with him," she said.

"You don't need to tell me that," I said.

"Just a little pro forma full disclosure," she said. "If you learn later that he and I slept together it would make the previous months that you and I worked with each other seem like a prolonged period of betrayal."

"I already have a job," I said. I clutched the padded arms of my chair; I squeezed them so hard I touched its underlying skeleton. *This mortal chair*, I thought. "A position. I'm sorry. What are you offering me?"

"I can't disclose the details," she said, "because Colophon is a control nut and insists on telling you himself. Also," she continued, "I suppose, if I were to be honest, I'm in a not-so-direct way warning *you* not to sleep with Colophon. According to my Jungian stepfather I'm pathologically territorial and view all females as competition, even for people or things I no longer want."

A woman emerged from the elevator sobbing quietly, her dignified sorrow amplified to hysterics by the lobby's acoustics.

Alwyn squeezed her temples between a thumb and forefinger.

"Could you help me up to my room?" she said. "I need to lie down."

I started to refuse. I had done for Alwyn what any sick stranger owed another sick stranger, and now I could go home. I imagined exiting the Regnor and walking past the shellacked roasts in the butcher's window, free from whatever complications a further relationship with Alwyn and Colophon Martin and a "project" concerning Dominique Varga would doubtless guarantee, until I remembered the tedious existence, momentarily upset by this woman and her engineered accident, my leaving would force me to resume. The return to my low-ceilinged apartment, the ceaseless strobe lights on the backs of my eyes, the steroid creams that smelled like mildewed bath towels, the friendlessness I'd cultivated

as a means of limiting my social shame to a circle of one, the pill routine, the stupid job, the loneliness, the fact that my life, at twenty-
six, had already notched onto a joyless track, the only derailment
option one I would never, given my family history, consider.

I caught an inadvertent glimpse of someone in the lobby mirror; I mistook that someone, me, for a frightened old lady, tensely
palpating the chair in which she sat, appearing like an Alzheimer's
victim who's emerged from a sundowner fugue with even less of an
idea than usual who or where she is.

A disruption to the given system.

Even knowing what I know now, I cannot blame myself for
making what would reveal itself to be a very poor decision.

I stayed.

Alwyn's room smelled of frequently vacuumed carpets. While I
poured the cappuccinos into a water pitcher and removed the contents of the minibar in order to chill it, she lay on the sofa and told
me about Colophon's involvement with the Lost Film Conference.

"I thought he was a control nut," I said of Colophon.

"He trusts me with his backstory," she said. "I'm his authorized
context provider."

"That's your job title?"

"Job title would imply I was paid," she said.

"I guess that's why he had sex with you," I said. "As a form of
compensation."

She smiled, revealing a chipped front tooth.

"I like you," she said. She seemed more impressed with herself
for liking me than with for me being likable.

"Thanks," I said.

"Seriously," she said. "I don't tend to get along with women."

Reclining on the sofa with a can of minibar beer pressed against her forehead, Alwyn told me how, while researching his book on Dominique Varga, Colophon had become acquainted with a man named Timothy Kincaid, a billionaire Cincinnati businessman plagued by Howard Hughes-ish behavioral oddities who was, more notably, the biggest private collector of Varga's films. Though Kincaid initially refused to share with Colophon his Varga collection, he'd been impressed by Colophon's résumé and hired him to help his company, TK Ltd., archive the film holdings generated by Kincaid's pet project, a suicide prevention service called vanish.org.

Best I could ascertain from Alwyn's description of it, vanish.org functioned as a type of witness protection program for people who weren't in danger of being killed by anyone but themselves.

"Kincaid studied the negative psychological effects of what he called 'disambiguation,'" Alwyn explained, "meaning the supposed clarity that follows the removal of ambiguity, which is the counter-productive goal of so much talk therapy these days."

"Disambiguation?" I said. My stepmother Blanche was an occasional disambiguator on Wikipedia; when she wasn't tamping her manias on the potting wheel, she was disambiguating a Wikipedia page on rice.

"Clarity, it turns out, is a death sentence," Alwyn said. "Kincaid decided that by introducing patients to 'reambiguation,' i.e., by removing a person from his or her ambiguity-free, suicide-provoking context, he could offer them a viable suicide alternative."

"How does a person reambiguate?" I asked.

"Kincaid prefers to call it vanishing," Alwyn said.

"How does a person vanish?" I said.

"They leave and never go home," she said. "It's a very simple process."

When Kincaid started the service, Alwyn said, each family

received a detailed personal letter explaining the loved one's reasons for vanishing. Unfortunately these letters were often mistaken for suicide notes, which led to confusion with the police and the morgues.

"They might as well be suicide notes," I said.

"How so?"

"To the survivors," I said, "they amount to the same thing."

"Technically there are no survivors," Alwyn corrected. "Nobody died."

"To the family members, then," I said. "These films are essentially suicide notes."

"Interesting," she said. "So you're saying you see no difference between your mother being dead and your mother being alive and living somewhere else?"

I stared at her. When she claimed that she and Colophon knew everything about me, she meant it.

"My mother didn't leave a note," I said.

"We're aware," Alwyn said.

"Of course I see a difference," I mumbled.

Kincaid, she continued, hired video artists to shoot footage of the vanishers. The subsequent collection of vanishing films was stored at the TK Ltd. warehouse in Cincinnati so that family members, friends, acquaintances could view the testimonies of their vanished beloveds. Kincaid described his warehouse as a living mortuary, a hopeful grief museum.

"Colophon decided that the films could serve a wider population—that the viewing of these films by people who'd lost a loved one to actual death or to suicide, could be therapeutic. Which is how he came up with the idea for the Lost Film Conference."

"That's kind of a misnomer," I said. "The films aren't lost. And neither are the people."

"The attendees are metaphorically lost, by and large. It's not a complete misnomer. You saw the weepers in the lobby. Most of them had loved ones who were killed on 9/11. The weepers hold out some hope that their husband or daughter made it out of the buildings, realized they could disappear without a trace, caught a bus west or north or south, and started a new life."

I still struggled to understand how this qualified as a preferable scenario.

Alwyn mentioned, in an offhanded way, that she herself had recently vanished. She complained about her mother and step-father, neither of whom had gone to see her vanishing film and who were wasting thousands of dollars each month on a private detective.

"You were suicidal?" I said. I tried to spot the talent in her—because it was a talent, self-killing. I didn't possess it. I'd tried to find evidence of my mother's talent in photographs, but anything can appear meaningful at a backward glance: Hands clamped beneath opposing armpits on a warm spring day. Lips pinched shut against (it can appear, in retrospect) the release of a nuclear misery. The innocence of every gesture read as a clue to a future murder no one foresaw.

But Alwyn—I couldn't see the killer in her. She was haphazard, missing buttons, one shoulder always half out of her cardigan and roots that grew pale, not dark.

Even then: Alwyn's story did not add up.

"If they'd bother to see my film," Alwyn said, "they'd respect my reasons for not wanting to be found, they'd stop trying to find me."

"But what if a person changes her mind after she vanishes?" I said.

"A very small percentage of people unvanish themselves after a few years. But not the majority. Though quite a lot of people choose to *re*vanish. That's common. Because disambiguation recurs, after a time. Your life becomes your life, and you need to leave it again."

This seemed less a comforting solution than a stressful warding off of the inevitable. I imagined the dread and hopelessness suffered by the person who'd vanished so many times that there was no place else to go. She was known to everyone. It was a fear not unlike the one suffered by Blanche, who took medication to combat her mood swings. After a year or two the drug stopped working, as though her body had figured out the trick being played upon it, and formulated a runaround. She'd visit her doctor, who'd prescribe a new drug, and she'd return home to await its failure. Her body registered cures as invaders, as an enemy to defeat. At some point there would be no more cures. Her body would be too familiar, or would know too much.

"Too bad," Alwyn said, "there was an unvanishing panel this morning you might have enjoyed."

She flapped a hand toward the conference program. Most of the events were unmoderated screenings, for example "Selected Vanishing Films January 1, 2007–August 31, 2008," interspersed by panel screenings with titles such as "The Therapeutic Value of Witnessing" and "The Trauma Survivor as Cultural Hero."

"I'd like to see one of these other panels," I said.

"Now?" Alwyn asked. "I was going to shower."

I recalled that a person with a maybe-concussion shouldn't shower alone. Then I recalled that it wasn't people with concussions but people prone to seizures. I hadn't been allowed to shower alone for the month following my seizure at Madame Ackermann's birthday party. Pam had sat on my toilet reading her course pack whenever I showered, so close to my naked body that I could smell her highlighter.

My phone alarm beeped, reminding me it was time to take my

6 p.m. pills. Also it reminded me: I had dinner plans with my father and Blanche.

"I've got to get going," I said.

"But you need to meet Colophon," Alwyn said. She sounded quite desperate. "He needs to tell you about the job."

"I can't," I said. "I have plans tonight."

"How about tomorrow night?" she countered. "We'll rendezvous in the hotel bar. They serve excellent whiskey sours."

"That would be nice," I said.

I pulled on my coat, shouldered my bag. I shook Alwyn's hand and promised not to forget our meeting.

"Looking forward to it," she said.

"Me too," I said, my eyelid pulsing its silent alarm. What my mind no longer foresaw, my body did.

———

Back on the street, the temperature had dropped with the sun, but there was no wind, and walking down Eighth Avenue felt akin to being cryo-frozen, a gradual halting of bodily time. When I reached the Japanese restaurant Blanche had chosen I was pleasantly all-over numbed, a sensation I reinforced by knocking back, at the velveteen-tarped entryway, a pair of Vicodins.

"Julia!" said Blanche. Her yellow hair had grayed at the temples, lending her a punkishly off-kilter vibe that interacted really excellently, I thought, with her Icelandic sweater and her clogs.

Blanche stood and hugged me. And hugged me and hugged me. In contrast to my father's duck-and-cover personality, Blanche was an energetic wrangler of other people's messes, capable of dusting and watering the elephants that inhabited the many rooms of our farmhouse in Monmouth, the one in which my mother had killed herself, the one my father, for reasons both evident and bewildering, refused to sell. Once he married Blanche, my father, with relief, ceded to her female expertise the duty of my physical and emotional upbringing, and thus she'd guided me, from the age of twelve, through a syllabus that focused on Trixie Belden mysteries, the New England arts of wood stacking, linoleum block printing, and chowder assembly, and the poetry of Sylvia Plath. She insisted that she and I memorize Plath's *Ariel*; the poems, she said, might help me understand why my mother had done what she'd done. They hadn't, but I'd liked them very much, and they'd provided for Blanche and me a form of jokey intimate patter, a coded way to bitch, in his presence, about my father's occasional fits of chauvinistic pique, for example when he came home to find Blanche and I wielding Exacto knives over a pile of concrete-colored lino tiles, arguing over the most appropriately nondenominational holiday card image, the dinner chicken unroasted, the house a booked and scarved and sweatered mess.

It can sew, it can cook, it can talk talk talk, Blanche would say after he'd stomped off to his study, to which I would rejoin, *Will you marry it, marry it marry it.*

She had married it. And thank God. When Blanche arrived, our years preceding her arrival appeared, by contrast, a weary slog, a tiptoe, a blueness. And yet, with Blanche, there were boundaries. Blanche had never had children because she'd never wanted children. As much as she loved me, she did not desire to be my mother, in deference to my real one, yes, but also in deference to her own inclination to provide, for the needy, the occasional break from their lonely routine. She was the hired help, a hospice worker by trade, beloved by her patients and their families. She existed for me, too, as a temporary caretaker whose generosity was limitless because the job was not.

Blanche's hug concluded and my father stood to take his turn. My father expressed physical affection like a bad mime. He threw himself at me and administered the Heimlich maneuver of hugs, then, after stripping my coat from my arms and forcing it on a passing busboy, situated me on a chair and pushed me so far into the table that my lower ribs rubbed against the edge when I exhaled.

He seated himself across from me and made a low, silence-filling grunt that I'd mistaken for years as the sound of him clearing his throat, and had only recently come to identify as the grinding of his back molars. This was no harmless de-gumming of vocal cords. This was damage I was hearing.

We stared at our menus and readjusted, in those minute physical and emotional ways, to being in close proximity to one another.

As we waited for our drinks, Blanche chatted about the ceramics exhibit they'd seen that afternoon, and showed me the autobiography of the artist, a book called *I Shock Myself.*

"That," I said, "is an amazing title."

The waiter delivered a pitcher of sake and three small wooden boxes. Alcohol was contraindicated for twenty-three of my twenty-three medications. I filled my box with water.

"Did we mention that we saw James the other day?" Blanche asked.

"How is James?" I said. James had been my boyfriend from our chaste note-writing romance in the third grade through college and up to the summer before I'd left for the Workshop, at which point I'd been with him for a longer period of time than my father had been married to my mother, and we both thought we should try out other people. Unbeknownst to James, during the intervening two years, I had done nothing but hold tryouts.

"He's seeing a Kathy," Blanche reported. "He had no idea you'd left school."

"We haven't been in touch," I said. "Not for any mad reasons."

"I told him you hadn't dated anyone since him," she said.

"I hope you also told him that I've had sex with about fifty people since him," I said.

My father origamied his paper chopstick sheath into a little staircase.

"Even if you did sleep with fifty people," Blanche said, "it's not in your nature to do so. There are thrilling harlots and there are steady old dogs. I'm sorry to report that you're the latter."

"You'd be surprised, Blanche," I said. "I shock myself."

Blanche and I knocked sake boxes.

We ordered, we endured the intensification of the restaurant sound track, one volume bump every five minutes, until we were pretty much screaming at one another, and my father rolled the cardboard cocktail flyer into an ear trumpet that he used in full view of the hostess, who was not the least bit guilted into turning down the music.

"I love this place," he said, after our various makis and dons had, an hour after ordering them, still failed to arrive, and we were all gassy on fried peas.

Finally our meals appeared. Because we'd worked our way through all of the noncontroversial topics, my father asked about my health.

"You got my candida article," Blanche said.

"I did," I lied.

"Maybe what you have is sexually transmitted," my father said into his rice bowl.

"That's chlamydia," Blanche corrected.

"Believe me, I've been tested for everything," I said.

"And how is your job?" my father asked.

"A soul-crushing bore," I said. "Otherwise great."

"That's life for most people," he said. "That's why you need to find something about which you are passionate."

"I had something I was passionate about," I said. "But I can't do it anymore."

"Maybe the Workshop wasn't your true calling," Blanche said. Blanche persisted in hoping I'd retrain my psychic abilities toward the pursuit of a more practical career; she thought I'd make an excellent member of a political advance team, danger-proofing foreign sites for upcoming diplomatic visits, preventing future harm instead of prying into the pasts of random strangers, for whom the damage was already done.

"But today something unusual happened," I said.

I told them about the girl who tripped on the rug, her maybe-concussion, my visit to the Regnor, the vanishing films.

"I've never heard of anything so cruel," Blanche said of the vanishing films, and of vanishing generally.

"Do you really think it's cruel?" I said. "Would you rather, Dad, that mom be dead than alive and living elsewhere?"

"That's not a question anyone should ever be asked," Blanche said.

"I was asked that question earlier today," I said.

"And how did you respond?" Blanche challenged. She was a steady old dog herself.

"She is dead," my father interjected. "Thus making this a futile conversation."

"Maybe a film is a bit much," I said. "But a note might have been nice, don't you think?" Once I'd asked my father why my mother hadn't left a suicide note, to which he'd replied, *We are not that sort of people.* To his mind, this oversight of hers was less a mark of insensitivity than of the tensile strength of her character.

"Most meaningful sentiments are cheapened by articulation," my father said.

"In America today . . ." Blanche began.

"In America today," I said. "How could you possibly finish that sentence?"

" . . . people overestimate the value of expression," Blanche said.

"Don't be bitchy to Blanche," my father said.

"Blanche can handle it," I said.

"It's your father who can't handle it," Blanche said. "Be nice to me for his sake."

"Maybe that was her problem," I said of my mother. "She never found something about which she was passionate." My mother, or so my father liked to tell me, was "always a bit drifty." The implication being that she might not have killed herself if she were less drifty, never mind that I considered suicide the least drifty act a person could commit.

"She had a passion," my father said defensively.

"What?" I said.

"She was a metalsmith," he said. "She won a fellowship to apprentice in Paris after we became engaged. She sold her jewelry on the street to make extra money. Then a gallery picked her up. She had some very rich clients. Famous clients. But you knew that."

I stared at him incredulously.

"How would I know that if you've never told me?"

"Don't be disingenuous," Blanche said. "We know what you got up to at that school."

"I don't go there," I said. "I mean that in the literal sense of the phrase."

I could tell: They didn't believe me.

"She lost her engagement ring while she was in Paris," my father said, apropos of God knows what.

"Which I wouldn't have minded so much," he added, "except that it cost me the bulk of my tiny savings at the time."

Then, changing his mind, he said, "I minded a lot. I was very angry with her. She wasn't one to talk about things, ever. I couldn't help but suspect that she lost the ring because she didn't want to marry me."

"But she did marry you," I reminded him.

"I suppose," he said, as if this remained debatable. "But only because she viewed me as good for her health. Our marriage was the medicine she forced herself to take daily."

I could see Blanche wondering whether or not she should attempt to reassure him about the probably honestly loving intentions of a person she'd never met.

"Well," Blanche said, opting instead to revert the conversation to me and my problems, "I think you're lucky, given your lack of qualifications, that you've found a job at all. The next step is finding a job you like."

"I might have a new job soon," I said. "A man I sort of know through the Workshop wants to hire me."

As I confessed this I realized: I had no intention of meeting Alwyn and Colophon tomorrow night at the Regnor's bar. Aside from the fact that any doings with Colophon, and more crucially doings with Dominique Varga, represented a serious health risk, two restaurant outings on two consecutive evenings was a form of exertion for which I'd end up paying.

"He's a . . . psychic?" my father asked.

"He's an academic," I said.

"Is he," said my father, more interested.

"He writes about film," I said.

"Ah," said my father, less interested.

"What sort of films?" Blanche inquired.

"Art films," I said. "Made by an artist named Dominique Varga."

My father's interest re-upped, but cautiously.

"Dominique Varga?" he said. "The French woman?"

"By birth she's half French and half Hungarian," I said. "But yes, I believe she lived most of her life in France."

"That's curious," said my father, who sounded totally incurious, even half scared.

"You've heard of her?" I said. I found this hard to believe. My father's area of professional interest—sinkholes and underground streams produced by the chemical erosion of carbonite rocks such as dolomite—singularly obsessed him. He was uninterested in art, politics, culture, people. While his brain burrowed through rock toward a very specific knowledge goal, mine preferred to warren the air; his brain operated a drill bit while mine launched a thousand aimless kites that tangled strings or bounced along the invisible currents, disconnected and alone. Cognitively, we were the gravitational negatives of each other. Sometimes I wished I had his brain. But only sometimes. He suffered due to his specialized excesses; he just suffered differently from me.

"Your mother knew her," he said. "When she lived in Paris, I mean."

"You're kidding," I said. "When was this?"

"Eighties," my father said. "That Varga woman bought a lot of her work. Practically supported her."

"What kind of stuff did she make?" I asked.

"I don't know what they're called," he said. "Necklaces?"

"Wow," I said, still too stunned to know what to make of this. "Do you own any of these necklaces?"

"*No*," he said, as though it would be unthinkable that he would hide such a thing from me. "She sold it all before she came back to the States. She was somebody else by then."

"What did they look like?" I asked of the necklaces.

"Very ugly," he said. "Very . . . angry."

He pinched his lips with his thumb and forefinger. He was done with this conversation.

I, however, was not.

"And you've met Dominique Varga," I said.

"Me?" he said. "Never. But I heard all about her. Your mother was quite . . . taken with her. And not in a good way."

"What does that mean?"

"She was not a positive influence," he said.

"Because why," I pressed.

"She . . ." He grew uncomfortable. "She was not a nice person. From what I could glean."

"Mom told you this?" I said.

"No," he said. "No. Your mother thought she was an inspiring person. A magnetic person. But she did not have your mother's weaknesses in mind. Or maybe she had them too much in mind."

"Meaning what?" I said.

My father snapped.

"Because that woman romanticized *death*. And she made your mother believe that death could be an artistic act. She exploited people who lacked a sense of self—not that your mother lacked a sense of self. I don't mean that. She lacked . . . resistance. She lacked resistance to bad ideas. And so she married me because she thought that I could help her, that I could boost her resistance. But I couldn't do it. I turned out not to be who she thought I was. I failed her, but not for lack of trying. I did try, I tried very hard, though she might tell you otherwise. I assumed she already *had* told you otherwise. That you knew how I'd failed her. In which case, you did not and you do not need to hear it from me."

He pulled off his glasses. He pushed his thumb and forefinger deep into his eye sockets.

"Sorry," he said. "We've had a long day."

"Don't be sorry," I said.

"I am, though. Sorry. No helping that."

He replaced his glasses and stood behind my chair, patting me twice on the head. I tried to reach for his hand, to give it a reassuring squeeze, but he'd already retracted it, shoved it in a pocket.

He struck out in search of, presumably, a restroom.

Blanche tracked him until he disappeared behind a translucent shoji screen.

"He doesn't hide things from you on purpose," Blanche said. "He just . . . thinks he doesn't need to tell you stuff. Because you can . . . because you already know it."

"That's kind of like assuming you don't need to tell your daughter about sex because she was raped by her uncle," I said.

Blanche speared a maki wheel with a chopstick.

"That's unfair," she said. "He honestly has had a very hard day. He doesn't like to leave home. And he's worried about you. We're both worried about you."

She peered around to see what had become of my father. She was also worried about *him*, and with good reason. My father had an unerring ability, when searching for a restaurant restroom, to fail to return for thirty minutes or more, and later claim to have lost himself in the kitchen.

But moreover my father was a man who nurtured an emotional void that Blanche, in her decision to stay married to him (and to live in the Monmouth house), had long ago accepted as a chasm she needed to navigate rather than one she might someday hope to fill. Because it had mass, this hole; it had a name. Elizabeth. Blanche hadn't known my mother, Elizabeth, any more than I had known her, but we'd both lived with her, or this void version of her. We had agreed to honor a vacancy we'd never experienced as occupied;

we tried our best, but we never fully succeeded, and this kept my father at a distance from us both, the fact that neither of us could miss her the way that he did. Neither of us could share his grief; in this he was alone, and thus whenever my father failed to return from one of his restroom forays, I could see the panic in Blanche's face, quavering like the thin crust of the earth before it crumbles into a perfectly circular dolomite nothingness: this time he wasn't coming back to us.

─────

The next morning I had a message from the Belgian-Iraqi woman, informing me that the Showroom was closed for cleaning.

I spent the balance of the day on my couch thinking about my mother and Dominique Varga. *What a crazy coincidence!* Blanche had said, as she, the lone conversationalist by that point, recounted to my father and me the highlights of our own evening while we shared a cab uptown. This coincidence must signify something important (not that she believed in such things, she insisted, but regardless)—this new job of mine, she said, could prove very meaningful to me.

"You can't deny that it's a crazy coincidence," Blanche repeated.

My father and I exchanged a baleful glance. Before my illness, this was another of my so-called abilities, what my father chose to see as an aptitude for engineering credulity-straining twists of fate. When I was ten he'd taken me to Hong Kong for a geology conference, and we'd met a photographer on the plane who told us about his assignment to track a nomadic eco-terrorist through "China" (he refused to be more specific), and since we, too, were headed to China—we planned to explore the caves in the Guilin karst region, those ulcers formed by salt water percolating through the limestone over a period of time measured by glaciers—we made plans to have dinner with the photographer in Hong Kong the next day, but the photographer never showed at the restaurant (we later learned he'd gotten food poisoning). Two weeks later my father and I flew to the tiny airport in Guilin, we took a four-hour boat trip down a river and then, when the river became too shallow, a flat-bottomed canoe, and as we approached the dock to our tiny stilted guesthouse we saw, standing at the end of the float, snapping photos of the birdless twilight sky, the photographer.

Coincidence, of course. But after a while you can begin to feel stalked by coincidence, or as though you can manipulate the world by expressing a narrative desire—this thread is loose, this thread inconclusive. It must be doubled back upon, it must recur. You can start to suspect, as I suspected, that I provided a gravitational center to which all lost people, past and present, were invisibly tethered, to which they were drawn. I know this sounds like the most profound sort of egoism. I don't know how to make it sound otherwise.

But while I wanted to disregard Blanche's exhortations to, as she put it, nurture life's random alignments, I had to admit that I, too, was piqued by the fact that Varga had known my mother, and that, despite having at my disposal a few new data points, my mother had become (if this were even possible) more of an unknown to me. The longer I turned these new facts in the cement mixer of my mind, the more I failed to spin from her vexing particulates a substance that could harden without trapping, within its interior, a billion weakening voids. What was this resistance she lacked, what were these bad ideas? I could not synchronize the woman who'd married my sinkhole-obsessed dad with the woman who had lived in Paris, pawned ugly jewelry on the street, and hung out with artistic pornographers. If my dead mother refused to visit me, perhaps I could visit Varga, wrest from her the account I would never get from my father, who hadn't been in Paris with her anyway.

For this reason, I met Alwyn and Colophon at the Regnor. If

he wanted me for his "Varga project," whatever that entailed, well, I could only assume our mutual goals would coincide, and I could quit my job at the showroom.

Though I wasn't due at the Regnor's bar until 6 p.m., I decided to go early and check out one of the Lost Film Conference panels. Alwyn had recommended "The End of Scarcity" since it was being moderated by Lydia, owner of the tweed coat.

The Regnor's lobby was empty save for a lone weeper crying into the handset of the lobby's busted courtesy phone, a sight that made me think, not wrongly, of me on my red phone in the showroom, a person speaking in public to the disconnected air.

I took the elevator to the third floor. Save for the flapping crepe paper sounds emitted by the floor vents, the hallways of the Regnor were silent, as though the building were host to a Zen meditation retreat rather than a film conference. I'd hoped that the door to Room 337 might be open to latecomers. It was not. I contemplated the door's faux-wood paint job, wondering if I should knock or just enter.

I knocked.

The door opened; a person hushed me inside. People sat cross-legged on the bed and on the floor or stood against the wall; the four panelists occupied folding chairs pushed against the drapes, which were drawn.

One panelist, a sexpot in fishnets and ankle boots, eyed my awkward attempts to puzzle myself against a wall blank. She, possibly Lydia, announced that, prior to the panel, she planned to screen a few vanishing films rated "inspirational" by focus groups.

She killed the lights and, using a remote, thrummed up the room's TV.

Each vanishing film began the same way: a black screen with a white identification number that cut to a person standing before a fake backdrop—of the Tokyo skyline, or of the Matterhorn, or of a Mars-scape roamed by mustangs.

A woman in her thirties, identified as 3298732-MU (backdrop: file closet interior), read an Elizabeth Bishop villanelle ("the art of losing isn't hard to master/so many things seem filled with the intent to be lost that their loss is no disaster") before reciting, for the remaining four minutes, the sentence "I thought that I could love you."

The blandly pretty 7865456-BK (backdrop: rain ticking down a window screen) told stories about her childhood summer lake vacations in Minnesota. All of the people in her stories came off as charming and decent, her parents and siblings, her cousins and grandparents, even the stepfather who, she maintained, had molested her when she was twelve, but not without her permission.

A twenty-something man with a chapped upper lip, 8764533-WE, told a story about himself in the third person when he was babysitting the neighbors' two-year-old son. The neighbor's son was prone to running into the road, and so he'd decided to strap the boy into a plastic toboggan on the lawn, but then the family's dog ran into the path of an oncoming car, and the car, in order to avoid the dog, swerved onto the lawn and crushed the boy, who was strapped into the toboggan and unable to save himself.

"But the truth was that the man had never liked that kid," he said of himself. "He'd even, on occasion, wished him dead."

We watched three more films, the most squirmy-making an homage to Buñuel's *Un Chien Andalou*, in which a man slit open a cow's eye with a razor blade while speaking dispassionately about the pains of his dyslexic childhood.

The films ended, the TV screen cataracted by a brilliant block of cobalt. The room shifted as the people readied themselves again to be seen. Possibly-Lydia cued the lights.

A hippie panelist with Asian coin earrings opened the discussion by raising the issue of scarcity. Was scarcity scarcer than ever?

"My specific question," she said, "is whether or not reproductions—of paintings, of people, but specifically I suppose I'm speaking about these films—create scarcity or negate it."

"But we're not talking reproductions," countered a panelist who resembled, with her asymmetrical bob, a brunette Cyndi Lauper. "It's not as though TK Ltd. is a wax museum. These are testimonies. These are not substitutes for actual people. You cannot touch them or hug them or fail to be hugged back."

I struggled to focus my attention, finding it difficult to hear the panelists speaking over the voices of the vanished people, their testimonies echo-calling to one another in my head, their individual explanations weaving together to form a suffocating textile through which I found it hard to breathe. A sharpness, like an exercise cramp, cinched the underside of my diaphragm. *Would you rather your mother be dead than alive and living somewhere else?*

My answer was ugly and unequivocal. Given the choice, I'd prefer her dead. To kill yourself was to say to your family members, *I can no longer live with myself.* To vanish was to say, *I can no longer live with you.*

"But you can't deny," Cyndi Lauper said, "that a wax museum carries a heavy death implication due to the embalmed quality attending even the best reproductions. Did you know that many so-called wax artists learn their tricks by apprenticing for morticians?"

The mention of "morticians" elicited a mousy sob from a woman on the bed.

Possibly-Lydia checked her bracelet watch—its loose chain necessitated a few staccato wrist rolls to bring the face into view—and said it was time to take questions from the audience.

"I found it interesting that you should raise the topic of wax museums," said a man in suede. "Scarcity could be viewed as a romantic way to refer to manufactured celebrity. We can't care about a person unless they're famous. So you could accuse the people who made these films, and the people who control their distribution, of manufacturing fame for profit."

"Not to mention emotional profit," said a woman in a head kerchief. "All those traumatized 'survivors.' The collateral gains reaped by the psychiatric industry shouldn't be underestimated."

"I don't understand," said the hippie panelist. "Are you implying that the psychiatric industry is in cahoots with TK Ltd.?"

"The world of commerce is a web of interconnected extortionists," the kerchief woman said.

A woman wearing an ethnic sweater-coat asked a question about something called "re-performance"; a theater group had secured the rights, from TK Ltd., to "re-perform" a handful of vanishing films. This had led to quite a bit of heated arguing at an earlier panel, said the sweater-coat woman.

"I was Vito Acconci's studio assistant in the seventies," she said. "When asked to re-perform *Seed Bed*, he responded, 'If a performance is teachable and repeatable, how does it differ from theater? How are the participants not actors?'"

"You raise an interesting point about acting our own memories out of existence," said Possibly-Lydia.

"It's been estimated," said the hippie panelist, "that seventy-five percent of the people who vanish suffer from Acquired Situational Narcissism, a syndrome that afflicts ninety-two percent of real celebrities."

"But what kind of celebrity are we talking about here?" asked Cyndi Lauper. "How many people see these films? The more films that exist, meaning the more successful a venture TK Ltd. is, the greater the chance that a film will remain unwatched—assuming it's not 're-performed' by some low-rent theater company. Is that fame, or is that the cruelest definition of obscurity?"

"It makes me think," said the woman who'd been crying on the bed, "of library books. I always look at the due dates stamped on the back. Sometimes, between readers, whole decades pass."

The woman in the sweater-coat asked if TK Ltd. had anything to do with the recent rash of "surgical impersonations" she'd read about in the papers.

"People who died tragically and often young," she explained to the room at large, "and suddenly a stranger shows up at the family's house, a stranger who's had his or her face surgically altered to look like the face of the dead person."

"Strangers can be so perceptive," said the formerly crying woman.

"TK Ltd. has nothing to do with those 'impersonations,'" the probable lesbian asserted. "Also, there's no proof that these imper- sonations have occurred. Most of the witnesses were severely dam- aged by the loss of their original loved one. Most had spent time in mental institutions."

I raised my hand, wanting to ask if these impersonators weren't impersonators at all, if perhaps they were restless astral imprints (a common byproduct of an accidental or a young death), returned to deal with unfinished business. But no one called on me, and it was just as well, in part because, though I publicly endorsed the theory of the young and unhappy dead, privately I'd chosen to believe that certain people might find great solace in being deceased.

Possibly-Lydia wrist-rolled her watch into view again and announced that the panel was over; she reminded people that her books were for sale in the lobby, where there would also be a cock- tail reception in half an hour.

The room's population surged toward the exit. I found myself crushed against the wall, butted by backpacks and messenger bags. I allowed myself to be pushed down the hallway and into the eleva- tor, our collective cozy mood calcifying under the brighter scrutiny of fluorescents. We mass-flowed into the lobby and paused by the revolving door to furtively unball scarves from coat sleeves, produce gloves from hats, as though we'd all emerged from a hotel room in which we'd conducted a love affair, and now every innocuous act was tainted by embarrassment and regret.

My kneecaps bleated; I searched for a place to sit but all of the sofas and chairs were occupied by weepers. I closed my eyes and tried to ignore the garish blinking on the underside of my lids. I, too, felt embarrassed, or regretful, on the verge of dissolve. Perhaps it was the repeated (if unintentional) bumping of bags against my body, which reminded me of certain massages I'd received from physical therapists who communicated, via their cold hands and blunt, stabbing gestures, that they believed me to be a psychosomatic faker who drained from their fingertips all traces of goodwill, leaving them face-to-face with their own empathic shortfalls as healers. Or perhaps it was the crying woman's mention of the unread library books, because truly there was nothing sadder, except a gift that a person has hand made for you, a scarf or a poncho, that, try as you might, you cannot ever see your way into wearing. This is when the cold indifference of the world envelops you, and makes you feel invigorated by emotion but also acutely alone. These moments of heartbreak for unwanted scarves and unread books can reveal to you, more than the inattention of any long dead mother, what it is to be alive.

––––––⸏⸏⸏⸏––––––

The Regnor's bar was located through a windowed protuberance I'd mistaken, the previous day, for a phone booth. I needed a drink, but no bartender materialized from behind the mirrored escarpment of liquor bottles.

I sat two stools over from the bar's only other occupant, a

vaguely familiar woman who held an unlit cigarette and wore a pendant that resembled a flattened mace. Perhaps, I thought, my mother's necklaces had looked like this. I hoped so. I fetishized black-and-white photos of women in ladylike clothing and barbaric jewelry. I'd always admired a photo of Sylvia Plath wearing a cardigan and a pendant that is either a gargoyle's face or a hazardous flower.

"Are you here for the film conference?" the woman asked. She had an Eastern European accent. With her doll eyes blinking from her scavenged face, she resembled a person buried inside another person.

"No," I said.

"I'm an actress," the woman offered. "Visiting from out of town."

I smiled a force field. I was in no mood for talking.

She played with her necklace, balancing it on her pointer finger.

"My mother gave this to me," she said. "She's a movie director. She told me I was her muse."

I squinted at her anew. This, perhaps, explained why she'd seemed familiar to me. No doubt she'd appeared in one of the many foreign films I'd watched since arriving in New York, my apartment located a block from a revival house that insisted on screening films without English subtitles or dubbing. I'd become gifted at extrapolating story lines without the aid of a single comprehensible line of dialogue. These movies also made me miss my psychic forays less, these oblique glimpses into the lives of cinema strangers functioning as a plausible substitute.

"Your necklace reminds me of one Sylvia Plath wore in a photo," I said.

"The one where she was also wearing the flowered dress and the sweater?"

"Exactly," I said.

"Sometimes her eyes look blue and sometimes black," she said. "And what was she thinking with the over-the-head braids? She might as well have tattooed the word *hausfrau* on her forehead, or what little you could see of it under those dustpan bangs."

"'He tells me how badly I photograph,'" I said, quoting from the poem "Death & Co." Of the many mysteries attending Plath (for example, whether or not she'd meant to kill herself—she'd stuck her head in the oven, true, but had left a note for her neighbor instructing him to "call Dr. Horder," a note she possibly expected him to find in time to save her), this was the one that most fascinated me—no matter how many photographs I'd seen of her, I had no idea what she looked like. Each new photograph undermined the believability of the others, as though she'd been, even while alive, unwilling to commit to her own face.

"Irenke," the woman said, failing to extend a hand.

"Julia," I said.

Finally the bartender appeared.

"Can I get you something?" he asked.

"I'll have what she's having," I said.

"I'll have what I'm having," Irenke said.

"Make it two," I said to the bartender.

"Two what?" he said.

"Whiskey sours," Irenke said.

The bartender grew very irritated.

"Well?" he said.

"Two whiskey sours?" I said. "Please?"

"All you got to do is ask," he said gruffly.

Irenke put on her coat.

"It's so cold in here," she complained.

"It's really cold," I agreed.

"Tell it to the management," the bartender said.

He throttled up a pair of whiskey sours and placed them both in front of me, as though Irenke weren't even there.

I slid a sour to her.

We sat without speaking. She snapped beer nuts between her front teeth and shot me sidelong glances when she thought I wouldn't notice.

"I think we are suffering in the same way," Irenke said finally.

"Huh," I said.

"We have both been jilted by people who might have loved us," she clarified.

"I practice a no-attachment policy with men," I said. "I'm all business."

"Oh," she said. "You're a call girl?"

"I used to call on people," I said. "But I was never paid."

"It's no big deal to be used by strangers," Irenke said. "It's when you're used by people you know that life becomes unfathomable."

She announced she had to visit the ladies' room.

"Need anything?" she asked.

"No thanks," I said. "Maybe a toilet."

She examined me at unabashed length.

"Don't worry," she said. "Your life is about to get better."

"It is?" I touched my cheek, always an alienating sensation. The anti-seizure meds numbed my skin; to touch my face was to enter a failed romance between body parts.

"You must have been such a pretty girl," she said. "We should get her back."

"Get who back?" I said.

She touched my droopy eyelid with a fingertip.

"The woman who did this to you," she said.

Her lids flung wider. Suddenly her madness, like the flecks of

lead sifting to the surface of her blue irises, was all that I could see
of her.

I shied away.

"Nobody did anything to me," I said.

"You did this to yourself?" she asked.

"I've contracted a virus," I said.

"Fascinating," Irenke said. "And how's that going?"

"How's what going?"

"Believing that."

As she dismounted her stool, she knocked my bag to the floor.
She shoved the pill bottles back inside. She handed it to me.

"When you're ready to fight," she said, consonants blurring,
"give me a call."

I amended my diagnosis. Irenke wasn't crazy, she was drunk.

"Thanks," I said.

"You know I'd do anything to help you," she said, flipping up
the collar of her coat. "I owe you that much."

"You owe me a lot more than that," I said, humoring her.

"You're right," she said. "I owe you much, much more than that."

There was no point in correcting her drunk's outsized commitment to our insta-barroom intimacy—we didn't know each other.
She owed me nothing.

"I mean it," she said. "When you decide you need my help, call
on me, call girl."

"I will," I said. "And same here. If you ever need my help. Don't
hesitate to call."

She steadied herself on the edge of the bar.

"Not to worry, Julia," she said. "There's no helping me."

Irenke disappeared through the door, over which an exit sign
buzzed. I swear I heard the sound of dirt raining onto a coffin lid.
I experienced, or thought I experienced, what might be described
as a muscle memory, if the brain could be considered, as psychics

considered it, a muscle—my gray matter straining to interact, for the first time in over a year, with those ulcerations in the astral plane. But then I realized that there was nothing psychic going on here, this was plain old human intuition kicking in—an arguably more useful talent for me to manifest. Because it didn't require any special talent to know: Irenke was doomed.

My phone alarm beeped. It was time to take my 6 p.m. pills. I swore to myself as I struggled with the tops. My pharmacist refused to give me non-childproof bottles even though I promised her I knew no children.

On the bar I lined up one Dramamine, three ibuprofens, two vitamin Cs, four folic acids, a Voltaren, and two psylliums. Handling pills, even after a year of copious pill taking, still gave me an illicit charge. I did not touch, but often visited, the prescription bottle I'd found in my father's bedside table when I was seven, a bottle with my mother's name on it containing a single, half-nibbled pill.

Weirdly, I couldn't find my bottle of diazepam. I emptied the contents of my bag onto the bar. I checked under the stools, searching the shadows where an errant bottle might have rolled when Irenke spilled my bag.

Then I understood: Irenke had stolen my diazepam. She didn't strike me as a drug addict, but as something worse—a creepy collector of souvenirs.

Her odd violation tiptoed me to the brink of dissolve again— really, what was wrong with me? If there was one victory I could claim to have achieved over the past thirteen and a half months of illness, it was my refusal—or inability—to wallow. Perhaps, I thought, my unsteadiness could be blamed on the whiskey warming my chest, and its bittersweet reminder of my carefree early Workshop days, when the only schedule I respected, after basking, hungover, on the campus green, was one that landed me each afternoon in the windowless reading corridor because I liked the packaged butter cookies the librarians served with the four o'clock tea, the silly daintiness of this ritual leavened by the violent death images on the reading corridor walls, painted by a forerunner of the Mexican mural movement.

Such nostalgia left me vulnerable, however, to the understanding that this person didn't exist, and not only because I'd left the Workshop. I didn't count my life in days anymore, I counted it in hours. I counted it in pills. That carefree person no longer functioned as the norm from which I'd deviated. As the months elapsed, my old self would be vanished by this new self. It was a mean variety of suicide that permitted you to keep living, and I wanted nothing to do with it.

Your life is about to get better.

I clinked Irenke's empty glass.

As I finished the last of my sour, the bar door opened—Irenke, I assumed, returning from the ladies' room. But no.

Alwyn entered, followed by a balding man in a charcoal muffler.

"*There* you are," said Alwyn, as though we hadn't agreed yesterday to meet exactly here.

"This is Colophon," she said, presenting a drawn man who most resembled, of the famous people I could think of, Virginia Woolf. He wore a gray suit beneath a gray overcoat, and could have passed for an overworked diplomat were it not for the felt beanie on his head.

Colophon announced that he was hungry and needed to eat. He did not appear interested in me, save to discover whether or not I was a fan of gnocchi.

Fine, I thought. We could be mutually indifferent to each other.

Alwyn insisted on charging my bar tab to her room. I left Irenke a napkin note that said, "You vanished. I'm off to eat Italian. I'll call on you." Of course Irenke hadn't given me her phone number, but I hoped she'd figure that I was drunk and forgot I had no way to contact her. Because the truth was this, I told myself: I was never going to call.

At the restaurant, Alwyn filled and refilled her tiny wineglass with Chianti, and occupied herself by holding the corners of her polyester napkin in the candle flame, watching the fabric wither to a nub. After we ordered our food, she engineered a tiff with Colophon.

"Did you mail the grant application?" she asked.

Colophon confirmed that he had mailed the grant application.

"Because it had to be postmarked by today," Alwyn said.

Colophon repeated that he had mailed the application.

"You always insist that postmarks don't matter," Alwyn said, "but I assure you that the committee is dying for a reason to throw your application in the trash."

"We've applied to Timothy Kincaid's foundation for a research grant," Colophon explained. His voice was subterranean and minor-keyed, mellow but not altogether relaxed.

Not that I wanted to sleep with him, but—I could sort of understand why Alwyn did.

"*We* are not trying to get a grant," Alwyn said.

"I am trying to get a grant and Alwyn, though she does not agree with my Varga theory—that her acts of political and professional immorality were performance pieces meant to critique such political and professional immoralities—will nonetheless benefit from the funding as my research assistant," Colophon explained.

"Porn is porn," Alwyn said. "Authorial intent does not make it less porny. That was her point."

"And what was your authorial intent?" Colophon asked. Then to me: "Alwyn had quite a porn career once upon a time."

"I don't know if I'd call it a career," she said. "More of an inspired hobby."

"Not so inspired," Colophon said. "How familiar are you with Dominique Varga?" he said to me, cutting to the chase. Colophon, I'd already registered, was not one for small talk unless it, too, was of the cutting variety.

"Not very," I said.

As Alwyn continued to drain glass after tiny glass of Chianti, Colophon told me all that I already knew, and much that I did not, about Dominique Varga. Born in 1942 to a Hungarian mother and a French father, Varga began her career as a morgue photographer in Paris, where she'd moved from Budapest in the late sixties at the age of twenty-six. One day Varga took a razor blade to the photographs she'd snapped of the female cadavers, excising them from their morgue surroundings. She pasted these into the editorial spreads of fashion magazines on the metro newsstands, situating them alongside the models like dead alter egos. When Varga was arrested and charged with vandalism, her career was born.

"From the very outset, however," Colophon said, "she positioned herself as an artist with a contradictory, even hostile belief system."

When Varga's work was championed by French feminist critics Simone Moreault and Lisette Bloch, for example, Varga responded by wearing funeral attire to the trial of Jules Fanon (a then-infamous dismemberer of prostitutes) and weeping on the courthouse steps for seventy-two straight hours following Fanon's sentencing to life in prison. Later she published a series of domestic photographs titled "Interior ReDecorator" wherein she simulated a self-administered abortion with a curtain rod; obscuring her head is a large photograph of "Let Them Live," the French 1970s anti-abortion group.

But according to Varga—a claim her oft-mocked critics, Colophon said, met with forgivable dubiousness—her cruelly whimsical attitude changed overnight when, in 1977, her mother died. After selling all of her belongings, including her prints and her negatives, and donating the proceeds to a political collective intent on installing the death penalty in France, she withdrew from the art scene for two years. By the time she reappeared, in 1979, she'd become one of the most prominent directors of underground pornographic films in Europe.

Yet the word *pornographic*, Colophon explained, didn't accurately capture the tenor of these films, which were less erotic than meditative, even serene. The films gained a fringe cachet among louche, aristocratic Europeans, in particular a wayward heiress who organized, at her Ibiza beach house, the first official festival dedicated to Varga's films, in June 1980. The second night of the festival, the heiress disappeared.

"Like vanished?" I asked.

"Like dead," Alwyn interjected.

"Or possibly not," Colophon said.

"Dead," Alwyn repeated, bored.

A month later, a gossip columnist in Paris received an anonymous phone call informing him of the existence of a film directed by Varga, one that starred the heiress lying on an Ibiza roadside. Her car, crunched against a cliff, smoked in the background as her body, thrown (or dragged) free of the wreckage, was lovingly fondled by masked women wielding prosthetic hands.

While many in the heiress's circle claimed to have seen this film, Colophon said, no hard copies were ever recovered. Soon, however, a series of six snuff films bearing Varga's signature dark aquarium lighting began circulating, again via underground channels, throughout Europe. Though no bodies were found, Varga was charged with the murder of the heiress and six other women. But at her sentencing, a female spectator removed her coat and lay, naked, in the aisles of the courtroom. Once in custody, the woman identified herself as the "snuffed" star of Varga's six films.

"Nobody died during the making of these films," Alwyn said, quoting Varga. "Nobody but me."

Following her acquittal, Colophon said, Varga again found herself both embraced and reviled by the French feminist establishment. Those who reviled her were invited by Varga to her film premieres and asked to speak to the audience about Varga's moral flaws while Varga wept audibly backstage. Those who persisted in supporting her, such as Simone Moreault, found themselves mercilessly parodied.

"She made a film called *Simone Moreault*," Colophon said, "in which a badly dressed academic uses a naked woman as a typewriter stand."

In 1982, criticism erupted over a series of films showing Varga having sex with young male artists who, afterward, professed to have slept with her only to gain a career foothold. None of these men knew they were being filmed. The results were exhibited in a show Varga curated at Blue Days, her then-gallery in Paris, called "Up-and-Comers, Coming, Going."

"Varga claimed, 'My grieving body is the most powerful sculpture any of them will ever create,'" Colophon said. "And here is where my scholarly interest in Varga begins."

According to photographs of this opening, an anti-fascist artist named Cortez was among the guests. Two weeks later, Varga announced she'd accepted an endowed chair at the Institut Physique du Globe de Paris; additionally, she'd been hired to shoot a propaganda film for Jean-Marie Le Pen and his Front National party that would, Varga said, "make *Triumph of the Will* look like a Looney Tunes animation," a claim that earned her the nickname, "the Leni Riefenstahl of France."

When Varga disappeared again in 1984, this time for good, no one, Colophon said, was surprised. Some people believed she'd been kidnapped and killed by either the leftist radicals who'd been sending her death threats or by a member of Le Pen's own security team, many of whom boasted backgrounds in organized crime; others believed that she committed suicide, a claim buttressed by Varga's last known film, *Not an Exit*, interpreted by some as a suicide note, in which Varga stars as a woman who's violated by an anonymous hand.

Colophon drank two glasses of wine in quick succession. Alwyn, entranced again by her napkin-burning project, seemed unaware that her lips were pursed and twitching, like a person unpleasantly dreaming.

"And what do you believe?" I said to him.

"He believes she ran off with Cortez," Alwyn said. "He believes the fact that the film reel was found in Cortez's safe proves that they were collaborating, and that Varga wasn't a fascist, or a pornographer, but a bold crusader against ideology. Her 'fascist' project was a performance art piece, aimed to undermine all ideologies."

"The love of clandestine perversions, of exploiting opposing sides of the political propaganda machine, is a familiar Vargian trope," Colophon retorted.

"Only if you think she was exploiting anything other than her own ability to be exploited and to exploit," Alwyn said.

"And what do you believe?" I asked Alwyn.

"Me?" she said.

"Is she alive or is she dead?" I said.

"I have no idea," Alwyn said.

I don't know why but I did think: *she's lying.*

"What I mean is," she clarified, "something happened to her."

"Clearly," Colophon said.

"She was emotionally derailed," Alwyn said. "Watch *Not an Exit* if you doubt me."

"Probably she had her heart crushed," Colophon said. "Don't let the porn hobby mislead you. Alwyn's a closet romantic."

"This from the person who refuses to consider the woman who directed films about pretend-dead girls being fucked by strangers to be a pornographer," Alwyn sniped. "She wasn't exploiting people, she was exploiting an ideology."

Alwyn excused herself to the ladies' room at the precise moment that the waiter delivered our meals. Colophon and I waited five minutes for her to return, then gave up and started eating.

"I don't suppose you have an opinion," he said.

"About whether or not she was exploiting an ideology?" I asked.

"About whether or not she's alive," he said. "You *were* Madame Ackermann's protégée. I'm assuming you exhibited some sort of . . . facility."

"I don't have an opinion about that, no," I said.

"Of course not," Colophon said. "Madame Ackermann mentioned you'd become sick. That you were taking 'time off.'"

Colophon, chewing, inspected me. Then he reached beneath the table and produced, from his briefcase, a familiar sheaf of ghost-grid paper describing Madame Ackermann's "trip" to the Tour Zamansky.

"I asked around to find out whose handwriting this was," he said.

"It's mine," I said. "I was her stenographer."

"Madame Ackermann's account of how she found the film safe number always struck me as suspicious," he said. "Among other things, she described the Tour Zamansky as Neo-Gothic, when really it was designed by a disciple of Le Corbusier."

"To her credit," I said, "Madame Ackermann's not a googler."

"I consulted an automatic handwriting expert," Colophon continued. "He said that there's a difference between writing produced from external aural prompts and internal aural prompts, which can be seen in the length of the ligatures. Ligatures refer to letters joined by links."

"I know what a ligature is," I said. I had no clue about ligatures.

"When a person is taking dictation, you see ligatures of three to four letters. But when they're taking what is known as 'auto-dictation,' i.e., transcribing an internal voice, the ligatures tend to be five to seven letters in length."

Using the clicker end of his ballpoint, he counted for me—five, six, five, seven, seven.

"According to the ligatures, you were not taking dictation from Madame Ackermann."

"Huh," I said, as though this were news to me.

Then he asked me how familiar I was with the phenomenon known as psychic attack.

I told him that I knew a little bit about psychic attacks, though I knew more than a little bit.

"I don't want to seem as though I'm diagnosing you," Colophon said. "But I believe that you're being psychically attacked by Madame Ackermann."

I thought he was joking. He was not.

"Why would she waste her energy on me?" I asked. "I'm a nothing."

"Well," Colophon said, wiping his mouth. "You are now."

Alwyn returned from wherever she'd been. With a spoon back, she methodically flattened her gnocchi one by one. It was like watching a child kill bugs, and did very little to warm me toward my own meal, a colorless dish scarred with prosciutto.

I was not a fan of gnocchi.

"So," Alwyn said. "Did you tell her?"

"I was in the midst," Colophon said.

"Just tell her already," she said.

"I'm getting to it," he said.

"Please," she said. "I may die first."

She turned to me.

"Madame Ackermann hates you because you were able to do what she failed to do, namely find the film safe number, and this humiliated her and made her feel old, obsolete, sexually diminished, etcetera, and so she's psychically attacking you, which means you're screwed because even though her career is on the wane, she's still more powerful than most people in your field, but Colophon, contrary to how he might have presented himself to you while I was out smoking, does not feel 'responsible' for what happened to you, and thus if he's offered to help you it's not because he's an altruistic guy, trust me, he's an academic, i.e., an egotistical bastard who's willing to pay for you to go to a pricey psychic attack recovery facility only if you agree, in exchange, once you're better and once you've regained whatever powers you possessed to the extent that you possessed any at all, to help him resuscitate his failing career by finding Dominique Varga, whom he believes to be alive, and if he can prove it his career will be pulled from the scholarly junk heap and maybe he'll get tenure somewhere decent and will no longer be forced to take visiting lectureships at agrarian schools in the Urals, but regardless he's hoping, given what he presumes to be your shared personal interest in ruining Madame Ackermann's reputation, that you'll accept his offer to help you avenge your bodily misfortune."

Alwyn forked a pair of gnocchi into her mouth.

"I might have phrased it a bit differently," Colophon said.

"Of course you would have," Alwyn said, chewing. "And yet here we are, meaning the same thing."

Colophon withdrew a brochure written in German, Hungar-

ian, and English (denoted, in case the language alone failed to signify, by nation-appropriate flags) from his briefcase. On the cover
was a photograph of an art nouveau building located, according to
the English copy, in a wooded district of Vienna, abutting a place
called Gutenberg Square.

"The Goergen specializes in curing victims of psychic attacks,"
Colophon said.

I noticed, on the brochure's bottom right corner, the TK Ltd.
logo.

"Currently the Goergen services two types of guests," he continued, "those wishing to recover in secret from plastic surgeries,
and victims of psychic attack who've been forced, in order to evade
their attackers and recover their health, to vanish."

"Point being," Alwyn said, "you could also get a nose job while
you're there."

Colophon examined my face for possibly the first time since
he'd met me.

"I like her nose," he said.

"Maybe truer to say that her nose is the least of her problems,"
Alwyn said. "Sometimes it's nice to fix what you can."

"Psychic attack victims vanish?" I said, ignoring Alwyn.

Colophon nodded. "Psychic attacking vanishings account for
a decent percentage of TK Ltd.'s business, one that increases by
the year. You are far from alone." Psychic attacks, he explained,
both the conscious and the unconscious varieties, had become
rampant among the non-psychic population—among members of
book groups, for example. People were attacking each other via
shared texts. Many more attacks were launched through social
media sites. The possibilities for connectedness, and for privacy
invasion, had unleashed what Colophon called "an epidemic of
opportunity."

"I still don't understand why you want to ruin Madame Ackermann's reputation," I said. "She lied to you, OK. But so what?"

"Oh," Colophon said. Then to Alwyn, "See? You overlooked a major detail."

"So stab me," she said.

After he'd received the ligature assessment from the automatic handwriting expert, Colophon explained, he'd accused Madame Ackermann of lying to him about her role in the recovery of the film safe serial number. She'd denied it. A week later, she'd informed him, via e-mail, that she wouldn't be able to further discuss her research methods with him due to the fact that *she'd* decided to write about Varga. She, too, was convinced that Varga was alive; she, too, had decided it would constitute a bold career move to find her.

"I understand Madame Ackermann has a habit of nicking other people's ideas," Colophon said. "Which is why, if you managed to do what it seems you somehow managed to do—find the correct serial number—then it would appear you have a talent that could help me, and we could be of mutual use to one another."

"Ah," I said. It was less a sound of revelation than of defeat. *Ah*.

Had it come to this? I thought. Was I this sick, this desperate that I'd embroil myself in a relative stranger's revenge fantasies against my former idol in order to punish her for misfortunes that were, best I could tell, nobody's fault but mine? And regarding Madame Ackermann's psychically attacking me, well . . . I couldn't see how I was worth the personal cost such an act would incur. Psychic attacks risked destroying the health of the victimizer as well as the victim.

I picked the prosciutto strips out of my meal. The stink of air-cured meat turned my stomach and reminded me of my first late August in the Workshop dorm, the air redolent with what amounted, in hindsight, to the ridiculous ambition to alter the molecular state of dead animal flesh with one's spastic, twenty-three-year-old attention span. I remembered thinking, as a first-year initiate, *this is the smell of my future.* I would be a giddy, sweating failure, but then I would, without question, succeed. When I matriculated at the Workshop I was under the impression, as was probably every untried and untested initiate, that I was fated to be famous. Every streetlamp I walked beneath and darkened was proof of this. The Workshop, thus, had always been, in my mind, a temporary resting point on my life's journey to greatness. But it hadn't happened that way. Nothing about my time at the Workshop was restful. And while greatness no longer seemed a destination within my reach, I no longer knew, even in the average scheme of things, where the hell I was going.

———

I couldn't sleep that night, even though I'd swallowed one Nembutal, two over-the-counter sleep aids, a glass of valerian-browned water. Finally I decided to kill the hours that remained until day watching the DVD Colophon had given me. As he'd chased a runny tiramisu around a plate, he'd emphasized: in order to cure myself of this psychic attack—in order to become well enough to humiliate and discredit Madame Ackermann by finding Dominique Varga before she did—I would first have to vanish.

There was no other way.

"And if you're going to make a vanishing film," he'd said, "you might as well be inspired by the master."

I slipped *Not an Exit* into my computer. I clicked "Play."

Varga's film was about five minutes long, and I watched it fifteen times in succession. I couldn't help but giggle at the title, until, by about the sixth watching, it no longer seemed funny, Varga and her mean love affair with an anonymous hand. Nor did the single line of dialogue, delivered by voiceover, possibly Varga as well, while a child cried in the background: *It's not the people you let into your vagina who can hurt you, it's the people you let out of it.*

Then I became depressed.

I removed the DVD, I drew a bath. As the tub filled I hunched on the toilet lid and considered the possibility that I was being psychically attacked by Madame Ackermann. Professor Blake had explained psychic attacks with one simple and incontestably true statement: People make other people sick. Blake tweaked that statement to suggest that sickness was purposefully, malevolently, caused by other people. After an hour of witnessing Blake at his twenty-foot-long slate board, layering chalk scribbles over fist-erased chalk scribbles, his hands by the end of class as dusty and swollen as a wrestler's, his ideas seemed the furthest thing from radical. They seemed obvious. They seemed like the only viable ideas.

I closed my eyes. I tried to sense Madame Ackermann inside of me, like the chatter of enemy bacteria I could sometimes hear when I had an ear infection. Surely there would be a trace of her; more than a confusion of symptoms, Madame Ackermann would want to leave her personal mark.

And she had. My pulse gonged in my ear canal as, eyes closed, I stared at it. And stared at it. And then marveled how, for all the hours I'd spent looking at the backs of my own eyelids, I had never until this moment realized what should have been apparent to me from the start—the annoying constellation of light pricks outlined the shape of a very familiar wolf.

I tested this suspicion. I opened and shut my lids rapidly. I tried to dislodge her design on me. But the pricks remained.

It was she.

I should have been alarmed. No, I should have panicked. I was being psychically attacked by the most powerful person in the field of parapsychological scholarship. But instead I was so relieved that I could almost hear the endorphin floodgates sliding open.

My sickness had a cause. What had been, for over a year, my free-floating, possibly fabricated (according to some doctors) state of misery had been validated and identified. I knew where it lived, what it ate for breakfast, what kind of parking tickets it amassed on vacation, the type of sheets it desired.

It even had a name.

I ran to my computer to e-mail Colophon. He'd been right. I had proof. But when I opened my inbox, I'd received another e-mail from aconcernedfriend—my third that day—with the same attachment of the woman on the bed. And then I nearly slapped myself in the head, it was so obvious: aconcernedfriend was Madame Ackermann. These e-mails constituted a form of psychic warfare, proving she'd hacked into my immune system and also my past. She'd been invited places that I'd never been invited to go. She'd been to my mother's death bed, and she'd filmed this dramatized artifact to taunt me.

I watched the attachment so many times that it started to collapse, in my mind, with Varga's vanishing film, the woman lying on the floor and the woman lying on the bed becoming one, and I could hear Varga's voice saying, *it's not the people you let into your vagina who can hurt you, it's the people you let out of it.*

I closed my eyes again. I savored the wolf.

This is your fault, I thought, thrillingly. *Your fault.*

I drew a bath. As the tub filled, I stared at my face in the mirror and dared it to care. It did not care. With a gummy razor I crosshatched, for the sake of experimentation, the topmost layer of skin on my wrists. I held my hand over the toilet and watched the blood drip into the bowl, a sight that made me remember my last menstrual cycle, now more than a year ago, with detached fondness. I would not say I was suicidal. I would never say that.

Besides, there was no point in punishing myself. Madame Ackermann was to blame for my misery. And I was going to make her sorry that she'd ever met me.

part Three

My favorite guest at the Goergen was a plastic surgery patient who identified herself, when I met her, as "Hungarian skin-care royalty." A widow named Borka, she showed zero respect for the anonymity rules by which we were instructed to abide.

At the Goergen, the first thing we'd learned was the peril of being known.

"It means 'foreigner,'" Borka told me of her name. "Always I have been a bedbug in my own family."

Reedy, turbaned, with a spooky Isak Dinesen expression paralyzing her features, Borka appeared to be in her late sixties, though this remained an uncorroborated guess. Her rheumatoid hands—swollen, hooked, beige—resembled ginger roots, suggesting she might be nearer to two hundred. We sat together at meals, including Silent Breakfast, during which she scribbled instructions on a pad. A typical jotting would read LOOK 11 O'CLOCK, and I would do so, only to witness something I did not need to see: a psychic attack victim flaking her psoriatic scabs with a fork tine, for example.

Before bed, Borka and I played backgammon in the lobby, where marble columns severed the vast square footage into many wall-less cubicles of space. We sat in scarred leather club chairs, our knees touching. Borka tried to psych me out whenever it was my move by intensely owling my face.

"You are a big déjà vu to me," she'd say, her smoker's rasp so throaty and mechanical it sounded as though it had been routed through a voice changer.

There were many discouragements at the Goergen, the strictest of which involved leaving it; we were threatened with not being allowed back in if we disregarded this particular admonishment. Given the skittish, high-profile clientele, paparazzi lurked across the street in Gutenberg Square with hopes of catching, as one famously did, the wife of an Austrian diplomat, her postoperative face coated with a salve that reflected the camera's flash and inspired a number of gossip columnists to speculate that she'd had a diamond surgically implanted in her cheek.

The Goergen thus resembled a more extreme version of my existence in New York, my travels circumscribed now to the interior of a single building, the positions I assumed in chairs—the club chairs in the lobby, the chaises in the thermal baths, the lyre-backed chair in my room—acts of sitting with no pressure attending my inertia, no tourists for whom to speak theatrical Arabic.

I found it, at least until Alwyn arrived five days after I did, relaxing.

Alwyn was not a guest at the Goergen but a quasi-employee; given Colophon's professional and financial entanglements with Timothy Kincaid (Kincaid's foundation had awarded Colophon his research grant), and given that TK Ltd. owned the Goergen, Kincaid made an exception to the Goergen's guest-only rule, allowing Alwyn to liaise with my psychic attack counselor, to make sure I abided by the many discouragements, and to guarantee, in the interests of everyone receiving a decent return on their investment, that I took my healing seriously.

In her spare time, Alwyn's job was to track Madame Ackermann's movements and keep abreast of any Varga progress she made that threatened to supersede ours.

Not that we, or I, had made any progress.

I met Alwyn in the lobby where, a mere five minutes after walking through the front door, she was already in a fight.

"Cell phones are discouraged," the concierge said. "If you do not give me your phone, I cannot give you your room key."

"Just to be clear," she said. "You're not discouraging me. You're forbidding me."

"I forbid nothing," he said. "You are free to sleep in the square with your precious phone."

"But I'm not one of them," she said, gesturing toward the club chairs occupied by surgical patients in bandages, psychic attack victims overcome by tics and rashes. "Tell him," she appealed to me.

"She's not one of us," I said.

"How can I say this as a compliment," said the concierge. "You will not always be a young or unloved girl."

Alwyn grudgingly relinquished her phone.

"What a puffin-stuff," she said, after procuring her key. "Walk me to the elevator."

She handed me her heaviest bag. She'd changed her hair while on her brief vacation in Paris, coloring it burgundy and snipping tiny bangs. She'd traded her sloppy cardigans for a collarless tweed jacket with expensively frayed cuffs and hems; around her neck she'd pinned a scarf patterned by miniature equestrian hardware, stirrups and bits.

Alwyn noticed me noticing her, and in return took my quick measure—my wool robe, my boiled-wool slippers, both presents from Blanche one Christmas when she'd themed all her gifts around the support of a local sheep cooperative.

"You look so convalescent après-ski," she said critically. "I got here just in time."

"I've been taking my healing very seriously," I assured her.

"No," she said. "I mean *I* got here just in time."

We slalomed her bags between lobby columns, past a quadrant of club chairs occupied by postsurgical patients in headscarves, cards fanned before their bruised faces, legs slung to the side as though riding horses through a copse of spectral trees.

Alwyn babbled, at an indiscreet decibel level that triggered the lobby's rat-a-tat acoustics, about the detective her mother and stepfather had hired, and how this detective had tracked her to Paris.

"My old prep school roommate, who lives in the Marais, started receiving phone calls from a man inquiring about me. Where was I staying in Paris? What were my travel plans? Fortunately, I told her I was headed to Sofia. Once a deceitful gossip, always a deceitful gossip. How are things with you?"

I told her about the Goergen's discouragement against sharing personal information.

"Anything you divulge could be used against you," I said, quoting the book of discouragements chained to the underside of my bedside table. "The less the other guests know about you, the fewer opportunities exist for them to collude, even unwittingly, with your attacker."

"Hmmm," Alwyn said.

"It's kind of a relief," I said.

"What is?" Alwyn said.

"Not having to be curious about other people."

Alwyn smirked.

"What?" I feigned. Because I knew what. Alwyn had made it her conversational goal, for the duration of our nine-hour flight to Paris (at which point I'd continued alone to Vienna), to prod me for details about my mother's life, of which I could provide, in her opinion, pathetically few, except that she'd grown up in a ragtag corner of Connecticut as the only child of a widowed father who'd never remarried and died of lung cancer when she was twenty-three; she'd been allergic to mohair and developed francophone pretensions as a means of armoring herself against the deleterious effects of her lower-middle-class upbringing; she'd resented her honeymoon to a buggy coast of Canada and hated the leather couches my father had inherited from an uncle and refused, because they were basically new, to exchange for something "classier"; she always took the bigger steak and became wickedly depressed when forced to sleep in houses less than one hundred years old; and while living in Monmouth she'd never had a close female friend or a decent winter coat or any sense of social reciprocity, all of which led the people of Monmouth to believe that she thought she was better than them.

It is possible she was.

Also she wore her long, black hair like Madame Ackermann's, parted in the middle, the ends narrowing to a point on her back like a damp paintbrush.

I did not tell Alwyn that, while apprenticing with a metalsmith in Paris, she'd sold her work to Dominique Varga, nor did I mention that she'd lost her engagement ring and married my father because he was good medicine. It did not, at this point, strike me as any of Alwyn's business.

We waited for the elevator to grind up from the basement.

"But with your abilities," Alwyn said, "how could you refrain?"

"Refrain from what?" I said.

"Knowing things," she said, returning to her plane fixation. "It's like you have unlimited access to the Facebook profiles of anyone who ever lived."

"Parapsychologists never use social networks," I said. "They're a boon for psychic attackers. For self-protective purposes, we confine ourselves to e-mail."

Then I tried to explain what I saw as a matter of respecting, psychically and otherwise, a person's privacy, in particular my mother's.

"I don't go where I'm not invited," I said.

"She forfeited her rights to privacy when she killed herself without leaving a note."

"Interesting theory," I said.

"I'm here to help," she said as she stepped into the elevator. "By the way, I spoke with your psychic attack counselor last week on the phone."

"My who?" I said. I held the elevator door open.

"Her name is Marta. Your first meeting with her is tomorrow."

"Oh," I said, miffed that Alwyn would have spoken to this counselor before I did.

"Marta said we have to assume that you've made yourself vulnerable to Madame Ackermann's attack."

"Because I deceived her?" I said.

"Everyone has vulnerabilities, everyone has a weak spot. It's my job to help you locate those weaknesses. These portals. The opening via which Madame Ackermann *got to you*."

"Too bad there's not an MRI for that kind of thing," I said.

Alwyn sighed testily.

"I thought you said you were taking this seriously," she said.

"I am," I assured her.

"Are you?" she said. "Ask yourself that. Ask yourself right now."

I removed my hand from the elevator door.

"Your sad life," she intoned, as the door pinched her from view, "when will you stare it in the face?"

I walked to my room beset by claustrophobia, the slurry of my slippers against the floor tiles echoing off the ceiling in a gossipy swirl. I stopped in front of an unclean window.

You, I said to the reflection. *When will you stare your sad life in the face?*

I pointed at her. She pointed at me. We stood, accused.

Then we shared a laugh that the acoustically hyperactive hallway magnified and sheared to a sharp bark, the kind that a dog emits when his tail is stepped upon, half blaming outrage, half hurt surprise.

En route to my room, I swung back through the lobby to check my e-mail. Though the Goergen discouraged computers and cellular devices, the concierge kept a terminal in his office that, depending on his mood, he allowed guests to use. Fortunately, he'd expended his daily ire quota on Alwyn; he waved me through.

I checked my e-mail even though, per the TK Ltd. vanishing protocols—which required me to dispose of all vestiges of my former self, including the online vestiges—I'd ditched my old account and opened, via TK Ltd., a secure one for the purposes of communicating with my vanishing coordinator in Cincinnati, and with Colophon, who was in Paris.

Colophon's plan, while Alwyn and I were at the Goergen, was this: He'd obtain objects that had once belonged to Varga in hopes that I might, once cured, be able to psychometrize them. Psychometry—"mastering the hostile object"—was one of the few areas of Workshop study I'd proven good at. We'd learned, in Professor Penry's seminar, how a flow of electrons moves between people and the things they touch, creating an electromagnetic imprint, a greasy emotional coating you could read like a piece of microfiche.

During the midterm exam, I'd been the only initiate to identify a thimble as belonging to a woman whose finger had once touched the mouth of the Mona Lisa.

But no word from Colophon. The only e-mail I'd received was from aconcernedfriend; Madame Ackermann, despite TK Ltd.'s boasted-about firewalls, had somehow tracked me down.

I stared at her attachment, the tiny canted paperclip visibly throbbing. I considered opening it, even though it was against the discouragements to do so ("Refuse any communication with your attacker while in residence; this includes postcards, e-mails, care packages, etc.").

I slid her e-mail into the trash.

Then I stared at my empty inbox, a rectangular void that finalized what had been under way for a year—I'd been forgotten by everyone.

Vanishing, in other words, proved a redundancy for me. As far as most people were concerned, I was already gone.

I did, however, feel pretty fucking guilty about vanishing on my father and Blanche; Blanche, over sushi that night in New York, had expressed her clear disapproval of both the act and the films, and my father, well, he'd already endured his fair share of sudden human absences. As I'd tried to explain in my film (which, so far, neither of them had seen—we received an e-mail from TK Ltd. whenever a visitor "checked out" our film), I viewed vanishing as an extreme medical necessity, akin to a form of radiation in which a partial killing takes place in order to promote a healing.

I promised to be in touch when I was better.

I was pretty certain this was not a lie.

Back in my room I lay on my bed, two skinny mattresses bridged by a length of V-shaped foam, and failed to sleep. In addition to my passport and cell phone, I'd surrendered to the concierge all of my pill bottles. Without my Nembutal, night was an ice age of unmoving time spent staring at the wolf, or trying to fall asleep with my lids open, eyeballs drying in the dark. Things glowed in my room that shouldn't: the light switch in the bathroom; the face of the alarm clock. I closed the bathroom door and shut the clock in the armoire. I heard clicking noises outside my window coming from Gutenberg Square, the little-bird-skull-popping sounds of the paparazzi snapping photos, I thought, until I realized it was my clock, echoing from inside the armoire, louder now that I'd enclosed it in a smaller space.

⸙

The first of my daily meetings with Marta, my psychic attack counselor, occurred, as scheduled, one week following my arrival.

After breakfast, Borka offered to escort me to Marta's office, stashed in a distant wing of the Goergen and impossible to locate the first time without a guide.

Borka said, "Whenever you are late, Marta will ask you, 'Why were you late?' To which you should respond, 'Why do you not want to be found?'"

We exited the elevator on the Goergen's gloomy topmost floor, the one obscured behind the building's mansard roof, its darkness moderately relieved by the high-up circular windows, each one permitting a beam of light to bore through the moted air. These many dull moons marked our travel, and made me feel, as we scuffed our slippers over the tiles, as though we were midnight skaters following a river of dusty ice.

I asked Borka why a plastic surgery patient such as herself should be meeting with a psychic attack counselor. She explained that due to her surgical history—she'd undergone extensive facial reconstruction decades ago, following a bad car accident—she had been deemed worthy of psychological evaluation.

"But the windshield did not ruin my face quite so much as the doctor who fixed it," she said.

I didn't want to agree with her, but it was true that hers was not a face that anyone would pay for. This explained why she always wore a hood-like headscarf even though she'd yet to have any procedures or suffer any discoloration or swelling that required, per the Goergen's unspoken dress codes, polite obscuring. Her face, uncut, was a weapon.

"Now I want to right the wrongs that were done to me," she griped. "And this indicates that I am insane."

"You want to be yourself again," I said.

"Please," she said. "For what it's costing, there are far more worthy people to be."

As we walked down a hallway that narrowed as we progressed toward its endpoint, Borka inquired about my attack.

I knew it was against the discouragements to tell her, but Borka was a harmless old lady and not the sort to hurt anyone. We were friends. Despite my experience with Madame Ackermann and my instinctual resistance to Alwyn, I was not so spiritually wrecked that I'd come to distrust all people.

I related to her a basic version of the events that had landed me in the Goergen.

"So you are like Eve in *All About Eve*," she said.

"No," I said. "I am like Dumbo in *Dumbo*."

I told her that I was looking for a Hungarian artist.

"Dominique Varga," I said. "Maybe you know her work."

Borka's body recoiled minutely, as though she'd inhaled a sharp odor; otherwise, she appeared not to have heard me.

She asked me where I'd grown up, what my full name was.

"Severn," she said. She practically chewed this information. "That is an aristocratic-sounding name."

"I think, like most aristocratic-sounding names, it used to be Slevovitz," I said. "Or Severnsky. Or Sevethanopopakis."

My father, I told her, was born to murky people—the only child of parents whom I remembered best for serving me sandwiches filled with a paste of ground bologna, mayonnaise, and pickles, a combination that suggested either high American Waspiness or one of its many immigrant opposites.

"And your father? What does he do?"

"He's a geologist obsessed with sinkholes," I said.

"Here we call them drains," she said, unimpressed.

"No . . . well . . ." I said.

I explained to her about sinkholes.

"They may be formed gradually or suddenly," I said. "But the sudden ones swallow cars, buildings, sometimes people. My father studies sinkholes caused by human activity, namely industrially produced waste."

Her stare grew keener.

"And your mother?" she said.

"My mother is dead," I said.

I expected her expression to stall in that gear of generic pity I'd come to so detest, and tried never to inspire.

But it didn't.

"No wonder your father is obsessed with holes caused by people," she said.

We arrived at Marta's office. The top half of her door was windowed by nubbled glass; on the other side, a dark shape bent and straightened, as though stretching before a hike.

"Put in a good word for me," Borka said. She scampered down the hallway as though scared of being spotted by Marta in my company.

Marta, a woman with Hunnishly high cheekbones and turquoise bifocals, did not shake my hand when I entered her office, gesturing me instead toward a tweeded loveseat.

Marta riffled through some documents in a desk drawer before sitting across from me in a matching armchair. She wore a patent belt high on her waist that forced her stomach outward and created a convenient podium on which to rest a manila file with my name ("Severn, Julia") written on the tab.

I recognized the Workshop insignia atop what appeared to be my school transcript.

"It is not specified by the discouragements," said Marta, "but in the same way that prayer is discouraged, so are regressions or any kind of psychic foray, unless supervised by me."

She asked me to explain my attack situation.

"In your own words," she said, as though she'd already heard my story from someone else, probably Alwyn.

I told her about Madame Ackermann, my stenographer demotion, Colophon Martin, and so on.

"You've had sex with this Mr. Martin," Marta said.

"No," I said.

"In your own words, please."

"No," I said. What had Alwyn been telling her?

"It's apparent to me that she's enacting some kind of revenge on you," said Marta.

"Alwyn?" I said.

"Madame Ackermann," she said. "A revenge driven by the fact that you rejected her as a mother substitute. But your rejection did not stop her from acting 'motherly' toward you, and resenting the fact that her powers were on the wane at the precise moment that yours were on the upswing. And by powers," Marta explained, "I mean her sexual attractiveness and her potency as a mystic, the mutual degenerations of which, alas, tend to coincide."

Marta played with the bridge of her bifocals, sliding them up-down, up-down, and staring alternately at my file and then at me, as though, of the two, I was the one refusing to appear plausibly 3-D to her.

Madame Ackermann, I informed Marta, had no shortage of willing sexual partners.

"Everyone wants to have sex with her," I said, unclear why I was so determined to defend her on this point, but it did seem a kind of blasphemy to deny Madame Ackermann, even to this woman who would never meet her, her epic allure.

Then I explained the significance, by way of debunking Marta's occult mastery decline theory, of the double torque Madame Ackermann threw at her forty-third birthday party.

"Hmmm," Marta said. "Perhaps this Madame Ackermann is a psychic vampire. Perhaps she siphoned your energies in order to attack you."

"Meaning I attacked myself?" I asked. Marta made it sound as though I suffered from a psychic autoimmune disorder.

She recommended I do some reading on the subject in the Goergen's library.

"We've scheduled a renowned psychic vampire expert to give a presentation here in a few weeks," she said. "I'll remind you to attend."

She slid my file into her desk drawer and announced that it was time for us to perform an exercise called Mundane Egg.

"Many people have fissures or holes in their eggshells," Marta said, "that allow the foreign entities to invade."

She instructed me to lie on her sofa and visualize my eggshell.

"Now imagine it's thicker," she said.

Marta asked me to inspect my shell for cracks or holes. I imagined running my hands over the bony smoothness until I found an irregularity—a tiny checkmark-shaped fissure.

Marta instructed me to patch it.

"We'll do this exercise every session," Marta said. She warned that I'd find new holes to patch as my abilities for espying imperfections in my shell grew sharper.

"In order to get better I must become more skilled at detecting how I'm sicker?" I said.

"If that's how you need to see it," Marta said. "Regardless, you cannot take these exercises lightly. I don't want you to make poor choices."

"Choices," I said.

"I want you to channel your energy inward, not outward," she said. "I stress to my psychic attack patients—revenge is not a compelling therapeutic goal."

"Revenge is a very compelling therapeutic goal," I said. "It's just not a very noble one."

"For a woman of your exceptional abilities, these exercises are far more dangerous," she cautioned. "What you do when you leave here is your business. But while you are in my care, I cannot assist you with your . . . unconscious warfare."

I promised Marta to engage in no unconscious warfare. In good faith, I promised her this. I was innocent, at the time, of the lengths to which my unconscious would go to mock my inability to know my own warfare intentions.

On my way to the elevator, I ran into Alwyn.

"Hey," I said.

Alwyn didn't recognize me at first, her eyes glancing off me with chilling indifference.

"Oh," she said, catching herself. "Hi."

Her smile unnerved me. I knew, now, what casually stony person hid beneath.

I followed her to the concierge's desk. En route she caught me up on what she'd learned about Madame Ackermann's movements. She'd been to a spa in New Mexico.

She also told me, displaying a recent *New York Times* article, that Madame Ackermann had been in the news in conjunction with the surgical impersonators case I'd first heard about at the Regnor panel. There'd been a sharp rise in reports of surgical impersonator sightings (i.e., people refashioning their faces to look like people who had died) in and around New York City, prompting a Manhattan criminologist to speculate that these impersonators were part of a terrorist group engaging in civilian psychological warfare. A number of notable American psychics, including Madame Ackermann, had become interested in the case—they assumed these impersonators to be astral imprints whose sudden abundance suggested there'd been a meaningful "rupture" in the astral membrane.

Hilariously, Alwyn said, the psychics had positioned themselves on the side of reason; Madame Ackermann was even quoted in the *Times* article as saying that a band of surgical impersonators acting at the behest of (and funded by) a terrorist leader was, comparatively speaking, "an unlikely scenario."

I noticed Borka across the lobby, reading a butcher-papered book. She waved to me. I waved back.

"Who is that woman?" Alwyn asked.

"She's skin-care royalty," I said.

"Really," Alwyn said.

"Her name means bedbug," I said. Then I started to correct myself—her name didn't mean bedbug—but I'd already forgotten what it was that it meant.

"She more resembles a praying mantis, don't you think?" Alwyn said.

"I guess," I said.

"She's astonishingly ugly," Alwyn said. "I hope she finds a better face soon. Don't you?"

"I like her," I said.

I was, I'd noticed, one of the few. Borka did not socialize with the other plastic surgery patients—the baronessas and the wives of import moguls, the members of the varied Austro-Hungarian aristocracies with whom she, in the outside world, presumably mingled. Whenever she passed the card-playing quartets in the lobby, mean whispers fizzed in her wake.

For some reason, however, Borka made me feel at home. Also she taxonomized humans using inscrutable animal metaphors that never failed to amuse me. People she didn't like were half-dachshunds, people she did like—for example, me—were beetles.

Alwyn suggested I join her for tea in the dining hall. I agreed, even though I was made nauseous by the tea they served between meals, called liver tea because it detoxified the liver, the organ most weakened by psychic attacks.

"So," Alwyn asked, "how's the work?"

I assumed she meant my first session with Marta. The airiness of her tone renewed my paranoia that she'd shared with Marta inaccurate information about me.

"It's fine," I said. "But I'm a little curious . . . I'm concerned . . . what I mean is, I'm wondering what it is that you tell Marta."

Alwyn regarded me, bemused.

"How can I say this," Alwyn said, "so that you don't take this the wrong way."

"By wondering if I'll take something the wrong way," I said, "you're guaranteeing that I won't."

"You're the last person to be trusted to portray an accurate version of yourself," she said.

"You, meanwhile, are the first person Marta should trust," I said.

Alwyn stopped mid-stride.

"I've never told her anything you wouldn't eventually have told her," she said.

"OK," I said.

"OK," she said, as though the matter were settled.

"But," I said, "I'm a little concerned that you might tell her something that I would never tell her because I don't believe it to be true."

"Such as?" she said.

"Such as the ridiculous theory that Madame Ackermann wanted me to use her as a mother substitute."

"Only you would find that theory ridiculous," Alwyn said. "Madame Ackermann is a medium. A person through whom dead people speak."

"Believe me," I muttered. "When I was with her, no one was speaking through that woman."

I circled back to my original worry.

"But you didn't tell Marta I had sex with Colophon."

Alwyn pulled at her little bangs as if they were a furled shade she might draw down over her face.

"What?" she said.

I repeated my question.

"Did you?" she asked.

"Have sex with Colophon? Or tell Marta that I did?"

"Please," she said. "I know you're way smarter than to do that."

Alwyn returned to walking, briskly this time. I marveled at how she was able to project a blanket of certainty over a conversation that was pure jumble, stunning her listeners into shamed muteness. I didn't dare press her to elaborate on what I'd failed to understand, even though a few crucial logic steps were missing from our exchange, steps wherein actually useful information might reside.

The dining hall was empty. We tapped the hot urns, filled our cups with liver tea.

"I know I keep saying this," Alwyn said, "but we really do have a lot in common."

She proceeded to recount in dull detail the gist of a paper published by the *Journal of Mental Science* in the mid-seventies, one that established a telepathic link between mothers and babies, and proved that babies in orphanages—separated from their mothers and deprived of their first, and most intense, human bond—were forced to search further and further afield for this connection.

"Those babies were twice as likely, by the age of three, to exhibit psychic predilections," she said. "Would you say that's when your abilities first appeared?"

"I can't remember," I said.

"What I don't get is why I didn't develop any psychic abilities," she said. "My mother might as well have been dead for all I saw of her when I was little. Part of me suspects she must have read *that* article; she's so competitive, she probably spent just enough time with me to make sure I wouldn't develop powers that she hadn't developed herself."

"I suppose that's possible," I said. It sounded totally insane.

"My stepfather told me she tried to abort me."

"Recently?"

"She denied it when I confronted her. I'd deny it if I were her. It's curious, though, right? I mean obviously *I'm* curious. Why did she want to abort me? Maybe she did have some kind of . . . power. Maybe she knew I'd grow up to disappoint her more than she disappointed herself."

"I thought she was an internationally famous shampoo model," I said.

"You say that so dismissively. She had iconic hair."

"I'm marveling at the inadequacy of the phrase," I said.

"Because it was a hair campaign her face was barely visible, thus people assumed she was an unattractive woman whose unattractiveness a skilled photographer was forced to obscure. Passersby on the street would say, 'You're the Breck Girl!' And then, 'But you're so pretty.' She was a famous model, and yet she spent her life convincing others she had a face that didn't need hiding."

"That is kind of tragic," I conceded.

Alwyn pulled a tabloid magazine from her bookbag.

"Odd that you should be asking so much about my mother today," she said.

She showed me a photo of a woman in an ivory ski ensemble standing in front of a gondola at Gstaad, her hair a blue-ish auburn that winged to the sides as though attached to wires.

"That's her?" I said. "You're prettier. Not that it's a competition or anything," I hastened to add. But it was true. Alwyn's beauty came and went depending on how much sleep she'd had, or how much water she'd drunk, or how many people she'd annoyed that day, and this made a person want to keep examining her face because it was never the same.

"She doesn't look like a woman whose daughter has vanished," Alwyn said. "Though what that would look like, I can't say. I only know it's not that."

She finger-jabbed the page, creasing her mother backward at the knees.

"She still hasn't flown to Cincinnati to see my film," Alwyn said. "Has she?"

"I don't know," I said. "Has she?"

Alwyn scrutinized me.

"Just testing," she said. "I wanted to make sure you were obeying the rules. No psychic activity."

That wasn't the only reason she'd asked. She was deeply both-ered by her mother's and stepfather's failure to see her vanishing film. (I wanted to assure her: on this front we did have something in common.) I recalled the crying woman at the Regnor panel and her comment about library books that remained unread for decades. Alwyn and I, by committing our absences to film, had become objects whose neglect could be quantified.

"You're lucky you're being attacked," Alwyn sulked. "Someone cares a lot about you."

"Your mother cares about you," I said. "She hired a detective."

"Mmmm."

"She probably wants to make sure that you're not in any trouble or danger," I said.

Alwyn laughed.

"If you'd had a mother," she said, "you'd understand what a forgiving interpretation of motive that is."

"I had a mother," I said. "But I was spared the rite of passage of hating her."

"Which is exactly your problem," Alwyn said.

"Maybe more of a matter of inexperience than a problem," I said.

"Hate is a form of emotional attachment," she said. "You're denying yourself the only maternal bond available to you. This is your weakness, in my opinion. This is why you're being attacked."

"Because I don't hate my mother?" I said.

"Like it's so outlandish," Alwyn said. "What kind of woman would kill herself when she had a month-old baby? I'm sorry, but that's monstrous."

I picked up my liver tea. I drank what, for me, counted as a lethal dose.

"It's not monstrous," I said. "It's fucking tragic."

"I suppose you're one of those people who feel worse for Sylvia Plath than for her two children," she said.

This was true.

"I don't understand how a woman could do such a thing," Alwyn said. "I don't understand it at all."

"Maybe that's *your* problem," I said coldly. "Thinking it can be understood."

Two weeks after my arrival at the Goergen, I received irrefutable proof that I was getting better. Or maybe it was proof that the pills I'd been taking in New York had been cleansed from my system thanks to the liver tea and the colonics to which I'd been subjected, and the bookbinding hobby I'd picked up, maybe too the Mundane Egg visualizations I did every day with Marta, even though I always left her office feeling dirty and ashamed.

Regardless of the cause, after more than a year of psychic blindness, I was able again to see.

On my fourteenth night at the Goergen, Helena, a plastic surgery patient from Budapest, blustered into the dining hall.

"My engagement ring is gone!" she announced. Her left hand spasmed above her head, lacking the ballast of the very large diamond she'd made certain we noticed, rattling the gem against table surfaces when she ate, her hand otherwise seemingly paralyzed by its amazing shackle, the fingers slack, the palm upturned, as though awaiting something—a kiss, a nail.

Perhaps I was reading too much into her. Borka had told me: Helena was not a lucky girl ("girl" employed by Borka as an emotional category—Helena was in her fifties). This engagement would be Helena's fourth marriage; her previous husbands had left her, two of them had beaten her. But on the plus side, said Borka, she'd started out as a secretary, and very poor, so at least she'd married her way to money.

"It's not all ditch water," Borka said.

An orderly hurried Helena into a chair and urged cold compresses upon her. Helena's three-day-old face-lift was in the delicate stage; intense emotions were contraindicated. A man in a white suit took notes while the rest of us hovered. Her ring, Helena told us, had been stolen from her locker while she soaked in the thermal baths.

"I'll post a reward," Helena said to us, the silently gathered. "To whomever finds the thief, I shall express my gratitude in a manner known as handsome."

I heard her tell another plastic surgery patient that she'd lost the engagement ring her first husband had given her, too. "Though it was impossible *not* to lose that ring," Helena confided. "The diamond was the size of a lentil!"

Back at our table, Borka and I gossiped.

"It probably fell down a drain," I said of the ring. The Goergen featured an unnerving number of drains, not only in the showers or puncturing the walkways between the thermal baths but in rooms usually immune to deluges—mine, for example. I'd found a drain underneath my bed, implying that the room would be hosed out once I left, my various residues cleansed. Maybe the drain was regulation. Who knew. I tried not to think about it. Whenever I lay on my bed, I repeated in my head this sentence: *I am contaminating the scene. I am contaminating the scene.*

"It is for the best that she not marry this man," Borka said.

"She's still going to marry him, I'd imagine," I said.

Borka appeared traumatized by this suggestion.

"She cannot," she said. "A lost engagement ring means the marriage cannot happen."

Borka drew a finger across her throat.

"If she marries him she'll die?" I said.

"Maybe only the living kind of dying," Borka said. In the Hungarian countryside, she informed me, people believed in the existence of beneficent meddlers who broke up bad marriages before they happened. In ancient times this was accomplished by the destruction of the dowry, for example the disappearance of a herd of livestock.

"But of course it is just a folktale to allow for the theft of jewelry and sheep," she said.

"My mother lost her engagement ring," I said.

Borka was unimpressed, much as she'd been when I'd told her that my mother was dead. I'd come to expect such reactions: she was slightly autistic, Borka was, but aware enough to know that she *should* respond differently. As a result, these confessions of mine made her tense; she seemed to register them as a rebuke.

"And she persisted in marrying my father," I said, trying to apply a happy spin, also to assure her—I expected her to be nobody other than who she was.

"Indeed," Borka said. "And look what happened to her."

"Well . . ." I said.

"When a woman is enchanted by unhappiness, there's little that anyone, even a beneficent meddler, can do to dissuade her," she said.

"I thought you said the beneficent meddlers didn't exist," I said.

"I said they were probably thieves," she replied, her tone embittered for reasons I couldn't connect to the loss of rings.

That night I had a vivid dream.

The locker room could have been any locker room in any former Eastern bloc country—tiled, steam-noisy, the locker doors painted noxious shades of citrus, the vibe vaguely gas-chamberish. A little girl stood naked while a naked woman—her mother, I guessed— dried her back, her breasts and haunches bobbling with the effort.

The mother disappeared to the lavatories; the girl pulled on her sweater, her too-short pants. Beside her, a young woman disrobed with professional efficiency, quick and fluid. At first I did not recognize her—Helena was a blonde now, and thirty-odd years older. She removed her engagement ring, its diamond minuscule, more of a chip than a stone, and placed it in her locker. Without padlocking the door, she, too, disappeared to the lavatories.

Sneaky as a shadow, the young girl slipped her hand into the locker. She posed in front of a long mirror, hand against her cheek, stolen quarry glinting on her finger.

"I" stood behind her.

As in my previous regressions, I did not appear in reflective surfaces. My consciousness was not embodied, though I inflicted on this world my ghostly void. When I stood before the locker room mirror, a white spot in the shape of a person appeared where I should have been, as though someone had taken an eraser to a charcoal drawing, rubbed me out.

The girl's mother called her. The girl stashed the ring in the shallow coin pocket of her pants, but as she hurried toward her mother's voice the ring jogged loose and rolled onto the tiles. It carved a wide ellipsis, its orbit narrowing and quickening toward the drain. The girl fell to her knees and, trying to intuit the ring's trajectory, snatched at the future space it might inhabit. But then she was distracted by something—me, it seemed—and missed her chance to grab the ring before it disappeared through the drain's vertical slots.

The girl stared at the drain before returning her gaze toward me, as though I were to blame for the ring's loss, as though I were the thief.

I awoke to my alarm at 6:30 a.m.

I dressed, ate very little breakfast, did Mundane Egg with Marta, ate very little lunch, took the elevator to the basement to soak in the thermal baths. I'd felt vague all day, my post-dream self like an organ transplant slow to take. I grabbed my towel from the bath attendant. I shakily undressed. I needed, after each slipper removal, to rest on the wooden bench that paralleled the lockers.

Even so, my sense of disequilibrium surged.

I lay on the floor, the tiles against my cheek like hot teeth. At this point, I believe I fell asleep. Again I dreamed, or thought I was dreaming, because again I saw the drain and the ring falling into it, over and over I saw this, I saw the younger Helena, I saw her returning to her locker to discover her ring missing, I saw her telling her fiancé outside a restaurant that she had lost his ring, and I saw him wanting very badly, were it not for the sidewalk spectators, to hit her. I saw all of this except that my eyes were open, and I could hear Borka berating the bath attendant for failing to call a doctor when a doctor was needed.

"But she looks so happy," the attendant said.

When the doctor arrived he asked me hyper-articulated questions most people could not fail to understand.

"Did you check the drains?" I asked. All I could see, still, was a drain, over which the doctor's features were superimposed.

The doctor shone a penlight in my pupils.

"Helena's ring," I said, "did you check the drains?"

"Of course they checked the drains," said Borka.

"Can you tell me the date of your menstrual cycle?" asked the doctor.

"All of them?" I asked.

"All of the drains were cleaned yesterday," the attendant said.

"Just the last cycle," the doctor said.

I flipped onto my stomach; I crawled across the floor.

"Even a rough estimate," said the doctor, following me.

I pried the drain's grate loose with a fingernail.

The string was very long; whoever tied it to the grate's under-side wanted to make sure that a flashlight beam, flashed into the drain, wouldn't snag Helena's diamond.

I pulled until the ring flipped onto the tile floor.

I smothered it in my fist.

"Has it been one month?" asked the doctor. "Two?"

"Who did this?" asked Borka, without a touch of curiosity.

"It's important that I know," the doctor said.

My body tingled with endorphins. The ring in my hand required no coddling to tell me its tale of future sadness, Helena married to a man who killed her daily.

"It doesn't matter," I said, pushing the ring away from me. The metal radiated a repulsive sliminess I did not dare absorb. "I haven't menstruated in over a year."

That night, we received a memo under our doors.

"Dear Guests," it read. "Your discretion and relaxation are our utmost treasures. Memory is unnecessary work. To forget is to respect the past, and to enable your pleasant future."

Soon everyone knew about my role in the recovery of Helena's ring. I could sense their knowing most forcefully in the lobby, a space unwisely constructed of palissandro bluette marble, a stone touted for its properties of thought amplification. The robed women in the club chairs emanated what I can only compare to a wireless signal that would have measured five full bars; via these frequencies we were bound.

Borka, meanwhile, installed herself as my bodyguard, escorting me to meals, protecting me from the other guests.

"Why did you hide from me the true you?" she said.

"There was nothing to hide," I assured her. "That part of me was dead."

"You must have missed yourself," she said.

"I did at first," I said. "But then I figured, what's gone is gone."

She owl-eyed me weightily.

"I'm sure you have a lot of experience in that area," she said.

"Me?" I said.

"Because of your mother," she said.

"Oh," I said. "I never experienced her as missing, though. I was so young, you see, when it happened."

"When what happened?" Borka asked.

"When she . . . died," I said. Borka's inability to process basic tragedies meant that she might not register the distinction between plain dying and suicide.

"But you have visited her," she said. "So now you can miss her."

"I've never visited her," I said. "I've never been able to."

"Because it is beyond your abilities?" she said.

"Because I am not invited," I said.

Borka's eyes teared up, though probably I mistook for tears the light from the lobby's chandelier silvering the ointment she rubbed on her lids, preparing her face for its eventual surgery.

Alwyn, when she caught wind of the ring kerfuffle, acted mad.

"I'm obligated to tell Colophon that you've broken the rules," she said.

Beneath her sternness, however, she seemed oddly energized by my breach.

"But I didn't *do* anything," I said. "It's because they don't allow any stupid pills in this place."

"If you don't abide by the discouragements, you won't get better," she said.

"Evidently I am better," I said.

"Trust me," she said. "You aren't."

I did try to abide by the discouragements. I did. It wasn't my fault that soon I was being propositioned in the lobby, the thermal baths, the lavatories. An Austrian woman wanted me to find out whether or not her husband was cheating on her while she recovered from the chin tuck she hadn't wanted but which he'd given her anyway for her birthday. A French woman kept a journal about her sexual activities with a coworker that she worried her teenage daughter was reading in her absence. A former model wanted to know if the tiny newborn she'd abandoned in the waiting room of a doctor's office seventeen years ago had found a happy home.

I rebuffed them all. What good had ever come from my abilities? I'd never been able to control them. Always someone suffered; often that someone was me. My good intentions meant nothing. Asleep, I proved powerless to refuse the voyages. I intruded upon a ski chalet where a man with a bald spot dumped spaghetti into a colander while another man with a bald spot massaged his neck. I visited a girl trying on a gaping orange G-string for an audience of three boys. I visited a little grave.

None of these visions were conclusive, or so I told myself. Nor were they even terribly vivid: the colors muddy, the image flickering like a movie screened on a projector with a hair stuck in the lens. They could have been dreams. But nor did I seek to corroborate them as valid regressions. I did not ask the woman with the chin tuck to show me a picture of her husband so that I could cross-reference him with the image of the bald men I kept in my head. I did not ask the French woman if she owned an orange G-string. I did not ask the former model if her tiny baby, when she'd left him in the doctor's office, was breathing.

Instead I provided answers to their questions with a fortune-teller's vagueness. You are the current cause of your husband's sexual fulfillment. You inspire others with your spirit of adventure. Happiness comes to those who are well-rested.

But while I soon became one of the most popular guests at the Goergen, I remained unimpressed, even disenchanted. My brain was flabby, clumsy, a geriatric detective that farted on the job. Even at my strongest point—at the Workshop, while regressing for Madame Ackermann—my successes were sheer accidents, flailing sword thrusts into the psychic ether.

So I decided—in the interests of reducing the harm I could cause by amateurishly bungling about in such matters—to do some secret exercises. This, I rationalized, was the responsible way to manage what was going to occur despite me.

First I stole a rump roast from the kitchen and stashed it atop my armoire, wrapped in an ammonia-soaked towel to hide the stink from the chambermaids. Three times a day I lay on my bed, arms and feet canted outward in a modified corpse pose, and tried to petrify the roast.

It became for me a little bit like praying.

I did not check my work for a week. When I unwrapped the meat—noting with a surge of hopefulness that I detected no putrifying stink whatsoever—I found a caramel-colored geode, half the size of the original rump and five times the weight. On one flank I'd created a crystallized ulcer that allowed me to see the jeweled interior, like the peephole into a Fabergé egg.

I tried not to be too proud of my work. Pride, Madame Ackermann used to say—not that we ever believed her—is a psychic's endgame. Still, I had reason to be impressed, at least a little bit. Also, coincidentally or not, my health, for the first time in fourteen months, improved. I suffered no migraines. The eczema on my hands receded. The wolf, when I blinked, was gone.

When Alwyn asked me how I was feeling, I told her, *I feel won-*

derful. My brain tingled as though it were bobbing in carbonated liquid. I viscerally recalled the way I'd felt when I'd been sitting in the Barcelona chair, regressing in order to save Madame Ackermann's reputation. I'd felt lightweight. I'd felt disembodied. I'd felt fiery and alive. I missed that person—a person eradicated by all the medications I'd been taking in New York, and to what end? My suffering wasn't minimized, and these cures had killed off the best part of me. The transgressor. The Peeping Tom. The spy.

Two days after I'd unwrapped the rump roast, I skipped lunch and visited, for the first time since I'd discovered Helena's ring, the baths.

I was alone, everyone else at lunch.

I chose the hottest bath—more of a swimming pool—and eased myself in one step at a time, the water to my shins, now my hips, now my shoulders. I floated on my back. I noticed for the first time that the skylight overhead was nearly identical to the skylight at the Regnor—same beveled corners, same twining snake-or-ivy.

It gave me an exercise idea that I felt, after my petrification success, skilled enough to attempt.

I centered myself beneath the skylight and tried to imagine myself back to the Regnor, a place I'd once been, a place where there'd be a fossilized placeholder for me to slip inside. This was the easiest form of regression because it allowed you to travel along the familiar byways of memory and required you to be no more foreign a person than a past version of yourself. However, risks were involved. We initiates were advised against using our own lives too frequently as practice fodder; revisiting one's memories could result, over time, in a form of self-erasure.

I gave it a try.

A busier skylight blotted out the Goergen's plainer one—it was like watching a text written in invisible ink exposed to heat, the hidden letters burning to the foreground. I saw a giant clock, the hour frozen at 2:29 p.m., the second hand poised, spear-like, over the belly of the six. I stared at that second hand. I tried to activate the space, break through the static barrier that froze this moment in time.

No success.

I imagined myself diving into water, but this felt wrong. Water could too easily, and without yielding apparent wreckage, accommodate a foreign object. Once, as Madame Ackermann lay on her futon couch, snoozing through another failed regression, she'd started crying in her sleep.

This is my only legacy, she'd whimpered. *I make scars in time.*

So I envisioned the barrier as layers of transparent muscle, fat, skin. (I'd been born by cesarean section, my umbilical cord wrapped three times around my neck.) I dove headfirst into the barrier. It stretched, it resisted. I dove a second time and the barrier tore. I heard amplified sounds: the electric buzz of the clock, the crick of a heater vent.

I opened my eyes. This lobby was not the lobby of the Regnor. There was an elevator, but a smaller one. A wall was covered with mirrored tiles that gridded the lobby's reflection into cocktail-napkin-sized squares of visual information. People in winter coats spoke French.

The elevator disgorged a trio of women, one of whom was crying.

I searched for someone I recognized and found one person. I knew her from somewhere—as Borka might say, she was a big déjà vu for me. I could see her in the gridded reflection, but when I turned, I could not locate her in the lobby. She existed only in the mirror.

I was comically slow to realize that this girl, she was me. Unlike during my previous regressions, I did not register in the mirror as a foggy blank.

I was there. Or rather *here*—wherever here was. Based on the outfits worn by the lobby loiterers, I guessed here was, temporally speaking, the early eighties.

The elevator opened again. Four women exited, including the actress I'd met at the Regnor's bar. She was the same age she'd been when I'd encountered her in New York, even though, based on our surroundings, we were now occupying a moment in time preceding that one by twenty or thirty years.

I recalled how the bartender had never acknowledged Irenke, how he'd placed both whiskey sours in front of me as though I were sitting at the bar alone.

From his perspective, maybe I was. Irenke was an astral imprint. Despite the fact that my medications should have blunted such incursions, she'd managed, somehow, to visit me.

Irenke sat on the couch opposite mine. She slung her coat across her lap. She tried to flag a waiter.

"Hey," I said. "Irenke, right?"

She lit a cigarette, eyed me along the barrel. She didn't appear to recognize me.

"Julia," I reminded her. "I don't mean to bother you—"

"Except that you do bother me," Irenke interrupted. "Every day."

"Really?" I said. I had no recollection of this. So far as I knew, I hadn't seen Irenke since the Regnor.

"Every day like clockwork," she said.

Her claim unnerved me. It also thrilled me. It suggested that I'd regressed without any knowledge or memory of doing so; I might even be a living-dead trancer. Without a stenographer present, who could say?

Irenke, fingers throttling her cigarette, was evidently in a mood.

"Let's try this again," I offered.

"Too late," she said. "We've been overridden. Or overrode. I never was very good at grammar."

"What do you mean, overridden?" I asked.

"You're the paranormal expert," she said. "Ask one of your professors. The past is not past if it is always present. Memory is an act of murder."

She loosened a buckle on her dress.

"I'm fat," she complained. "I shouldn't eat cream soup. Do you know what this is called? A self-belt. Such an ugly term. Sylvia Plath should have written a poem called 'Self Belt.' She liked those staccato word punches: Black shoe. Fat black stake. God-ball. The villagers never liked you. *Achoo*."

"We spoke about Sylvia Plath the last time we met," I said. "Or rather, the time I met you in New York."

She wasn't, I noticed, wearing her pendant.

"You must have me mistaken for another girl," she said. "I've never been to New York."

She stood, smoothed her skirt, tossed her empty cigarette packet on the coffee table.

"Be right back," she said.

A weeping woman strode past Irenke, clipping her elbow. Irenke glared at her.

In my head I recited the final lines of "Death & Co."

The dead bell,
The dead bell.
Somebody's done for.

A waiter appeared.

"Drink for the madame?" he asked in French.

"Whiskey sour," I said.

"And for the madame's friend?"

"Make it two," I said.

Irenke returned before our drinks arrived. She unfoiled a new pack of cigarettes.

Two more weeping women exited the elevator.

"Guess they didn't get the part," Irenke said.

"What part?"

"The part of the dead girl," Irenke said. "There's a casting call upstairs."

"Huh," I said. "Well, there's probably an upside to not getting *that* role."

"My mother's the director," Irenke said. "I've heard she can be very abusive to people who disappoint her. Which is why I'm nervous about auditioning."

I recalled that Irenke had told me about her mother at the Regnor, how this mother had given her the necklace and called Irenke her "muse."

"Don't worry," I said. "You're a shoo-in."

"A what?" she said.

"You're her muse," I said. "How could she give the role to anyone else?"

Irenke appeared horrified by this suggestion.

"You think a mother should cast her own daughter in a porn film?" she said.

"Your mother directs porn films?" I said.

I knew, then, who this mother was.

Was this why Irenke had visited me—or rather, why I had visited her?

I cased Irenke for proof that she was Dominique Varga's daughter. I'd only seen Varga once, in *Not an Exit*; my brain conjured a woman with a jutting, aggressive face, one unwilling to succumb to the victimization of an anonymous hand, even as her motionless body did. Irenke's face, meanwhile, melted downward, failing to refute the melancholy gravity that pulled at it.

"But she doesn't know she's my mother," Irenke clarified. "I only found out recently myself."

"And so . . . you're here to tell her?" I asked.

Irenke laughed.

"That would be a mistake, don't you think?"

Probably, I thought.

"You're here to spy on her, then," I said.

"I'm here to *audition*," Irenke said. "I want to see if she knows who I am. Don't you think a mother should recognize her own daughter? Even if she abandoned her at birth?"

"I didn't know that Dominique Varga had a daughter," I said.

"Of course you didn't," Irenke said. "She erased me. She over-rode me. A woman like her couldn't be a mother."

The waiter appeared with our whiskey sours.

"I didn't order this," Irenke said.

"I did," I said.

"What is it?" she said.

She took a sip.

"It's good," she said. "I like it."

We clinked glasses. Irenke withdrew a camera from her purse and asked me to take her picture.

"I want to remember this day," she said. She wheeled a com-pact from her coat pocket and reapplied her lipstick.

She tried, with mixed results, to smile.

I took her picture anyway.

"Beautiful," I said.

"So," Irenke said. "Have you decided yet?"

"Decided what?" I said.

"Do you want me to help you punish her or not?" she asked.

"Punish who?" I said.

"I'm an expert at ruining people's lives," she continued. "It's the one talent I possess."

She flashed her drink, already half gone.

The elevator dinged. Two red-eyed women exited, followed by a woman obscured by long, black hair. Her step, unlike that of her dejected elevator mates, was springy, elated. She noticed Irenke, absorbed again in her makeup compact, picking at her lashes. The woman's shoulders flicked together. She sped her gait and cut to the left, skimming so near to my armchair that her hand glanced off my cheek as she passed.

She hurried past the doorman, who followed her with his eyes. *Madame Ackermann*. For certain, it was she, her hair shivering thickly across her back as she strode into the street without checking for traffic, hailed a cab, was gone.

My cheek burned where she'd touched it.

She'd been upstairs, I thought. She'd possibly met Varga. Apparently, too, she knew Irenke, or at least *of* her, and had chosen, for whatever reason, to avoid her. What did she know that I didn't? Quite a lot. We'd funneled our way back through the same regression wormhole, Madame Ackermann and I, but she was leagues ahead of me.

I considered chasing after her, confronting her, threatening her, even (*I'm onto you*), but decided against it. Psychics died doing this sort of thing. We were data collectors, not participants. Madame Ackermann's mentor, for example, had drowned as an astral stowaway on a doomed Great Lakes cruise ship in search of a grandfather she'd hoped to save. Madame Ackermann, as her stenographer, had recorded her final, shrieking words before the water sucked her down.

"You know," I said to Irenke. "I *could* use your help with a different matter."

I told her that I wanted to accompany her on her audition. I wanted to meet her mother.

"That's impossible," Irenke said. This request spooked her. "I'm sorry, no. She doesn't want to see you."

"Your mother?" I said. "But she doesn't even know me."

Irenke fell silent.

"Why do you want to ruin people's lives?" I asked her.

"This isn't about what I want," Irenke said. "It's about what *you* want."

"But I don't want to ruin anyone's life."

Agitated, she drained her sour.

"Look," Irenke said, calming herself. "I'm trying to make it up to you in the only way I can. Please. For my sake. Accept my help."

I had no idea what she was talking about, but she wasn't going to help me in the way I wanted to be helped until I relented. What was the harm in saying yes? I could pretend to accept her offer, I'd let her think that she was doing me this favor. Because then maybe she'd be more amenable to doing me an *actual* favor, and introduce me to her mother.

"Thank you," I said. "I'd love your help."

After dinner, I stopped by the concierge's office to check my e-mail. I had one message, from aconcernedfriend; though it was against the discouragements I clicked on Madame Ackermann's video. What hurts you makes you stronger, I rationalized. And I needed to be stronger. I'd seen Madame Ackermann in a hotel lobby in Paris, circa 1980-something. We were fated to collide in the astral ether; I wanted to be up to our future encounters.

The fog registered as green-toned, though perhaps this was due to the concierge's crappy monitor. I watched the entire attachment. It centered me.

Then I wrote Colophon a quick note. *Did Dominique Varga have a daughter?*

Then—though it violated the vanishing contract I'd signed— I wrote an e-mail to Professor Hales. Professor Hales, I reminded myself, was so freakishly self-involved that he couldn't be bothered to care that I'd vanished. He likely hadn't noticed I'd left the Workshop.

Dear Professor Hales, I wrote. *Wondering if you could tell me a bit more about regressions via memory byways, and if you've ever heard of a phenomenon called "override." I ask because I'm interning as a fact-checker at a new parapsychology journal based in the former Yugoslavia called* Mundane Egg.

I reread what I'd written. This notion of override was interesting. Though not the word used by my father, *override* might well have been the reason cited for his refusal to hypothesize about my mother, a request I made frequently as a girl. For example: we are on a beach, he and I. We watch a boy build a sandcastle alone while his mother sunbathes on a towel with a book, we watch a pair of sisters digging holes while their mother hauls buckets of water from the shore. Which mother would she have been, I ask him, the tuned-out sunbather or the hauler of buckets?

This would elicit from him an evasive response, the gist of which was this: Of course it would make sense for me to claim that she would have been the hauler of buckets, because what's the harm in conjuring a mother of exquisite selflessness? My response would not be a truthful attempt to answer your question, it would be an attempt to compensate for your loss by creating an ideal person whose absence you can mourn unreservedly. However, this puts me in the position of making her into someone she was possibly not; it forces me to falsely represent her to you, and in doing so I become, not the keeper of her memory, but the re-creator of her past, and that role makes me uncomfortable; also I believe it is, in the long run, a disservice to her, because you will grow up missing a mother that you would never have experienced, had she not died. And this strikes me as a second kind of death, a more complete and horrible death, to be annihilated and replaced by a hypothetical person who is not remotely you, thus I think it is better that she remain a quasi-mystery, a pleasant unknown, than an absence filled with compensatory narratives supplied by your guilty father.

Of course he never said this, but he did, in his way, say this. How, as a child of five, of seven, I came to understand what he meant without his ever articulating it was less a measure of my psychic abilities than of my skill for interpolation, a skill that motherless children, raised in a preverbal communication void, come to master. Because he was telling me too, without telling me: She would not have been a hauler of buckets. She was not selfless. She would have been an absence even if she'd been there. And while it was true that he didn't want to do a disservice to her memory, his reasons were maybe less noble than he was comfortable admitting to himself. He didn't want her turned into a saint because she didn't deserve sainthood. He was not so generous that he could allow her a posthumous glory she had not earned.

I respected his caution. Some things, once done, can never be completely undone. Only a trace remains of the original, a scar in time.

Before sending the e-mail to Professor Hales, I added a sentence about my boss at *Mundane Egg*, an attractive brunette who was a huge fan of his last book.

I checked my account one last time; Colophon had responded. *no daughter.*

—∞—

The halls were empty. Dinner had ended long ago. Alwyn, thankfully, hadn't shown—she'd had a meeting with the head of the Goergen's privacy division, because her detective had tracked her to Vienna and was sending her menacing postcards—so I was spared having to lie to her about what I'd done all day. Lately Alwyn emitted a carcinogenic unhappiness that rendered me so anxious that I'd found myself, at one point, making an odd grunting noise with my back teeth like my father sometimes did when he was around me.

From behind the guest room doors came sitcom laughter. The Goergen, at this hour, resembled the interior of an insane person's medicated brain, the halls like vacant neural pathways lit by the occasional lunatic spark of activity.

I didn't want to go to my room. I'd started to find discomforting the height of the ceilings. To recline on my bed was not unlike lying at the bottom of a well.

Instead I took the elevator to the fifth floor and stopped by Borka's suite, for which she'd paid extra, but she didn't answer when I knocked, and no wonder—when I unlocked my door I found her sitting on my bed wearing her coat and a headscarf.

"I have a treat for you," she said.

Borka unhangered my parka; she zipped me into it like I was her child.

"Where are we going?" I asked.

"We are going not-here," she said.

"But that's discouraged," I said.

Borka rolled her eyes.

"Distinguishing us from the other guests," she said, "is that we are not cows."

From the street, Gutenberg Square appeared shabbier than it did from my window; the apartment building entrances were graffitied, the square itself populated by drug addicts and paparazzi. Borka called them nodders and snappers.

"There's one snapper in particular," she said. "He's followed me for decades. Now I find I miss him when he isn't there. You know how these hateful people can become a daily part of normal."

Borka pulled me through the shadows of the buildings and along the cooler perimeter of the nearby woods. As I swayed down the sidewalk, Borka sped along at a hasty clip ahead of me. She wouldn't take a taxi because, she said, the taxi drivers were spies, and besides, the metro led to the house her husband had purchased right before he died.

I asked why he'd wanted to leave their hometown of Budapest.

"Because Budapest is the City of Egrets," she said.

She means the City of Regrets, I thought, then reminded myself— this was Borka.

City of egrets, city of tall, thin, spooky, watchful people.

We emerged from the metro in a neighborhood where apartment buildings yielded to stand-alone houses. The air was dirtier, the heated smog hovering at the height of the rain gutters in a tobacco-colored band.

Borka rang the doorbell of a stone house. A silhouette scurried back and forth in front of the parlor windows.

"My maid," Borka said. "She loves to sit in my chair when I'm out and read her smutty papers."

Finally a woman in a robe unlocked the door.

"This," Borka said to me, "is Sun. It means hedgehog in Magyar."

"That's her given name?" I asked.

"Of course it is given," Borka said. "I gave it to her."

Sun led us to a living room with walls painted the black-blue of an aquarium for nocturnal fish. Borka prowled around a wing chair—testing the spring of the cushions, brushing her palms over the armrests, inspecting it for illegal use.

Sun asked Borka a question to which Borka testily responded.

"I told her we don't want dinner," Borka said. "Only some tea."

"I'd like some dinner," I said.

"It will have to be cold," Borka said. "I cannot tolerate food smells in the evening."

"Cold is fine," I said.

Borka sat in the wing chair and busied herself by reading one of Sun's newspapers.

I ate the cold dinner Sun delivered while Borka flipped through her paper with the rage of old people in charge of television remotes. Finally she settled on a page, her blinkless Strigiforme eyes seeming to literally absorb its contents. Folding the paper, she showed me an article accompanied by two photos, one of a man caught on a short-circuit video camera, one of a second man, or maybe it was the same man, wearing a tie and smiling.

"He is pretending to be this young fellow," she pointed to the tie guy, "who jumped in front of a train."

"Why would he do that?" I said.

"Because he was sad," she said. "Though I can't say why. He had a beautiful wife and three boys. He managed a hedge fund and had recently bought a house in New Jersey."

"The sad man's pretending to be the happier man?" I said.

"No," she said. "The man who jumped in front of the train was sad. And this one had his face fixed to look like the sad man's face."

"Oh," I said, more interested now. "He's a surgical impersonator."

I examined the photographs. The two men looked alike but also not.

"So these impersonators exist," I said.

"Of course they exist. It's only people like you who believe ghosts are the more sensible explanation."

She continued reading, her lips moving.

"But what I don't understand," she said, "is why the dead man's wife is upset. Her husband killed himself. And she remarried to forget about him. And now she doesn't have to forget about him. What is so terrible about this?"

"Well," I began. As usual, Borka proved immune to standard emotional logic; it seemed injurious to her person to correct her understanding.

"If someone asked you to change your face to look like someone they loved, would you do it?" she said.

"Would *you*?" I said.

"Of course," she said. "I am heartless that way."

"You mean selfless," I said.

"Maybe it is because I do not have any special attachment to my face," she said. She poked her cheek. "This one is not even mine."

Borka folded the newspaper; she lay it atop the other papers stacked beside the room's tiny fireplace, over which loomed a massive marble mantle, as though any heat the fire might provide was an afterthought, really what she needed was a surface on which to place knickknacks. And knickknacks she had, a hamlet's worth of little china people holding shepherd crooks and parasols, trailing detritus in the porcelain aura that encased their feet—a family of ducks, a dog, a dropped bonnet.

Borka did not seem like the sort of woman to collect these sugary inanities, but perhaps she was compensating for the fact that mantles beg for photographs, and she had none. Not anywhere. I did not find this absence peculiar, however, because I knew from experience how unsettling it could be not to resemble the person once known as you. Whatever new face the car accident and the shitty surgeon had given her, it had required, for sanity's sake, the total eradication of the old one, even in pictures.

"Come," Borka said.

She led me to an upstairs study. From a desk drawer, she removed a perforated metal box.

"I wanted to show you this," she said.

"It's pretty," I said. It wasn't. "What is it?"

"A Japanese cricket cage," she said brusquely, as though, given my supposed gifts, this were a question I should be able to answer myself.

She withdrew from the interior a key attached to an elongated diamond of green Bakelite, embossed with the number thirteen.

Sitting at the desk, Borka wrote on a piece of blank card stock, her marks filling the entire white space, her penmanship buoyed by irregular aerial loops.

New York City. 152 West 53rd Street. Room 13. October 24, 1984. 4 p.m.–9 p.m.

"What's this?" I asked.

"You are invited," she said.

She closed my hand around the key. The chilly metal heated to skin temperature, then grew rapidly hotter until I was palming the equivalent of a live ash.

I dropped the key back into its cage.

"I'm sorry," I said. "I shouldn't."

"But it is no big deal for you," Borka said.

"I'm not allowed," I said. "I'm working for other people at the moment."

Borka appeared not to hear me.

"We can help each other," she said desperately. "I can give you what you most want to find. I can help you see her."

"Who?" I said. "Dominique Varga?"

Her eyes slid toward the floor.

"She's alive?" I said.

Borka nodded.

"How do you know?" I said.

"You don't trust me?" she said. "You should. I have your heart in mind."

She searched my face for something that she appeared both relieved and saddened not to find.

"Why do you care so much about her?" she said.

"Varga knew my mother," I said. "So maybe she could tell me about her. Since my mother will not let herself be known to me."

"You might learn things you'd prefer you hadn't," she said.

"I'm willing to chance it," I said.

"Also Varga's unreliable," said Borka. "She's an international liar."

"A lie is more valuable than nothing," I said.

Borka's eyes were the strangest color, brown with a ring of pale blue encroaching upon her pupils like a milk fungus.

She pressed my hand between hers.

"That's very true," she said. "In some cases, a lie can be more valuable than the truth."

"In some cases," I agreed.

She smoothed my hair with her hand.

"I will help you," she vowed.

"You will?" I said.

She handed me the cricket cage.

"We will help each other," she said, blinking.

Inwardly, I smiled. Classic Borka. She never gave something for nothing, not even a lie.

I removed the key from the cricket cage. Again the metal rocketed from cold to branding-iron hot. I dropped it into the pocket of my sweater.

I tried to return the cricket cage.

"No," Borka said. "You keep it. A gift."

"A bribe," I clarified.

Borka hugged me, smearing my hair with the softening ointment she rubbed on her face. She pressed her mouth against my skull so forcefully that I could feel her teeth.

"Silly Beetle," she said into my head. "As if there is a difference."

———— ⚬⚬⚬ ————

When Borka and I returned to the Goergen, nobody appeared to have noticed that we'd left.

I found this interesting.

The next morning I decided to go outside again. I spun through the revolving front doors, hunched against the sprung alarm, the bark of security dogs—but nothing.

Ha, I thought, as though I had gotten away with something sneaky. Then I realized I'd proved that we *were* cows, balking at a few white lines painted across a road. The discouragements were bullshit; maybe they existed as some form of thought experiment. Or thoughtless experiment, proving we'd failed to think for ourselves. How thoughtless can people be?

People can be remarkably thoughtless.

The park was empty at this hour, no nodders, no snappers. I sat on a bench to eat a roll and to better inspect, in the daylight, Borka's cage and key.

A sunglassed man entered the square. He wore coveralls and carried a canvas bag full of what sounded, when he set them on the octagonal paving stones, like tools. I decided that there was something suspicious about him, as though he'd determined which precise shade of brown promised to fade into most city backgrounds and render its wearer unmemorable, failing to register with witnesses save as a beigy blur.

Perhaps this man was Alwyn's detective. She'd barely left her room in the past three days, convinced that the detective was posing as a snapper in the square, one with a very powerful telephoto lens that might catch her, through the giant windows, in a first-floor common room.

It seemed, for once, that Alwyn was not being dramatic or paranoid.

The probable detective asked me a question in German.

I smiled.

"I said," the man said in English, "got a problem?"

"Thanks for noticing," I said.

The man finished his cigarette, checked his watch, opened his bag, and removed three telescoped metal tubes, which he lengthened and attached to one another via a flat, rotating platform.

"So you're a detective," I said.

"Huh?" the man said. He pulled a camera from his bag and affixed it to the top of the tripod he'd assembled. He loaded it with a Polaroid cartridge and photographed the pigeons at his feet. He yanked the Polaroid from the camera, shook it, peeled away the black skin. He stared at it. He showed it to me.

It was a Polaroid of pigeons.

"Do you mind?" he asked, pointing the camera at me. "I need a human being."

No question it was a bad idea to have my photo snapped by a probable detective in Gutenberg Square.

He dialed the focus. "Think about someone," he instructed.

"What kind of someone?"

"I tell people before I take their picture to think of a person they love. Then the picture will not only be a picture of their face. Because who cares about a face? A face is a hole in the landscape. How ugly," he said, pointing to the cricket cage. "Please, will you hold it?"

I held the cricket cage in my lap. I tried to think of a person I loved, but no one person stuck. Faces spun in blurry sequence. A sped-up odometer of faces.

"Another?" he asked. "Over there."

I shifted to a different bench. For some reason he used a flash, even though it was bright and getting brighter, the sun threatening to clear the roof of the easternmost building on Gutenberg Square.

I closed my eyes.

I opened them to total darkness. I couldn't see the buildings or the bench or the man or the pigeons.

Beside me was an animal; its hairs prickled against my forearm. It swung as though attached to a meat hook, then collapsed in a heap by my legs.

A coat.

I felt to the other side of me. A second coat.

My feet, when I moved them, encountered a battalion of shoes.

I was in a closet.

Then I heard voices.

"You're so proud to be a bastard," said a woman.

"A boy shouldn't ignore his talents," said a man.

Bed springs depressed.

"Tell me," the woman struggled to say as the man kissed her. "Tell me why you don't love me."

The man didn't respond.

"Tell me why or this stops now," the woman said.

The noises ceased. The man laughed.

"Because you're soulless," the man said. "And pathetic."

The noises resumed. There was wetness and gasping.

"I should be blamed for permitting you to fuck me," the woman said.

"No, for that you should be pitied," the man said.

"Pity me," the woman moaned. "Please."

The act was quick. Afterward there was silence, followed by crying.

I slid my hands along the door molding, feeling for the knob. I turned it.

Through an arched doorway I could see bodies on a bed, clothing askew.

I recognized this room.

The man still wore his shoes.

"Stay," the woman said. She clung to the man. "I love you."

The man unpeeled her hands from his torso.

"You're such a parasite," the woman said, voice rising. "A nothing."

Now I was certain: I had been in this room before, during one of my Barcelona chair regressions. I recognized the drapes, behind which, I knew, hid a young girl with a video camera. I recognized the intimidated and repulsed young man; I recognized the woman's hands, the ones that appeared to have squeezed many necks. Her face, however, remained a blur, as though she were a pedestrian caught in the periphery of a reality TV show, her head digitally smudged to avoid a lawsuit.

"The question we should be asking ourselves," the young man said, "is why I agreed to this."

"Because I'm the only contact you'll ever have with fame," the woman retorted. "I am the one successful work of art you'll ever make."

She reached toward him as he sat on the edge of the bed, cinched a shoelace.

"Pity me again," she said. "Please."

The man stood. He straightened his belt. He stepped on the woman's discarded clothing: a pair of jeans, a striped sailor shirt.

He yanked his jacket off a chair and left.

The woman curled herself around the absence on the bed, dredging from her body hideous scraping noises.

This went on for quite a while.

Then the woman was overcome by a case of hiccups, or what I initially mistook for hiccups.

In fact, the woman was laughing.

Clutching the bedsheet around her like a towel, she yanked the drapes open to reveal the young woman and a video camera on a tripod. The young woman appeared as a silhouette to me. She shivered; her dark boundaries blurred. Even so, I couldn't fail to recognize her. This was why, when I'd met Irenke at the Regnor, she'd struck me as familiar. I'd seen her before.

The woman kissed Irenke on the cheek, played with her hair.

"Let me get you a sweater," the woman said.

She walked toward my closet, sheet dragging over the floor-boards and toppling a spire of books. She flung wide the closet door and her face snapped into focus, her features sharp, unsheathed.

Up close, there was no mistaking who she was.

Dominique Varga reached toward me with a hand. I closed my eyes, I waited for her fingers to close around my throat and begin to squeeze.

"Stop squinting," the man said. "Smile a little."

He kneeled on the pavers, his camera against his face.

I reclined on the bench, overcome by wooziness. I felt as though I'd leapt from a speeding motorcycle. The sensation of sideways falling was impossible to shake.

I asked the concierge if he had a camera I could borrow.

He told me that cameras were not allowed at the Goergen for reasons that were likely very obvious to me.

"How about a flashlight?" I asked.

Back in my room, I shut myself into my wardrobe and beamed myself in the face with his flashlight, hoping to prompt another regression.

No regressions occurred.

I returned the flashlight and wrote an e-mail to Colophon. *Intriguing progress to report.*

I described to him my "encounter" with Dominique Varga and a woman named Irenke, while stressing to him that my regression had been accidental (I'd been, as Alwyn had surely reported to him, mostly pretty respectful of the discouragements). Then I watched the latest attachment from Madame Ackermann. She'd sent me a new version, one less obscured by fog. I could see the woman on the bed more plainly, she had long black hair and resembled, as she was meant to resemble, my mother—though "she" was no doubt Madame Ackermann.

I could imagine the dramatic arc of these attachments (and frankly I was impressed by the amount of time, money, and creative energy she was willing to dedicate to my attack). Madame Ackermann would become more and more visible, until the figure on the bed was unmistakably her, at which point she would address the camera with fake concern and say, *you poor thing, you look like you've seen a wolf.*

Then she'd laugh until she passed out. Or she'd tempt the video artist from behind his camera and have sex with him on the bed.

She was capable of any degree of blasphemy.

I dragged her e-mail into the trash.

Colophon, meanwhile, had e-mailed me back.

sounds like you witnessed the filming of "up-and-comers, coming, going" and who is this irenke

She was an actress, I wrote back. *She claims to be Varga's daughter.*

Colophon responded instantly.

varga had no daughter but if you talk to her again maybe she could help us however be careful she is probably unstable many women were obsessed with varga she had that effect

I told him I'd do my best. I waited for his next parry, a "congratulations" or some expression of enthusiasm or gratitude for what was a pretty significant breakthrough. Nothing.

Then I met Borka in the baths.

As we retrieved towels from the attendant, Borka badgered me about the key.

"Did you do it yet?" she asked.

I told her I had not done it yet. I needed more context. The key was not leading me anywhere.

"But this is the beauty of you, Beetle," she said. "You get your own context."

"Can't you tell me to whom this key belonged?" I asked.

"It's a hotel room key," she said. "It belonged to no one. And if I tell you what I'm looking for, you'll tell me what I'm looking for."

"That's the point of all this, I thought," I said.

She told me a little bit about her past, one that had nothing to do with the key, and truthfully seemed to have nothing to do with her. She told me about her dead husband, a gambling shut-in whom she'd cheated on. He'd given her the cricket cage as a present.

"He was a weak man," she said. "He wasn't up to the task."

"Of being your husband?"

"Of living," she said.

"And the key?"

"It was once in the possession of someone I might have loved," she said.

"Not your husband," I clarified.

She appeared pained. "Correct," she said.

I asked if she and her husband had had children. Borka adjusted the knot on her headscarf, hauling up on her jaw as though she had a toothache.

"No child," she said, "would have us."

Her expression suggested: this was not the truth.

In the locker room, as we undressed, I investigated the sags and droops of her body for signs of motherhood. Even if the heart says no, the body keeps a record of these biological capitulations to others. Or this is how I thought it should be. Those who can't make scars in time, they make scars in people.

But Borka's body was unreadable. She was distressingly thin; what flesh remained on her body had slung forward and looked like the pathetic rucksacks in which a person who owned practically nothing had consolidated her possessions. What could have been the stress of a long-ago pregnancy was indistinguishable from the hard wear of years.

"You find me disgusting?" Borka asked, catching me.

"Of course not," I lied. These regressions took their toll. I wanted to hide in my room with the shades drawn, blot my head beneath a pillow.

"It is not always a tragedy to be unrecognizable as your former self," she said.

"Why not?" I said.

"Because," she said. "You might be mistaken for someone better."

She wrapped a towel around her body, forgetting that her face was the scariest thing about her.

~∞~

My sixth week at the Goergen, I regained yet another talent I thought I'd forever lost.

I awoke one morning to find my pulse quickened, my peripheral vision tinseled. I'd come to understand these symptoms differently since I'd become sick, as dreaded harbingers of a migraine. Prior to my illness I'd welcomed these symptoms; prior to my illness they'd predicted the onset of one of my coincidences. *I would learn something.* Now, however, they promised an unenlightening journey, one that mimicked the movement of an oil drill, a claustrophobic spiraling into a hole.

I hurried to the lobby where I tried and failed to convince the concierge to slip me my bottle of vicodin.

"You are inhuman," I whispered.

"You are inhuman," he replied, and handed me a paperclip.

I spun around; I walked straight into Alwyn.

"Breaking the rules again?" she said. Her face was pale and her hair was a mess, her bangs thrusting upward like the fine tines of a comb.

"I needed an aspirin," I said. "You also look like you need an aspirin."

"That's not what I was referring to," she said.

I guessed she'd heard from Colophon about my encounter with Dominique Varga. I hadn't kept this from Alwyn on purpose; I'd figured that Colophon would tell her if he wanted her to know.

"Colophon is fine with me regressing," I offered in my defense.

"I'm not talking about Colophon. Though he already told me about your visit to the *Up-and-Comers* set. Very nice, by the way. I'm talking about Marta."

"What does Marta have to do with this?"

"Marta told me," she said, "what you've been telling her."

"I don't tell Marta anything," I said. "All we do is Mundane Egg."

"Interesting," Alwyn said. "That's not what I hear from Marta."

"And what do you hear from Marta?"

"Nothing you haven't presumably heard yourself," Alwyn said, "given it came out of your own mouth."

She switched the topic to Madame Ackermann, who'd visited three luxury spas.

"Does she always take so many vacations?" she asked.

"I have no idea," I said. "Actually," I backtracked, recalling what I'd learned of her habits in the crawlspace, "she doesn't."

"I'm beginning to worry," Alwyn said, "that she's got a lead on Varga."

"That she works as a masseuse at Canyon Ranch?" I said.

"Could be," Alwyn said, missing the jibe.

I went to my 10 a.m. Marta meeting, during which we did the usual boring stuff while I waited for my migraine to thunk into gear. Toward the end, I asked her if I could read the notes she'd kept of our sessions.

"That would be against policy," she said.

"Just what I've said to you. I wouldn't expect access to your notations."

"No," she said. "I'm very sorry."

"But what I've told you belongs to me," I said.

"That is an interesting interpretation," Marta said.

I shot a look at her clipboard. Marta tipped it closer to her chest.

"Who is Irenke?" she asked.

"Irenke?" I said.

"You wanted to know what you talk about during your sessions. Often you talk about her."

"I do?"

Marta's brows cinched.

"Now's not the ideal time to become involved with people like Irenke."

"Why?" I asked. I wanted to know what she thought about Irenke. Who was she? Why was she pretending to be Dominique Varga's daughter?

"You are a medium," Marta said. "Although so is everybody a medium, an involuntary host to free-floating misery. But you're a more available one."

"Available," I said.

"You are more easily used," she said.

After our session, I hid in a darkened hallway. I waited until I heard Marta's door open and shut, her gum soles suctioning over the tiles.

But her door was locked. I glared through the nubbled glass at the inert shapes of furniture, desperate to get inside. What had I told her? Again, I proved a victim of my own inexpertise. I was a clearinghouse for other people's misery, but lacked the requisite gravity to assert, over these doomy voices, any mastery or control. Mediums, or so Madame Ackermann liked to say, were not merely containers, they were decoders. They imparted meaning and shape to the meaningless and the shapeless. They pulled sense from the sorrowed air.

Me, I was an unreflective repository for people's sorrow. A trash can of sorrow.

I tried and I tried to get inside Marta's office.

No surprise. I failed.

⸺∞⸺

I took the elevator to the lobby. Empty. Even the concierge was gone. I went outside again and waited for my migraine in Gutenberg Square. Maybe I'd tempt another snapper to take my photograph.

Two nodders, a man and a woman, kneeled in a flowerbed, slow-motion weeding, or maybe they were holding on to the weeds to steady themselves. Closer by, an old man slept, a Leica over his crotch. His beard was so white it had begun to yellow, like a peeled apple exposed to air.

I sat on the bench across from him. I coughed. The old snapper awoke.

We made small talk. I told him I was staying at the Goergen.

"Your face-lift has healed nicely," he said.

"I'm being attacked," I corrected him.

"Age is a warrior," he said.

He aimed his camera toward the Goergen. A delivery truck had pulled up; a man unloaded crates of vegetables.

"Why do you care about turnips?" I asked.

The snapper reached into his vest pocket and removed a tin of chewing tobacco.

"I'm here to photograph a woman named Borka Erdos," he said.

Ah, I thought. *I've heard about you.*

"I am her conscience," he said wistfully. "Or maybe she is mine."

"She must have been very beautiful once," I said, meaning prior to her car accident.

"Only my pictures can say," the old snapper declaimed.

He offered to take me to his flat to show me these pictures. He bragged, as further incentive, that his flat contained "the underground snapper archives of Europe."

"I own photographs of everyone who was everyone," he said.

"Do you own photographs of Dominique Varga?" I asked.

He appeared miffed.

"Lady," he said. "Of course I do."

We drove a short distance to his flat—one vast room—that

indeed appeared to house the snapper archives of Europe. Side-by-side filing cabinets obscured every inch of available wall.

He withdrew a file folder and placed it on a table.

"Who is this?" I asked of a young woman in a shift patterned by saucer-sized dots.

"Borka," he said.

If I strained I saw the resemblance—mostly in the nose, but the rest of the features belonged to a woman I'd never seen before. When Borka had said her face was not her own, she hadn't been exaggerating.

The old snapper made coffee while I perused. The youthful photographs—Borka in her thirties—were followed by photos of a much older Borka, a Borka I could more easily square with the post-car-accident Borka I knew. The snapper owned no photos, however, of the intervening twenty-odd years.

He returned with two coil mugs handmade by a child, or at least their weighty lumpenness suggested this to be the case. To the touch mine was greasy, as though coated with a sorrowful residue like Helena's ring. I set the mug down, determined not to touch it again. This snapper, I did not want to know about his life.

"I'm out of sugar," he apologized.

I asked him about the gap in his file, the decades between the two Borkas.

"Tell me what I should have done," he said, interpreting my question as a criticism. "The world thought she was dead."

He told me that Borka, at the age of forty, had gone missing while on vacation in Ibiza.

"Ibiza?" I said. In my head I heard the words *heiress* and *masked women* and *prosthetic hands*. I was stunned, but I wasn't. What a moron I'd been not to have put the pieces together already.

"People believed she was killed in a car accident," the old snapper said. "That she drove her Mercedes into a cliff. But I promise you, it was no accident. She did it for Dominique Varga. She did it for art."

He sighed.

"The girls in those days," he said. "What wouldn't they sacrifice for Varga? I'm lucky my Rita never met her."

"And Borka didn't die," I said, finishing his previous thought.

"Not in the usual sense," he said.

Little surprise, then, that Borka would claim to have information about Varga's current whereabouts. She not only knew the woman, she'd ruined her face for her. Also, I felt a tiny bit chastened by this irony, or this coincidence, or this perversity: my most fruitful Varga research source didn't require me to regress anywhere. All I had to do was take the elevator upstairs to Borka's room.

"No doubt the family was relieved she was gone," the old snapper continued. "Borka was no picnic. Always needing to be the center of attention, and eventually she becomes a sort of movie star but she pays for the privilege with her face. So she disappears. The husband never remarries. And then, twenty years later the husband dies, and there is no one to take over the business, and Borka comes back from wherever she's been, not dead at all."

"How odd," I said. But upon reflection it wasn't so odd. Borka had vanished herself and unvanished herself. This was no longer an alien paradigm.

The old snapper shrugged. "Sometimes pretending to be dead is best for all involved."

"Speaking of which," I said. I asked him to show me his photos of Dominique Varga.

He scrutinized me, possibly trying to divine if I, too, were the sort of weak girl who might fall sway to her unhealthy influence.

He deemed me immune.

His Varga file proved lean. Inside were stills of Varga on the sets of her various films, such as *Simone Moreault*. Also, not that

I was expecting it, but I realized upon not finding it that I'd been hoping—maybe there would be a picture of my mother.

"That's it?" I asked.

The old snapper bristled.

"I mean," I said, "they're wonderful."

"But I haven't shown you the best ones," he said. "I keep them in a special place. Someday I will sell them and make an honest fortune."

The snapper retrieved two photos from his bedroom. The first was of a woman's face slashed to bits and surrounded by glass.

"A still," he said. "Of Borka. No one ever found copies of the car accident film, but I have proof—it did exist."

Borka, I had to admit, appeared pretty convincingly dead, her face a pulverized fruit. I better appreciated what a good job her initial plastic surgeon had done, given the original mess.

"But that is not the most valuable," said the old snapper. "This one is the most valuable."

He handed me a photo of a young Dominique Varga—she looked like a teenager—face shadowed beneath a straw visor, breastfeeding a baby.

"Which film is this from?" I asked.

"No film," he said. "That is from life."

"She had a baby?" I asked.

"A daughter," he said.

Irenke. So she hadn't been lying. Varga did have a daughter. But whether Irenke was that daughter remained unsubstantiated. Given the number of desperate acolytes Varga attracted, and Irenke's doomy vibe, it seemed prudent to wonder.

"What happened to her?" I asked.

"She is dead like my Rita," the old snapper said. "Pottery was Rita's life. That's her kiln in the corner."

"Which one is dead?" I asked.

"Everybody is dead," said the old snapper, extending his arms to indicate all the inhabitants of his loft, the 2-D people morgued in the file cabinets.

It struck me that he was a little bit senile, my old snapper.

"The child, too?" I asked.

"A face is like a rune stone," he said. "A face says to me 'long life' or 'happy marriage' or 'early death by wrong raising.' But she was such a terrible potter, my wife," he sighed. "That she was considered the artist in the family, it was a bad joke we could never, for the health of the marriage, laugh about."

His eyes bobbled unsteadily, as if he were seeing his wife in the room before him, and maybe he was; the line between senile and psychic was fine, even nonexistent. My father's father, when he entered his dementia endgame, had let me, then aged twelve, tag along on his sundowner fugues, the two of us traveling together to a World War II naval ship stationed in the Yellow Sea, to a two-story apartment building in Lowell, Mass., his birthplace.

"I guess that's love," I said.

"No," he said, turning back to the photo of Varga and the baby. "*That's* love."

The snapper's thumb landed on the infant's head, blotting it out.

That sudden redaction (thumb over face) provoked me. I passed a hand over the photo. The veins on the underside of my wrist twanged, a taut pulling of melancholy threads. Then it happened. This regression wasn't painless or dreamy, it was the physiological equivalent of being reduced to a mess of protons and accelerated through the Hadron collider, of being looped at light speed and crashed into other protons that had also, once, been part of me.

I coagulated into a crunchy mass in the Parisian hotel lobby, my body a casing for glass shards. I sat in my usual chair. I made grinding, particle noises whenever I moved.

Across from me, Irenke, drink in hand, wept.

I clutched my head.

Irenke threw her glass against the floor, shattering it.

Then the floor disappeared.

"That bitch," Irenke raged. She tore at the neckline of her dress.

"Who?" I said. I'd never been scared in a regression before; this time, I was scared. I'd arrived at a forbidden place.

"I wanted to be her muse," she said. "But instead I am her cameraman. She hides me behind the drapes and makes me watch."

"But you are her muse. She gave you—or rather she will give you—a necklace and tell you exactly that."

"She'll give me nothing," Irenke said. "Anything I own of hers, I had to steal."

She sobbed into her elbow crook. Her other hand grabbed my wrist.

"I'm sorry," she said. "I've done horrible things."

"You don't have to be sorry," I said. I patted her arm. A glass shard poked through my skin, then another and another. I touched one. They were numb as teeth. "Whatever it is you did, I forgive you."

"I'm not asking you to forgive me," she said. "She deserved it. She used me to get what she wanted and then she dumped me, pretended I'd never existed. I had to make her suffer for what she did. She was a bad person, you see. You're lucky you never met her."

"Your mother?" I asked.

She raised her head. To stare into her pupils was to stare straight at the subatomic engine room of the universe's collective human misery, its self-annihilating, Hadron-collider core.

"No," she said. "Yours."

———

The old snapper drove me back to the Goergen. I gripped my wrist—the one Irenke had held—but I couldn't stem the vacuum suck that threatened to empty my veins. I worried that I might psychically bleed out onto the car seats.

The concierge greeted me with his usual indifference. I sat in his desk chair—an off-kilter walnut spin that boinged on its base like those playground horses I rode as a kid, the ones attached to a thick metal spring, the ones that tried to buck you, head first, onto the cement.

Irenke was fucking crazy. She was a deranged astral imprint and nobody's daughter. Possibly she'd known my mother, but more likely she was a psychic stalker who'd, for whatever reason, chosen to pick on me. Maybe Irenke was a psychic henchman of Madame Ackermann's, an infiltrator tasked to further sicken and confuse me. This would explain why Madame Ackermann had hurried past us in the Paris hotel lobby. She didn't want to have to pretend to "meet" Irenke, and risk my cottoning on to their plan.

But regardless of who she was or wasn't, I needed to break off all contact with her. I'd ask Marta for help.

This plan calmed me.

Then I checked my e-mail. I'd received a reply from Professor Hales.

Dear Julia, he wrote.

Attached please find an essay I would like to submit to Mundane Egg *for publication. I wrote it to accompany the monograph of a spirit photographer whose photographs, quite frankly, I despised. The photographer rejected the essay because it had nothing to do with her work. Instead I wrote an essay about Indre Shira's "Brown Lady" photograph, because I had the good fortune, last summer when I was in England, to visit Raynham Hall. I paid the pound equivalent of US$300 to sit on the actual staircase where the Brown Lady photograph was taken, but as you will see from my essay, the expenditure was not a foolish one,* *especially if* Mundane Egg *sees fit to publish my findings. Please tell your boss that I'm a fanatical reader of her publication.*

I tried to open Professor Hales's attachment, but the concierge's computer didn't recognize the software. Needless to say, I knew there'd be nothing in there relating to my initial question to him concerning overrides.

I did a quick "overrides" Google search and ended up on a Wikipedia page about computer programming that made me realize: anything can strike a person as menacingly apt. *(The implementation in the subclass overrides the implementation in the superclass by providing a method that has the same name, the same parameters or signature, and same return type as the method in the parent class. If an object of the parent class is used to invoke the method, then the version in the parent class will be executed, but if an object in the subclass is used to invoke the method, then the version in the child class will be executed.)*

I copied the link and pasted it into an e-mail to Professor Wibley, whose advanced senility rendered him safe to correspond with, assuming he'd heard of e-mail. I dispensed with the pretense of soliciting fact-checking advice for *Mundane Egg*; I asked him about overrides, and left it at that.

Then I wrote to Colophon.

Varga had a child; possibly her name was Irenke. But we don't need her. I've found a better source.

He did not write back.

I did not reveal that I'd met the heiress who'd organized the first official festival of Varga's films, the heiress who'd once been the suspected victim of a Varga-directed snuff but who'd crashed her car on purpose, and who'd mostly survived her mistake.

I cannot say why I did not tell him this.

On my way to the elevator, I ran into Alwyn. She looked like crap, her hair flattened on one side as though she'd been napping all day. Stylistically, too, she'd backslid; gone were the scarves and the little tweed jackets, replaced by holey cardigans, yoga pants, a pair of blue babouches unthreading from their grubby soles.

"Where've you been?" Alwyn asked. Even her voice sounded compressed. "I've been looking for you for hours."

"Baths," I said.

"I checked the baths," she said.

"I meant the sauna," I said.

Alwyn worried a pimple on her chin. Her overall vibe was one of depletion, of exhaustion.

I remembered it well.

"Here," I said, steering her toward a club chair. "Sit."

She handed me her bag.

"Pull out that file, will you?" she asked.

I withdrew the Madame Ackermann file. Amidst the dot-matrix printouts I found a number of paparazzi magazines, a few of the pages dog-eared.

I held one up.

"This constitutes research?" I said.

"I like to know where my mother is," she said. "Last week she was in Stockholm for a charity ball."

"Oh," I said. "She still hasn't seen your vanishing film?"

Alwyn confirmed that she hadn't.

"I mean obviously she's busy, right?" she asked.

She stared at me.

"What?" I said.

"She's busy," she said.

"I guess," I said.

"You guess?" she said sarcastically.

She engaged in an intense calculation that involved me, but didn't.

"What?" I asked.

"Nothing," she said. "I know better than to ask anything of you."

I wasn't certain what I'd done or failed to do. I left it alone.

Then Alwyn confessed that she'd encountered a "bit of a dry spell" with respect to her Madame Ackermann research.

"What does that mean?" I said.

"It means I don't know where she is," she said.

"Did you call the Workshop?"

"I was informed that she was on medical leave," she said.

"Well," I said. "She likes to be seen. You'll find her."

"Oh, and before I forget," Alwyn said, "Marta requested a meeting with you at three. Also, tonight's that presentation by the psychic vampire expert. Marta and I both think you should attend."

"Am I in trouble?" I asked. Marta had never scheduled any extra meetings with me before.

"I don't know," Alwyn said. "Are you?"

"Maybe," I said.

I confessed that I'd broken the discouragements again; that I'd gone to the flat belonging to one of the paparazzi in Gutenberg Square; that I'd discovered Dominique Varga had had a daughter, and that I'd met a woman pretending to be this daughter, and that this woman, a liar, was a disturbed astral imprint, in fact I worried that she was psychically stalking me, maybe at the behest of Madame Ackermann.

"I know that sounds a little crazy," I said.

"I *knew* it," Alwyn said.

"I'm sorry," I said. "This is what I get for not listening to you."

"I knew it," she repeated. "I told Colophon that Varga had a baby. Of course he never believed *me*."

"Wait . . . you knew?"

"Gut feeling," she said. "It's not so special what you do. Everyone's a latent psychic. They just don't make a big deal about it. They don't get degrees in it."

"I don't think I make a big deal about it," I said.

"And let me guess: she abandoned the baby, right? Because being a mother marked her as sexless and ambitionless?"

"Given what we know about Varga," I said, "I'd wager she did her daughter a favor by giving her away."

Alwyn kicked a dust bunny. The Goergen's floors were always gauzy underfoot.

"Of course *you* would think that."

"Of course I would think *what*," I said.

Alwyn scrutinized a pair of surgical patients playing backgammon. They resembled—given their gigantic white head-bandages, and the underwater slowness with which they moved the backgammon pieces—very relaxed astronauts.

"I'm honestly curious," she began.

She hefted herself to a standing position.

"Yes?" I said.

"What does a woman have to do," she said, "to be classified by you as a monster?"

She put a hand on my bicep and gave it a mean squeeze, though it's possible she was using me to adjust her balance. She stomped off toward the elevators.

I collapsed into her chair. I wondered, too, what a woman had to do.

At 2:50, I initiated the long wend to Marta's office.

Marta ushered me inside without a greeting. She eyed me skeptically.

"I'm afraid I cannot be an accessory to your rage any longer," she said.

"My what?"

"You and this Irenke," she said. "You are both so angry."

"She's the angry one," I said. "Believe me, I don't want anything to do with her."

"You've both lashed out at the people you think are to blame for your misfortunes," Marta continued. "But the blame, you must accept, begins with you."

"I'm aware of that," I said.

"You aren't aware," she said. "You blame Madame Ackermann. You think it's her fault."

"Isn't it?" I said.

"Even if it is," she said. "It doesn't justify what you're doing. You cannot do to others what they have done to you."

"It's do to others what you would have them do to you," I corrected.

"So you think it is fair to attack a person because she has attacked you."

"I'm not attacking anyone," I said.

"Hmmm," she said. "Regardless, we're going to stop these sessions for the time being."

"But I need your help," I said. "I don't want to visit Irenke anymore."

"Then," Marta said coolly, "don't."

There were ten of us at Dr. Papp's talk.

Borka did not attend. She had not been at dinner. It was as though she somehow knew that I knew about her past with Varga. She did not want to be asked why she'd hidden this from me.

As Dr. Papp spoke, he bounced a ball of kitchen twine in one hand.

"Have you ever heard of the expression 'bubbling over with

happiness'?" asked Dr. Papp, winding the twine around the neck of each guest, connecting us chain-gang style. "Your emotions are like water; they pour onto the people around you."

Dr. Papp explained, as he distributed pairs of nail scissors, how throwing bad energy caused rips in a person's psychic carapace, thereby leaving the attacker vulnerable to retaliation.

"This affects all of you," Dr. Papp said. "You," he said, pointing at a countess who'd had a face-lift, braiding the fringe of her head scarf. "You've sliced open your carapace. Do you think it's only germs that can find their way into the wound?"

A crucial part of daily hygiene, Dr. Papp said, was to survey our emotional attachments and cut the unhealthy ties.

He instructed us to identify an unhealthy attachment growing from our carapace. Then, using the scissors, we were to cut the string that bound us to the neighbor on our right.

I identified Irenke as my attachment.

Before we cut our string, however, Dr. Papp recommended we imagine our attachment in the basket of a hot-air balloon.

"Revenge is a counterproductive therapeutic goal," Dr. Papp said, echoing Marta. "Pretend you are sending your attachment on a nice vacation."

I wedged my fingers into the scissors' tiny metal loops; the edges were dull, the blades chewed at the string one fiber at a time. The action made me sleepy. Finally the string snapped and I watched my balloon rise. The basket, however, appeared empty. Where was Irenke? I'd launched an empty balloon.

Then I saw her.

She called my name.

Julia, she said. *I tried to say I was sorry.*

What happened next happened, I later concluded, because my brain was overtaxed by the many exercises and regressions I'd subjected it to. The carpet morphed underfoot to a bed of nails that gouged my legs, and made them bleed and bleed and bleed, until I had to hold my chin up so that I didn't drown in it, my own rising red death.

Then a storm started. The wind scooted along the surface of the blood, carving it into sharp ridges until the blood was no longer blood, it was an ocean of fire that the wind fanned higher and higher, the waves flicking the balloon's fabric, saturating it red, then orange, then black.

From the basket I heard screaming.

"Stop now!" Dr. Papp yelled in order to be heard above Irenke's screaming (which, in theory, only I could hear). Then I understood: I was screaming.

"Bring it in for a landing!" Dr. Papp commanded.

It was too late. The flaming balloon refused to land, powered by its own manic gusts of heat. It made a swipe at me, zooming so close that I could feel its furnace exhale against my cheek. I looked into the eyes of the passenger's terrified face.

Her face, however, did not belong to Irenke.

I couldn't watch what happened next, but this seemed worse than cowardly. I forced myself to stare at that burning ball, I forced myself to watch as my mother climbed to the edge of the basket, stared down at my red ocean, and jumped.

<hr />

Here is what I learned in bed.

The Danube flows through, and partially forms the borders of, ten countries.

After a serious illness, Goya spent five years recuperating and reading French revolutionary philosophers, in particular Rousseau, who taught him that imagination divorced from reason produces monsters.

There are such things as irregular flowers.

I also learned that there'd been a spate of surgical imperson-ator sightings in European cities such as Paris and Düsseldorf, and that plastic surgeons had been asked to report to the authorities patients who approached them with "unrealistic" plastic surgery goals.

Things I did not learn in bed. I did not learn how I was moved to the top floor of the Goergen where, it turned out, the keypass-only medical facilities were located, and which included a hallway of private recovery rooms and a vast surgical theater. I did not learn the name of the specialist who attended me, a formal man whose hospital jacket had been tailored to fit his wide shoulders and nar-row waist (in those first hazy days, I thought my pulse was being monitored by a waiter in a white tuxedo), and who did not speak English. I did not learn the name of the pills given to me, sapphire blue capsules that, when left for too long on the white napkin that covered my bed tray, stained the fabric red. I did not learn how I'd acquired a hand-shaped burn on my face, one that spanned the pre-cise spot I'd been touched, during my trip to the Paris hotel lobby, by Madame Ackermann.

When Marta came to visit, she encouraged me not to think about the incident with the balloon basket.

"We have a saying," she said. "The wound heals better without the fork."

When Alwyn came to visit, I told her that Marta believed I was attacking Madame Ackermann.

"I'm aware," Alwyn said.

"But I'm not," I said.

"I wouldn't blame you if you were," she hedged.

"And I told Marta that I don't want to visit Irenke anymore," I said.

"Don't worry," she said. "I know you can't help yourself."

Regardless, Alwyn insisted, the counterproductive result of my regressing was this: I'd become sicker than ever.

I couldn't disagree with her. Since the night of Dr. Papp's presentation the wolf had returned with a high-wattage vengeance. Every time I closed my eyes. There it was.

"You are your own worst enemy," Alwyn observed, as a nurse changed my face dressing. "Have you heard of Dr. Kluge? He's a very famous electrobiologist. He was also once engaged to my mother."

Dr. Kluge, she informed me, discovered that a stone called quartzite, due to its density and a property called laser-woven particle distribution, prevented the transmission of certain energy frequencies. He'd helped develop a spa facility made of quartzite slabs to block these frequencies; this building was the perfect place to stall the aging process.

"It also works as a treatment for schizophrenics," she said. "They hear fewer voices when they're in 'the bunker.'"

I didn't object to being classified as schizophrenic. In the metaphoric sense of the word, or maybe the literal sense, no one could dispute that I'd become an unwitting ventriloquist for various hostile others.

But for my "wellness purposes," Alwyn clarified, I'd be unable to psychically reach out to or be reached by Irenke, or Madame Ackermann, or anyone else for that matter. This spa, to which she and Marta proposed I be moved, was, best I could tell, a building-sized version of the Faraday cage that Madame Ackermann kept in her basement.

"Usually there's a yearlong waiting list," Alwyn said, "but I've arranged with Kluge, because we've remained on friendly terms, for you to hop the queue. He guarantees you'll show measurable improvements within a week."

Alwyn fiddled with the cord to my blinds, raising and lowering them until the sunlight stopped at my neck, my head decapitated by shadow.

She admitted, then, that she'd taken it upon herself to do a little extra research "for the sake of our work."

She handed me a glossy fax that persisted, in the annoying manner of faxes, to curl up on itself rather than lay flat, as though protecting its contents from dissemination. I pinned it open on my bed tray. Written in French, it was a bill of sale from a gallery in Paris called Les Einsteins, dated May 1980, and included a photo of the necklace Irenke had been wearing at the Regnor. According to this bill of sale, the purchaser was Dominique Varga.

Which struck me as curious, but not overly. It confirmed what I already knew to be true. The necklace had once belonged to Varga.

But it grew more curious.

The bill of sale split the necklace's proceeds into various commissions—the finances of Les Einsteins were modeled more on those of a socialist consignment shop than an art gallery—the figures diminishing into smaller and smaller amounts until everyone who'd had any contact with the necklace, it seemed, received a cut, including, almost as an afterthought, the artist herself, whose name was Elizabeth Severn.

I saw threads, wet dark threads, swirling and knotting and leading definitively nowhere. My mother had made Irenke's necklace. This fact did not strike me with the force it might have; the minute dose of morphine my doctor prescribed protected me from astonishment. Maybe, too, I had already made this connection in the swampy backwater of my brain, but had failed to fish it to the conscious surface. Did this mean Irenke *had* known my mother? Did this prove Irenke was Dominique Varga's daughter? Perhaps the only thing it proved was that, yes, Irenke had acquired, and possibly stolen, this necklace from Varga, which Varga had bought from my mother.

But whether or not Varga was Irenke's mother, and whether or not my mother was, in Irenke's words, "a truly bad person," well, this necklace illuminated little more on these fronts, save the stark reality that nothing in my life, no object, no person, spun beyond the orbit of gravely, perversely mattering.

Perhaps I should have wondered how Alwyn, while doing "a little research," had tracked down the one bit of information I'd thus far kept from her—that Varga and my mother had been friends.

I did not wonder.

"Les Einsteins was Varga's gallery," Alwyn said. "Maybe Varga was simply a fan of her work. Regardless, I think it's safe to presume they met each other."

Beneath her allotted pittance, my mother had signed her name. I traced her handwriting's erratic and inscrutable leaps. Not to use these letters as a portal, not to go anywhere. I wanted a thing, not a doorway.

"Also," she said, "I spoke with the gallery owner. I said that he must have found your mother's work impressive, given he'd agreed to represent her. To which he said, *ah*."

I didn't know what *ah* meant. I did not want to know.

"Do you think Dominique Varga would have allowed any old person to regress into her past? She knew your mother. Maybe she respected her for being . . . similarly cutthroat. Whatever the reason, Varga's partial to you. This is a big advantage we need to exploit. You need to let her use you."

Alwyn, I noticed, had worried the pimple on her chin into a scab. She floated her fingertips over this scab, savoring the time when she could return to her room, pry it off, continue her excavation in private.

"OK," I said. "How?"

"She's partial to you," Alwyn said again. She seemed sort of pissed about this. "Just . . . do what she asks."

"That depends on what she wants," I said.

"She probably wants what everyone wants from you," Alwyn said meanly. "Information."

I tossed the fax at her. I was in no mood for Alwyn's jibes.

Alwyn retrieved the fax from the floor. She set it on my bedside table.

"Don't you find it interesting," she said, "how you're allowed to regress or whatever it is you do into my life, but I'm not allowed to pry into yours?"

"I've never pried into your life," I said.

"Exactly," she said, as though she'd been aiming to trick me into this very answer. "And why not?"

"Because I'm taking my healing seriously," I said.

"Right," she said, disgusted. "You're . . . how do I say this. You're undiscerning. You're a psychic slut. Any stranger who's in proximity, you 'can't help yourself.' So why could you help yourself with me? Why weren't you interested in me?"

"Because we are work colleagues," I said, not knowing what else to say—why was it I hadn't pried into Alwyn's life? "I figured it was better to respect your privacy."

"How thoughtful," she said. She pulled on her bangs so roughly I worried she'd tear them from her scalp.

I put a hand on her forearm. She tensed under me, unwilling to submit to my lame overture.

"Maybe it's related to the surgeries," she said dully.

"What is?" I said.

"You're drawn to infiltrate a weak spot. All of these surgery patients, they've made holes in themselves. How could you resist invading?"

"Maybe," I said, thinking that this category of person did not exclude Alwyn.

"And anyway," she said, "I suppose I shouldn't expect you to care about me the same way I care about you. I shouldn't expect *you* to do for *me* what I do every day for you."

She stared at me defiantly. Suddenly we were having a coded conversation and I was meant to provide my own key.

I could not.

Just as quickly as she'd turned abrasive, Alwyn recalcified into business mode. She'd already arranged, she said, for my train ticket and admission to the Breganz-Belken spa; she, meanwhile, would be staying at the Goergen.

We'd both meet up with Colophon in Paris in one week's time.

"I'm not coming back here?" I asked.

She told me I was not.

"I think you'll find your stay at the Breganz-Belken enlightening," she said.

"Enlightening?" I said. A sealed-off stone bunker, I thought, should promote the opposite of enlightenment: Endarkenment.

"Who knows," Alwyn said, "you might be forced to learn something you were never curious to learn."

"About myself?" I said. Given I'd be in a psychic safe house, more or less, mine would be the sole consciousness I'd have access to.

"Well," she said dryly, "if there's one person you're less interested in than me, it's you."

Borka arrived as Alwyn was departing. They practically collided in the small aperture to my room.

"*Excuse you,*" Borka said.

Alwyn did not cede her position. Borka pushed her scarf back. She brandished her face like a gun.

Alwyn caved, permitting Borka to enter. Borka did not thank her or acknowledge her for giving way, causing Alwyn to simmer, not that Borka noticed, or would have understood the implicit meaning if she had. Had they become better friends, or rather better enemies, since I'd been in the medical wing? Something was up. That something appeared to involve me. But I was too sapped to care what or how.

Alwyn tried again to leave, and was blocked by an orderly, a polite man who allowed her to huff through. The orderly bound my arm in a Velcro cuff and took a ridiculously long time to measure my blood pressure. I asked him if I had a pulse, and he answered, *I'm not sure.*

He stopped trying. He checked the progress of my burn, now mostly healed, he wrote something on my chart, he pronounced me well enough to return to my regular room.

"Fantastic," I said.

As Borka helped me pack my stuff, she noticed the fax on my bedside table.

"What is this?" she asked, pointing.

"Oh," I said. It was too difficult to explain. Also, I still hadn't confessed to Borka what I'd learned of her connection to Varga; this would inevitably arise if I showed her the bill of sale with Varga's name on it. A part of me enjoyed knowing something about Borka that she didn't know I knew. She'd made it clear—we were friends, but we were members of an information economy, too. A part of me intuited that I'd be wise to preserve this bargaining chit until I needed it.

"It's nothing," I said. "Alwyn gave it to me."

Borka stared at it disapprovingly.

"That girl is a half-dachshund," Borka said. "She will make you sick."

"Someone beat her to it," I said.

"She's your friend?" Borka asked.

I scrutinized the empty doorway. It wasn't that I didn't want Alwyn as a friend; I simply thought, given how little interest I'd shown in her, that I couldn't rightly claim her as one.

"No," I said.

"You're right," Borka confirmed, as though she'd been testing me. "She's not."

The night before my train was set to leave, I stopped by the concierge's desk to check my e-mail for the first time since Dr. Papp's presentation. I'd received no word from Colophon and ten video attachments from aconcernedfriend, none of which, due to the Goergen's gluggier than usual connection, I could open, and an e-mail from my father, forwarded from TK Ltd.

I saw your film, it said. And that was all. Maybe he'd hated it, but that he'd bothered to see the film in the first place was a loving overture I couldn't disregard. I wanted to write him back but knew this was not allowed, and suddenly these rules I'd been (sort of) respecting seemed self-defeating and sickness-enhancing and plain idiotic.

I wrote to my father.

I told him that I was in Vienna. I told him not to worry. I told him I planned to come home after I'd completed the job for which I'd been hired, because this vanishing business wasn't for me. I told him that I was just now (as I was typing this note) coming to realize that the reason I wasn't so crazy about vanishing was because I'd met people who seemed strangely in line with his ways of thinking about emotional management—also, for that matter, the Workshop's. Sealing your psychic shell against intruders. Keeping your personal story to yourself for fear that somebody might use it to hurt you, or for fear that you might use it to hurt someone else, even a dead someone else. Is that why he'd never told me how he'd suffered after his wife had killed herself, why he'd never told me what it was like for him to raise an infant alone—a creature that grievously howled as a matter of plain communication—how I must have functioned as a balm against her loss as well as a cease-less reminder that she was gone? Did he hate her for this? Did he hate me? Did he hate her for making him, on dark occasion, hate me? Did he, after he watched my vanishing film, experience the same guilty rush I had when I realized: I was happy she was dead, because if she were alive, it would mean that we were somehow to blame for her leaving? That her being dead was preferable to watch-ing a film in which she claimed that we were bad medicine, that we were making her sick? And as for experiencing her death as a relief, why should we feel guilty? If we secretly rejoiced and even bonded over our gladness of her death, *so what*? She hadn't left us any less vicious way to commemorate her.

Love, Julia, I typed.

I moused over the "Send" icon. But I didn't send. I veered toward the delete icon. I deleted.

I wrote to Madame Ackermann.

Dear Madame Ackermann, I wrote. *Wondering if we can call a truce. Forever your student, Julia.*

This one I sent.

I checked my e-mail one final time before logging out. I'd received a message from The Workshop.

It read:

The faculty member you are trying to contact is on leave. If you're looking for general information about the Workshop, please contact Dr. Karen Yuen at kyuen@theworkshop.edu. If you're trying to contact this faculty member in particular, we don't know what to say. Your e-mail will be forwarded to his or her personal account, but we cannot guaran-tee its receipt, nor, if received, that it will ever be read. Of course this is always the case with missives, virtual or otherwise; we're just pointing this out, should you be under the impression that any form of com-munication is fail-safe. Regardless, if you do not hear from this faculty member, the Workshop is not to blame.

That Madame Ackermann was unreachable was not news to me, but nonetheless this auto-reply ignited a tiny pilot light of panic in my sternum. I was not safe here.

I'm so fucking happy to be leaving, I thought. The Goergen's loose windowpanes, the gaps between the floors and the walls, the hundreds of drains, the women with the holes in their heads, every-where I looked I saw opportunities for infiltration and loss.

After packing, I went to Borka's room to tell her I was transfer-ring to a spa for old people and schizophrenics. Also I wanted to return the key and cricket cage. I'd failed to regress to 152 West 53rd Street, Room 13, on October 24, 1984, between the hours of 4 p.m. and 9 p.m., and now I was headed to a maximum-security building where it would be pointless to even try. Whatever infor-mation Borka possessed about Varga, she would have to give it to me without the promise of anything in return.

I found her in the rare giddy state; Marta had approved her surgical objectives. It appeared she'd already had a procedure or two—her eyelids were swollen, her upper lip distended.

"I can't wait until you see me again," she said.

I didn't bother telling her: I was never going to see her again.

Though I tried to discourage her, she insisted that I take her money.

"For sad mood days," she said, pressing a hamster-sized roll of bills into my hand.

When I returned the cricket cage and key, however, her mood hairpinned.

"You're giving up?" she said. "After all I've done for you?"

"I've tried," I said. "I can't."

She grabbed my hand.

"Tell me what you need to know," she said. "I'm ready to help you now."

"I don't know if that would make a difference . . ."

"Someone died in that room," she blurted.

I blinked at her.

"Who?" I said.

"A stranger," she said. "But her conceits were sent to me."

"Conceits?" I said.

"Clothing," she said. "Belongings."

"Why would a stranger send you her belongings?" I asked.

"There was a note," she said, "instructing the concierge. Should anything happen to her, I was to receive her conceits."

"What else did the note say?"

"Nothing," she said bitterly. "It said nothing."

"So you want to know why this stranger sent you her things?" I said.

She nodded.

"I want to know if I am somehow to blame," she said.

"Why would you be to blame?" I asked.

She pushed her fingers into her eyeballs. Literally, her fingers disappeared to the first knuckle, her old face like a snakeskin beginning to molt.

"These people," she said. "These people who die and you never knew them. What are you supposed to feel?"

She really wanted me to tell her. She really thought that I would know.

"Nothing," I said, tossing the key on her bed. "You're not supposed to feel anything."

She removed her fingers from her eyes, and it was, I swear, as though she'd pulled her fingers from holes in a dyke that had previously held back a flood. It struck me with the force of a riot hose.

"Oh *really*," she hissed. "Hasn't your blighted, miserable life taught you anything? You're just like her. Doomed to fail because you're too scared to try."

"Who?" I said. "Who am I like?"

My mother, I thought. Since she'd been in cahoots with Varga, maybe Borka had known my mother, too.

It was possible.

"My mother?" I said. "Did you know her?"

Borka laughed meanly.

"No," she said. "I did not."

I didn't push her to explain; to do so would be pointless. She wasn't giving me anything I didn't earn first. But I wanted her to understand: I had information, too.

"I discovered your Varga secret," I said. "I know about your 'death.'"

I didn't say: I know you disfigured yourself on purpose, that you drove your car into a cliff because you were an attention-hungry rich girl who wanted to be a celebrity, or maybe because you despised, with an intensity that drove you to violence, your face.

She scrutinized me as though I were a math problem, an x-value that remained momentarily, and terrifyingly, beyond her comprehension.

But whatever she divined reassured her. The wrathful floodwaters withdrew; she tamped her real self back to invisibility. Again, she was only ugly on the outside.

She smiled and held out her arms to me. I allowed her, one last time, to smooth my hair.

"Silly Beetle," she said. "You know so much nothing."

She forced the key into my robe pocket.

"But we still have our deal, right?" she said.

I didn't tell her that I had no intention of touching this key ever again. Whatever she wanted me to discover in that hotel room, it was a fool's errand. No matter what I found out, no matter whose face she had, it would not stop her from hating herself.

"We have our deal," I lied.

⁕

Back in my room, I opened my French doors and stepped onto my room's small patio. I took a mental snapshot of the view—the distant lights of the various bridges stretching over the Danube, and the blackened void of the Vienna Woods; the immediate quiet of Gutenberg Square, and the lighted flat windows across the square, revealing the collapsed cushions of easy chairs and dirty plates on tables but never people.

Soon, my presence was detected; below me, the camera flashes popped. I canted my face downward so the snappers could get a clear shot of my face. I waved. I smiled. I hoped that Madame Ackermann would see these photos and be lured to the Goergen in search of me. Let her come, I thought, because I will be long gone.

The flashes weakened, flickered, extinguished. Now there was only night down there. What I'd taken for flashes were the flames of many individual lighters as the nodders fired up their pipes. In the newly keen silence I listened to the wind that, when I closed my eyes, became the sound of the nodders' gaseous brains leaking from their bodies, whirling around Gutenberg Square, filling whatever lonely vacancies.

part Four

From Vienna I took a train through the Carpathians. The scenery was stunning but I barely registered it, instead spending most of the trip recovering from a fright I'd had at the station when a woman wearing a familiar Pucci scarf cut in front of me in the ticket queue. Her black ponytail hair lashed my cheek as she pushed behind a businessman, knocking his briefcase from his hand.

It was her. I willed myself not to move, to cease breathing. Perhaps she'd fail to detect me, purchase her ticket, swan off toward her gate. But then I had to sneeze, and I tried not to, and the pressure built and built until what emerged from my body sounded less like a sneeze than a rock striking another rock.

She turned.

She was not Madame Ackermann.

Still, I took this mistake as a warning. I "saw" people before I saw them, their arrival preannounced by a doppelgänger stranger.

Thank God for the bunker. I'd started to think of my new venue not just as a health necessity but as an architectural narcotic, even a potential vacation.

Before boarding the train, I checked my e-mail at a "free" Internet café, one that required me to purchase a pastry, and demonstrably enjoy it, before I was allowed to touch a keyboard.

I'd received my daily attachment from Madame Ackermann and a very long response to my override query from senile Professor Wibley.

"Concerning overrides," he began, and thank goodness he did, because the e-mail did not seem to be about overrides at all, but about the dangers of method acting, and how actors, in using their own pasts to animate the emotions of a nonexistent character, replaced their memories with the memories of a performance in which they'd employed these memories, the result being, after a number of "usages," that these memories became the province of myriad fictional others, and the actor could only access them by worming his way backward through the various roles he'd played, but that his past, once he reached it, was no longer, in theory, only his.

Wibley then veered into a riff involving T. S. Eliot's artistic quest for a degree of depersonalization "that approaches the condition of science," and how Eliot and other modernist writers at the turn of the last century viewed it as their ultimate goal to achieve the continual extinction of their personality, resulting in an idealized state that was adopted by the psychics of the time and renamed, in psychic circles at least, "clairvoidancy."

"Though these days I am suffering," wrote Professor Wibley, "more from voidancy than clairvoidancy. See me as a cautionary tale. I was colonized by the Mind of Europe even though I superannuated Shakespeare, Homer, and the Magdalenian draughtsmen. Regardless, it is not my intention to depress the youth. I simply hope that I have been of some small consolation to you, whoever you are."

He'd included, at the bottom of his e-mail, the following boilerplate:

"Some can absorb knowledge, the luckier must sweat for it."

A few hours past lunchtime, my train pulled into the tollbooth-sized station at Breganz-Belken.

A man in a pale sage uniform greeted everyone who disembarked—myself and two older couples—he took our luggage, he led us to a golf cart. Soon we arrived at a honed monolith that protruded from the ground at a slight angle as though it had been haphazardly dropped from outer space.

Whereas the Goergen was fluted and cartouched and polished to a high gleam, the Breganz-Belken was a Brutalist cave, the surfaces so matte they looked powdered.

I told the woman at the front desk that I had a reservation.

"Julia Severn," I said.

She had such good skin, this woman. She was so flushed with health that she appeared feverish.

"I'm afraid there's no guest here by that name," the woman said, as though we were discussing a third and presently absent person. I showed her the postcard on which Alwyn had written my confirmation number, as if this constituted convincing proof that her database was incorrect.

She inputted the number and her face flickered. Evidently I did have a reservation, but she refused to outright admit this.

"Additional postcards can be found in the night table," she said, initiating some rapid key commands. "Should you choose to use them, they will appear on your week's-end bill as 'additional room charge.' May I have your credit card?"

I handed her Alwyn's credit card.

"Also, I'm scheduled to see Kluge," I said.

"Kluge," she said. "I believe he's in Tehran, skiing. But I'm happy to know that women of your generation are taking the aging process so seriously. It's never too early to start the fight."

"No," I said, "actually—"

"However, I can't enroll you in the Kluge therapy until you've been approved by one of our diagnosticians," she said.

She told me she'd slotted me in for "a ten o'clock Mike."

Her computer beeped.

"I'm sorry," she said to Alwyn's card. "Declined. Do you have another?"

I told her I did not.

"We are not above accepting cash," she sniffed.

I sloughed a wad of bills from Borka's Sad Mood stash.

A sage-uniformed porter unlocked my room with a key card made of wood. After he left, I lay in the bed and, nose against the window, peered down the rubbly slope on which the backside of the spa was perched, the vertiginous view a freeze-frame of falling. From somewhere in the nearby woods, I heard wolves. Then I realized it was a recording of wolves, piped through tiny speakers scattered like spores throughout the room.

When I called the Goergen to tell Alwyn I'd arrived, I was told that she was unavailable. I left a message saying that she might want to pay her credit card bill.

She did not call me back.

That evening I ate in the spa's restaurant. My fellow diners were male-female couples in their fifties or sixties, seated across from one another at broad two-tops. Nobody spoke. Their faces remained slack, incommunicative blanks. Perhaps given my recent experiences—with silence-mandated meals, with postsurgical dining partners discouraged from facial displays of emotion—this did not strike me as unusual.

To my knowledge, I saw no schizophrenics.

After dinner I wandered back to my room, taking the scenic route past the thermal pools, clustered at the bottom of a windowless silo at the spa's center, its bubbling cauldron core. Maybe it was the pleasing aftereffects of the Grüner Veltliner I'd had with my entrée, or that I'd been inside this frequency-impermeable bunker for five hours, but I felt safe, entombed. Best of all, when I closed my eyes, I wasn't plagued by Fenrir on the backs of my eyelids; he left me alone, as though scared off by the stereo sounds of other wolves.

⸺∞⸺

As recommended, I ate a light breakfast in preparation for Mike. I drank three cups of coffee brewed from toasted millet that left a husky residue on my vocal cords. Voice aside, I presented an alarming picture of health. My face, when I caught an accidental glimpse of it in my bathroom mirror, resembled those photographs of me I no longer consulted to measure my decline.

I tried to check my e-mail but the woman behind the desk told me that the Communications Suite was under construction. She spoke of its future existence the way some people speak of the pronouncements of Nostradamus, as curious predictions they suspect will never come to pass.

At 9:58 a.m., Mike knocked on my door.

Mike, an American in his forties, resembled in looks and demeanor a surfer who'd been kept too long from the sea. He wheeled a gurney into my room.

With his hands he commenced a methodical sweeping of my body, hovering, on occasion, over a presumed trouble spot.

"So," he said, after about twenty minutes, "I'm guessing you were struck by lightning."

"Me?" I said. "No."

"Perhaps you don't remember," he said.

"I'm pretty sure I would remember that," I said.

"Your circuitry's been scrambled," he said. "Do you work in the nuclear physics sector?"

I told him I was most recently employed as a receptionist who answered a disconnected phone.

"And you're here alone," he said.

"I've noticed I'm one of the few."

"The spa's running a couples' retreat this weekend," he said.

"What kind of couples' retreat?" I asked.

Mike didn't respond. Instead he asked me if I was sexually active.

I told him I was not.

"Good," he said.

"Is that your way of saying you don't want to sleep with me?" I said.

"I don't want to sleep with you," Mike replied. "I never sleep with damaged people."

"*Damaged*," I said.

"Damaged people can fuck up your energy," said Mike, "especially if you're fucking them."

Mike inserted the tip of an elbow between two ribs; he ran the tip along the groove between the bones, back and forth, digging a little deeper with each pass.

"You're fused together," Mike said. "This is why I'm pretty sure you got struck by lightning; hypercalcification is initiated by exposure to high-voltage electrical currents."

Mike asked about my medical history. I told him that I'd had a complicated relationship with an old mentor.

"I'm thinking you've misread my toxic relationship with this woman as a lightning strike," I said. "An easy error to make."

"I disagree," Mike said. "What zapped you isn't human."

"You've never met Madame Ackermann," I said. "She prefers to work through a mythical Norse wolf proxy."

Mike's fingers recoiled from my hip bones; I could sense, in that infinitesimally wider space, the conflicted thrum of his trying not to lock me into a doomed diagnostic category. *Fuck*, I thought. I'd failed the test, revealed myself as a hopeless lunatic unworthy of his energies. This had happened to me in New York; at Blanche's suggestion, I'd volunteered to be a test patient at the Manhattan Psychoanalytic Institute, but the interviewer, when I'd mooned to her about my lost psychic abilities, had deemed me too deluded to be helped.

Mike busied himself behind me. Filling out my rejection slip, I figured. I abided bluely, listening to the judgmental scratch of his pencil.

Then he returned to the gurney and pressed downward onto my shoulders—a stretch that was also a restriction—and announced that he was recommending me for the Kluge therapy.

"What?" I said.

Mike elaborated on what he called the "not onerous stipulations" involved with enrollment: I was not allowed to go outside, nor was I to stand within ten feet of any windows. The reasons for these stipulations, Mike said, were obvious—in order to be spared the wear and tear of certain frequencies, patients had to surrender, without interruption, to no less than a weeklong quarantine.

"Not to mention," Mike warned, "when you've been protected from all random frequencies for even periods of time as brief as forty-eight hours, abrupt reentry can cause unpleasant side effects."

He speed-muttered a list of at least thirty side effects from which I heard "self-disfigurement" and "animal hallucinations."

I promised him I would stay inside.

"I've spent my life inside," I assured him, thinking of my New York days, of my Goergen days. "Lives," I modified.

"You'll find it relaxing to have the voices in your head silenced," Mike said.

How intuitive, I thought. Mike really was a special healer. He discerned, without me needing to tell him, my unique variety of exhaustion. Maybe he could tell by pressing on my skeleton—I did not always live in my body. I was like an astronaut whose every weightless minute came at a physical cost that could be measured in bone density loss.

"But to be honest I'm not convinced the voices *are* in my head," I said, thinking of Irenke. "Sometimes I think I'm a voice in someone else's head. Like a free-floating consciousness."

"You won't be allowed to go anywhere," he reassured me. "Your mind's staying put."

"Great," I said, honestly relieved. "Great."

"Also you'll be put on a special diet. For the most part, however, you're instructed simply *to be*."

"Yes," I said, "but who?"

I meant this as a joke; I was so many people. But I also meant it seriously. Who was I when I was only me?

I laughed to indicate, to Mike at least, that I'd been kidding. Mike, folding his gurney into thirds, matched my laugh, decibel for decibel, and both of us laughed until all of a sudden we didn't.

My stomach growled, ready for lunch. Only after Mike left did I realize that he was not an especially intuitive man; my bones had told him nothing. He'd recommended me for the Kluge therapy because, somewhere between the wolf mention and the multiple lives, he'd diagnosed me as schizophrenic.

<hr />

I spent the rest of the day in the thermal baths—so different from the Goergen's and yet, as with everything at the Breganz-Belken, so the same—soaking in water heated to the exact temperature of the human body, then leap-frogging through the higher-temperature pools until I reached the hottest one, a crack in the stone floor that mimicked a violent splitting-open of the earth's crust. When I couldn't stand the heat any longer, I dunked myself in the neighboring ice pool. Shivering, I'd hurry back to the human body pool and begin the sequence again. I worked this loop for hours. I couldn't make sense of this need, but later, reduced like a sauce to my most gelatinous essence and lying on my bed listening to the stereo wolves, I made sense of it this way: for the first time in over a year, I was choreographing my own pain experiences.

Then I slept the stone sleep of the happily dead.

I awoke at 6 a.m., ravenous. I sat alone in the dining hall and read a paperback mystery abandoned in my nightstand. Eventually another couple appeared. I didn't take much interest in them until they started arguing.

In German, the woman berated the man with what sounded like a litany of pent-up complaints, each one threading into the next as though she'd been awake all night lying beside him, writing and rewriting this little monologue in her head. The man, meanwhile, stared at the woman with the drowning O mouth of people trying to survive a conversation that is not a conversation but a tsunami of relentless criticism.

The woman finished. She stared at the man, daring him to respond; he thumbed a spot of juice from her chin, did not kiss her, left.

A waiter approached the woman's table to remove the man's plate. She faked for him a bright and believable smile.

I squinted at her face, its features tiny and modular like an actress's, each piece capable of behaving independently of the others. She registered to me as someone I knew from somewhere, though given her generic attractiveness, this could have been the reaction she inspired in everyone.

Her waiter returned, this time with a magazine, which he placed on the table alongside a pen, and a small digital camera. The woman untwined the hasty morning bun in which she'd stashed her hair, combing it out with her fingernails. When condensed her hair was a chestnut color but now, de-roped and catching the dawn slanting through the dining hall windows, it appeared more reddish-blue, as though it had been dunked to the roots in blood.

Then I knew exactly who she was. The resemblance was unmistakable. Plus I'd seen a picture of her skiing at Gstaad.

This was all too strange—like psychically spying on someone without the psychic part. Clearly, too, I'd been sent here by Alwyn for reasons other than my health. Since I'd refused (in Alwyn's mind) to use my abilities to help her, she'd dispatched me on a personal errand, possibly to find out why her mother and stepfather had yet to see her vanishing films. Recalling the paparazzi magazines in her Madame Ackermann folder, I suspected she'd spent far more time tracking her mother than she'd spent tracking Madame Ackermann. No wonder Madame Ackermann "disappeared"; disappearing wasn't very hard when nobody was looking for you.

And yet. In a strange way, I suspected I owed Alwyn; I did feel guilty that I'd never experienced even an unconscious curiosity about her.

I approached her mother's table.

"Pardon me," I said. "Are you the Breck Girl?"

She smiled that smile that accompanies blushing, but this woman, she did not blush.

"I'm sorry to disturb you," I said. "But I was wondering if I could get your autograph."

I handed her my paperback, flipped to a blank end page.

"You're not disturbing me," she said. She cast a glance toward the door through which her husband had exited.

I scrutinized the magazine photo of Alwyn's mother, the one

she'd autographed for the waiter. She was posed as Alwyn had described her, the photo really a photo of the back of a woman's head, her face obscured in a way that suggested it was better left unseen.

"Would you like to sit?" she said. "I've been abandoned by my grumpy dining companion."

"Wrong side of the bed?" I offered.

"But what are the odds," she said, "of his getting it wrong every single day?"

I sat. She inspected me in the way that older beautiful women inspect younger women, check-marking the areas in which she managed to succeed, despite predating me by thirty years, in being more ravishing.

"And you live where?"

"New York City," I said.

"Ah," she said. "I once read an interview with a man who could see into the future. As a Jewish child in thirties Germany he intuited that the world was going to hell, and pushed his parents to move the family to New York. The interviewer asked him, 'So was that your first paranormal experience?'"

She chuckled.

"I always want to ask people who move to New York that question. 'Was that your first paranormal experience?'"

"It wasn't," I said. "If you're asking."

"I don't think I was asking," she said.

She searched the room for a waiter. I was about to lose her. Her energy was terrier-like and distractible; it was easy to imagine Alwyn's childhood as a vain daily struggle to hold this woman's attention for longer than an eye-blink.

I considered confessing to her that I knew her daughter, but suspected that this would snap our exchange to an immediate close.

Instead I inquired if she'd ever heard of a phenomenon called psychic attack. I told her how I was being attacked by my former mentor, a woman named Madame Ackermann.

"How fascinating," she said. "And how does one know that she's being psychically attacked? Is there a blood test?"

"Often people have no idea," I said. "Often people are sick for years, and visit every conceivable Western and Eastern doctor, and then they commit suicide."

"So weakness is a sign," she said.

"More like unexplained aches and pains," I said. "Rashes. Exhaustion. Loss of hair, pigmentation, appetite, hope."

"Maybe these people are simply depressed," she observed.

"Chicken and egg," I said. "Are they sick because they're depressed? Or depressed because they're sick?"

"Depressed people," she said, "are a bore."

I took this as a warning.

"And this 'Madame Ackermann,'" Alwyn's mother said. "You're hiding from her here?"

"Sort of," I said.

I told her about Dominique Varga, and how we were both searching for her. I thought perhaps, since her daughter had written her college thesis about Dominique Varga, that the name might spark some recognition. It didn't.

"So you're not in any real danger," she said, "save the danger of losing a race to find a possibly dead person."

"Well," I said. "That's ignoring the fact that I've been physically debilitated by Madame Ackermann for over a year."

"Which is maybe not Madame Ackermann's fault," she said. "Maybe your 'debilitation' is stress related. I'd be stressed, too, if I were wasting time at a spa when I had work to do."

"Yes," I said, "except—"

"Your generation is always so quick to blame other women for its problems," she interrupted. "You girls and your ideological penchant for matricide. Kill the mother. Kill the mother. No wonder you're all so lost."

"Some of our mothers killed themselves," I said.

"I'm sure it's comforting to think that," she said.

She focused on the serrated skyline of firs ascending the slope beyond the windows.

"I'm assuming you don't have any children," she said.

I confirmed that I did not.

"No one ever admits that a mother's greatest heartbreak is when she begins to see her child as the embodiment of her own worst self. Literally, it is as if her worst self—that shameful part she's able, most days, to quarantine—has been loosed upon the world and refuses any longer to take orders from her."

"Your daughter's probably too old to take orders from you," I said. "Not that you're old," I added.

"I scarcely know my daughter," she said. "She lies to me about tiny things, insignificant things. She'll say 'I'm studying math' when she's studying film. She'll say her favorite color is blue when really it's green. It's far more insulting than if she had a secret worth concealing."

A waiter making coffee rounds refilled our cups.

"I've been chosen to participate in the therapy designed by Dr. Kluge," I said. "I . . . read in the tabloids that you almost married him."

She didn't quite roll her eyes, but she might as well have.

"Kluge," she said. "He recently hit on me in a hot tub in Gstaad. He also seduced my daughter once. You probably didn't read that in the tabloids. Or maybe you did." She sighed. "There are no boundaries these days."

"Your daughter slept with your ex-fiancé?" I said. This news surprised me, until I realized it did not surprise me at all.

"This was how I tried to retard his hot tub advances. When you remind a man that he's slept with your daughter, most decent ones will desist in their efforts to have sex with you. But not Kluge. I broke his heart when I refused to marry him."

"But how could you?" I said. "How could you marry a man who did that to your daughter?"

"My daughter had nothing to do with my decision," she said. "I don't blame him for what he did."

"Because you think your daughter instigated it?" I asked.

She sighed weightily.

"If you met her you'd understand," she said. "My daughter can only 'manipulate' a man for whom she is a stepping-stone to greater things."

She blotted her eyes with her napkin. Because she pitied Alwyn? Because she was ashamed of her?

I had no idea. Perhaps, to her mind, there wasn't a difference.

She autographed the air, signaling to the waiter that she wanted her check.

She was done with me.

What was more insulting, I wondered: to be lied to about little things, or to be entrusted too quickly with personal disclosures and just as quickly discarded?

The waiter hurried over with her check.

"Well," she said, "I hope you enjoy your stay."

I tracked her as she exited through the dining room, pausing to examine her reflection in the mirror behind the host stand. She didn't pretend she was doing anything but.

"I'm so glad I got to meet you in person," I said before she was beyond earshot. "All these years I thought you were an ugly woman with a face that needed hiding."

I tried to steal her teaspoon—this woman, she interested me now—but the waiter had swept the table of every object of psychometric use, right down to the pepper mill.

I'd failed even to get her signature. When I turned to the page that I'd asked her to sign, I saw that she'd left it blank.

———

I spent the rest of the morning going crazy.

I attributed my brain's mean squirrelliness to the fantastic sleep I'd been getting, the low-glycemic-index spa food I'd been eating, the minerals I'd been osmosing in the thermal baths, the metallic mountain air. Health, I'd forgotten, was a chore of options.

From my room I called Colophon's number in Paris.

No answer.

I tried to reach Alwyn at the Goergen, but was informed that she'd checked out last night.

To test that there were, in fact, no cracks in this fortress, I removed Borka's key from my suitcase. I lay on the bed and clutched it in my hand. Nothing. It didn't increase in temperature by a single degree. Using the spa-branded pencil I drew on the spa-branded paper pad, thinking I might doodle my way to a regression. I doodled a tree, I doodled a city skyline, I doodled a mountain range, I doodled any shape that might lend itself to inadvertent language, to communication, to a message. I stopped to see what I'd written.

A tree, a skyline, a mountain range.

I felt as though I'd suffered an amputation. I felt as though I'd been buried underground.

It didn't help that I had no e-mail.

I returned to the lobby and, standing at a safe distance from the windows, stared longingly outside. All I had to do was enter it, but like a regression I couldn't activate, it warded me off, an impenetrable scene protected by triple-paned glass, a diorama of a world, not a world.

Then I saw the man.

I did not immediately recognize him, kitted out in khaki shorts and hiking boots. He examined the shard-shaped pieces of wood nailed to the top of a stake and indicating, with their pointiest points, directions to various local attractions. When he turned toward the lobby I saw that it was Alwyn's stepfather.

I exited through the side doors. The day was warm and overcast, the air alkaline. The paths that led to the saunas had been groomed of stones and roots, the soil packed and swept by the attendants.

I caught up to him.

"Heading to the saunas?" I asked.

My presence, from which he initially recoiled, modulated once he saw what I was: in the spa scheme of things, a moderately attractive young woman.

"I'm hiking to the sister spa," he said, in German-accented English.

"Me too," I said. "Going for my treatment."

"Treatment?" he said. "What treatment?"

"Oh," I said. "I don't know."

He pinched his chin.

"That's part of the treatment," I said, "not knowing what it is. I was told that preconceptions risk negatively impacting the results of whatever treatment it is that I'm getting."

He resumed his uphill lumbering. I took this resumption as acceptance of my companionship.

I asked him what he did for a living and he told me what I already knew—that he was a Jungian psychotherapist from Berne.

"How far is it to the sister spa?" I asked.

"About three kilometers," he said. "This was the original spa, what they now call the sister spa. I used to come here with my grandfather when I was very small. We had to hike from the railway station. There were none of these silly carts to drive you about.

There was nobody idiotic enough to sweep paths with a broom. It's going to rain."

Two seconds later, it started to rain.

We hustled the last partial kilometer, the path concluding at a large granite bowl that swooped between two peaks. A small, gunmetal lake at its center glistened like a clogged drain. As we neared the front door of the sister spa, located on the lake's edge, I clocked that it was not an active spa at all but a scenic Alpine ruin. The windows had been de-glassed. What remained of the roof was upholstered in yellow lichen.

Near a giant stone hearth we found a pile of logs, with which Alwyn's stepfather built a little tepee in the fireplace.

He pulled a matchbook from his shorts and set the wood ablaze.

"So tell me more about this treatment you're getting," he said.

I considered running with my original lie—this was the treatment, what kind of preconception buster is better than this, to send a person to a spa that is not a working spa—but decided instead to come clean.

"I know your stepdaughter," I said.

He grunted.

"Given my experience, that strikes me as impossible," he said.

"Maybe you haven't tried hard enough," I said.

This was an accusation he'd heard before.

"She's a troubled one," said Alwyn's stepfather. "Me, I see only the manifestation of her demonic animus."

"Because she slept with Kluge?" I said.

He did not seem surprised that I should know about Kluge.

"Kluge and my wife were involved years ago. Alwyn is very competitive with her mother. Ergo, she slept with her mother's former lover."

"You make it sound so logical," I said.

"I once believed it was logical," he said. "I once believed that Alwyn's father had molested her as a young girl, and that this had created a sexually competitive relationship between the daughter and the mother, with unhappy results for both."

"You don't believe that now?" I asked.

He poked at the fire.

"People accuse therapists of seeing abuse where there isn't any; of fabricating memories for their patients. Maybe this is true. But if so, it's because neurosis without a perceptible cause is very hard to accept. How does one fix a problem that arose from nothing?"

I shivered in my wet dress. He removed his sweater—also wet—and wrapped the arms around my shoulders.

But problems don't arise from nothing, I thought. This man, this professional interpreter of the source codes of neuroses, was blind to the contributions Alwyn's mother had made to the emotional construction of Alwyn. Though I was primed, via my Workshop courses, to mock and reject psychological causality, in Alwyn's case, such causality seemed inescapably apt. After spending a matter of weeks with Alwyn and a mere ten minutes with her mother, theirs struck me as a behavioral muddle with a tragically easy explanation—Alwyn's mother could not square her identity as a sexualized woman with that of being a mother, thus her neglected daughter's sole option was to de-daughterize herself by becoming a sexualized woman, and subsequently a competitor worthy of her mother's attention.

I inspected Alwyn's stepdad, his new hiking boots, his expensive watch. Maybe this variety of blindness was his husbandly mandate; maybe, like my father, it was not his role to understand his remote wife, or to act as her spokesperson to her offspring. Still, it seemed undeniably evident that his wife had played a role in Alwyn's Alwyn-ness in that she'd refused to play a role. She'd been an emotional absence, a neglectful null.

I corrected my original thinking. Indeed, problems do arise from nothing, arguably the most vicious ones do.

We have a lot in common, you and I.

It turned out that Alwyn and I did.

Alwyn's stepfather and I stared into the fire. He was a nice man, not just because he'd given me his sweater, or because he reminded me of my own dad in a way, a man who interpreted his "protector" role as an internal affair. He was not protecting his family members from outside threats; he was protecting them from each other.

"My mother killed herself when I was a month old," I said.

He took this in professional stride.

"I'm sorry to hear that," he said.

"There's no need to be sorry," I said. "That's why I don't tell people."

He asked for the details: I told him that she'd taken a bottle of sleeping pills while I'd been napping in the next room. The fact that she'd killed herself in such close proximity to me was often cited by our town gossips as proof of her derangement: What kind of person could have killed herself with her infant so nearby?

But *why*? I'd always wanted to ask. Was death contagious? Did it release a toxin into the air? Why did I need to be protected from her, from it? Because wasn't it *more* caring for her to die with me asleep in the next room? Wasn't this the more compelling expression of maternal love, of her inability to be apart from me, even as she guaranteed that she would forever be apart from me? I preferred to route my understanding of the situation through Sylvia Plath's children, for whom plates of toast had been left and an insulating towel wedged beneath the bedroom door while their mother went about her business in the kitchen below, these details meant to signal to them, when they awoke, both her maternal commitment and her level of pitiable derangement, also the sad ways that a mother's love can be amplified or reduced to acts both monumentally considerate and monumentally selfish. A towel. An oven. A plate of toast.

"She must have been suffering from postpartum psychosis," he said.

"So it's my fault," I joked.

"I'm sure you've spent a great portion of your life wondering if it was," he said.

"No," I said. "Or rather, yes. But not in a way that I take personally, if that makes any sense."

"Maybe she believed she'd do more harm to you alive than dead," he said.

"Maybe," I said. *She was a bad person, you see.* Maybe she understood herself as a form of human contagion. Thus she eradicated herself, and my father helped, via his periodic small disclosures, to regularly inoculate me against any trace remnants of her unique disease, in hopes that I would not catch it.

"Whatever the reason," I said, "she did what she thought was necessary, despite the hideous personal cost. Thus I refuse to experience her absence as some great tragedy I must spend my life overcoming."

Alwyn's stepfather examined me dubiously.

"I'd like to think," he said, "despite any polite hopes that my daughters—I have two from a previous marriage—" he clarified, "could live happy lives without me, that my death would also, in some irreparable way, ruin them."

"How candid," I said.

"I thought that's what we were being," he said.

"OK," I said. "In the interests of candor, let me ask you this: why haven't you or your wife seen Alwyn's vanishing film?"

He squinted at me.

"Is that what she's calling it?" he said.

"You might find it therapeutic," I said.

"Might I," he said. "Somehow I can't imagine that watching one's stepdaughter engage in pornographic acts with strangers qualifies as therapeutic under any circumstance."

"You have the wrong idea," I said. I guessed he'd seen one of Alwyn's porn homages to Varga.

"I don't think I have," he said. "Do you know what it's like to be in a hotel room on a business trip, and to be flipping through the television channels, and to stumble across a film of your stepdaughter, from whom you've heard not a single word in a year, performing fellatio? Although *perform* isn't the right word. Being penetrated, via the mouth, while she lies there unmoving. I watched long enough to determine that she wasn't dead."

(A sidebar me was impressed that Alwyn's work had been so widely distributed; these porn films were not just "hobbies.")

"In her defense," I said, "she saw these films as art."

His eyes watered. He poked at the fire.

"When Alwyn deigned to contact us, it was to invite us to a screening of another of these repugnant films. For the sake of our mental health, I counseled my wife to refuse to be an audience to Alwyn's narcissistic theatricality. She believes her daughter made a heartfelt confessional film. She has no idea."

She did make a heartfelt confessional film, I almost said. But I didn't. I had no idea what kind of vanishing film Alwyn had made. Maybe hers was as stiff and unrevealing as mine had been—an attempt to explain what was not explainable or forgivable. Would her mother and stepfather have learned any more about her by watching it? Maybe not. Maybe the porn films she'd made were the more accidentally revealing documents.

"If that's how you felt," I said, "then why did you hire the detective?"

"Excuse me?" he said.

"You and your wife hired a detective. And yet it seems you have no interest in finding her."

This, for whatever reason, stunned him.

"She told you we'd hired a detective?" he said.

I confirmed this; meanwhile, a heavy dread settled in my gut.

"Well," her stepfather said hoarsely. "I'd find that lie comical if it weren't so utterly heartrending."

He cleared his throat, scrubbed his cheek with his knuckles.

There was nothing left for us to say.

He handed me a coal hod and asked me to fill it with dirt so he could smother the fire.

Outside, the rain had thinned to a mist. I turned my face upward, allowing the moisture to settle on my skin. My hands jittered, my stomach adrenaline-queasy. I recalled Alwyn's professed envy over the fact that someone hated me enough to attack me. Hate, she'd said, is a form of emotional attachment. How had I missed that Alwyn had been lying to me about the detective, how had I missed that she was maybe really suffering? She'd vanished herself, after all. She'd been suicidal, once. It was my error not to understand: anyone can find themselves on the brink. Anyone can wake up one morning and decide against living. Every single day, the very healthiest among us might be seen to have a fifty-fifty chance of survival.

The ground swamped and sagged under my feet. I'd eaten something that didn't agree with me for breakfast, I thought. I was dehydrated. But then the post-quarantine side effects Mike warned me about—the reason he'd recommended a gradual reentry—started to take hold. Or at least that seemed the most logical explanation for what happened next. Sounds torqued and amplified—each leaf rustle and twig skitter a sonic boom. Each millibar of dropping air pressure a thunderclap. I heard a horrible sandpapery grating I could not place, but which seemed to occur every time I blinked. I experienced a vertigo so intense it was as though I had been gutted by a suction nozzle.

Then everything went quiet.

Even I went quiet. Quiet in the head, quiet in the nerve endings. Snowstorm quiet.

And I felt the presence. I was not alone. It's impossible to describe this sensation to those who are numb to such things, but there's an involuntary quality to certain experiences, like the skin tingling that precedes vomiting. You can't *help* but feel.

When I opened my eyes, the wolf stood about six feet from me. It looked more or less like the pictures I'd seen of wolves, save this one seemed shorter and more compact, almost dog-like. It gripped the ground with four giant paws, its fur quilled along its spine as though it had just emerged from the lake.

We stood there, the wolf and I. I kept my gaze on the ground, angled so that it appeared in my peripheral vision. I did not want to die surprised.

Staring at the wolf this way, however, I noticed that it was surrounded by a spiraling nimbus, one that coagulated for the span of an eye blink into the astral imprint of a black-haired woman.

Madame Ackermann.

I should have been terrified. I wasn't. I was pissed. Her appearance registered as a physical space violation, as "unfair," even though psychic attacks, to my knowledge, had no rules of engagement, there were no Geneva Convention guidelines to humanely shape one person's cruelty toward another. Fine to kill me from the inside. But a wolf, an actual wolf, struck me as beyond the pale.

The wolf growled. It took two steps closer. It growled again.

"Go the fuck away," I yelled. "Go the fuck away, *leave me the fuck alone.*"

The wolf pawed at the ground so viciously I heard the thick canvas sound of its footpads tearing.

"*Leave me alone,*" I said, holding my ground. "*Leave me alone, you bitch.*"

The wolf lurched—it intended to remove a chunk of my throat, I thought—but no. It bowed its head to the ground and made horrible noises, roiling gags that threatened to bring up an organ.

Jesus, I thought, watching it convulse. This was no monster; this was barely more than a plain animal, shivering in the astringent wind that, once freed from the toothy firs, gusted unobstructed across the stone.

To think I've been afraid of this, I thought. *To think I've been afraid of* you.

The astral swirl of Madame Ackermann was barely visible now, her hair dissipating into the air like smoke from an extinguished fire.

I reached out to touch its fur—whatever "it" was. Not to pet it, not to comfort it. Just to ascertain to what degree it was really there.

But the wolf backed away, reversing a few frightened paces. We stared at each other. The eyes—it would be wrong to say that I recognized them, more accurate to say that I recognized something *in* them. A flash of myself, a trapped and desperate filament of me.

I reached toward it again.

"Come here," I said.

The wolf seemed caught between instincts, uncertain whether or not to flee.

"Come," I repeated. "I'm not going to hurt you."

I'd like to think I meant it.

"What's happening out here?" said Alwyn's stepfather, exiting the ruin.

He saw the wolf. He froze.

"Don't move," he said.

He grabbed a crutch-length walking stick, whittled by a bored hiker and abandoned beside the doorway. He wielded it like a lance. *"Gehen Sie zuruck zu ihrem holz!"* he yelled. He jabbed the stick toward the wolf's muzzle.

"Careful!" I said. "It's sick."

The wolf reared back on its hind legs.

"Zuruck zu ihrem holz!" Alwyn's stepfather yelled again.

The wolf turned, its body rolling over its ribs with a serpentine smoothness, and disappeared into the woods.

I experienced a tugging sensation in my chest; then a snapping, a sharp elastic recoil, followed by a dull pain.

I knelt on the granite. Tiny puddles of blood marked the wolf's departure. I touched a wet, oblong spatter. The ache behind my ribs sped to a state of fibrillation, a symptom taking flight.

The ache subsided. And then I felt emptier than ever.

"My God," said Alwyn's stepfather. "How long was it standing there?"

"I'm not sure," I said.

He helped me up. As we started back down the mountain, I repeatedly swung my eyes backward. I wanted to see the wolf again.

"So," I said. "What would Jung say?"

"Jung?"

"About the wolf."

"Often the self is represented as a helpful animal," he said. "But I imagine Jung would say you were lucky not to be killed."

"By my own subconscious?"

I glanced behind us. Nothing followed us but wind.

"Wolves," he muttered. "Wolves are the footmen of the weak."

⸺∞⸺

At the spa we were greeted with disbelief.

"There are no wolves in Breganz-Belken," said the man who'd driven me from the train. He was, or so I guessed, the closest thing the spa had to a security guard.

Alwyn's stepfather assured the man that we'd indeed seen a wolf.

"How big?" the man asked.

We estimated the size with our hands.

"As I said, we do not have wolves in Breganz-Belken," he said. "The altitude is too much for them."

I asked him about the wolf sounds that were piped into my room. Certainly this suggested that wolves were native to the area?

"Those are not wolves," he said. "Those are lynxes."

"It was sick," I said.

"Rabies," said the man. "Only a wolf that had *lost its mind* would come to Breganz-Belken."

He regarded me meaningfully. I guessed that he'd been apprised of my schizophrenia diagnosis.

The man issued German orders to an underling with acne so severe it would seem grounds for firing.

The underling unlocked a nearby broom closet. He removed from it a long rifle.

The woman with the pearlized skin found me by the windows, watching the underling hike up-mountain with his gun.

"Do *you* believe I saw a wolf?" I asked her.

"As opposed to a lynx?" she asked.

"No, I mean . . . the exposure to energy frequencies after leaving the spa, I was wondering if maybe the wolf wasn't an actual wolf."

"You think it was a mirage," she said.

"Yes," I said, though the phrase in my head was *visible thought forms.* I recalled a comment Alwyn's mother had made: *your worst self loosed upon the world.*

Had this wolf come for me or from me? I'd assumed the wolf was connected to Madame Ackermann; now I wasn't so sure.

"But Herr Schweitzer, he saw the wolf as well," she said.

"Who?"

"Your friend," she said.

"Oh, yes," I said. I'd never learned Alwyn's stepfather's name.

"Herr Schweitzer is not enrolled in the same therapy," she said. "So I would think that your wolf was a wolf."

"Except that there are no wolves at this altitude," I said.

"Well," she said, "it would be more true to say that there are not a lot of wolves at this altitude. We wouldn't want to discourage the hikers."

She withdrew some papers from her briefcase.

"As disappointed as I am that you were unable to honor the terms you agreed to," she said, "I think that we can reach a fair termination resolution."

The terms were this. I'd be expected to pay half of what I owed so long as I departed immediately and promised never to mention the wolf.

The pearlized-skin woman also agreed to give me a week's worth of the supplements prescribed to successful test subjects.

"These will ease the discomfort of reentry," she said.

I visited the front desk to settle my bill and book my train to Paris. I'd be arriving earlier than Colophon or Alwyn expected me to arrive, but no matter. After my Madame Ackermann encounter—if that's what it had been—I felt desperate, unhinged.

"Oh," said the woman behind the desk. "This arrived with the morning mail."

She handed me a postcard mailed from Vienna, the front of

which featured a photograph of a building unprettily named the Szechenyi Austro-Hungarian Gallery Archives.

I recognized Borka's script.

"YOU WILL FIND HER HERE," she'd written. "ASK FOR FILES ON DOMINIQUE VARGA."

Given my repeated failures to intuit when danger awaited me, it should come as no surprise to learn: I went.

part Five

I paid the taxi driver with Borka's money. After settling the Breganz-Belken bill, I was down to my last few euros. I tipped him amply, honoring the tradition of reckless generosity exhibited by the soon-to-be-destitute.

When asked to pay an entrance fee at the Szechenyi Austro-Hungarian Gallery Archives, I made a great show of looking for a fanny pack that had been stolen. The first guard summoned a second guard. I thought that everyone who'd ever met an American tourist knew of the term fanny pack, but this wasn't the case with these two. Much more attention was paid to the bewildering phrase "fanny pack" than to the pretend fanny pack's theft.

"So the pocket is on the outside," said the second guard. "It is a fanny pocket." He patted his rear.

"Yes," I said, "except I wore mine in the front."

"And where is it now, your fanny pocket?" he asked.

I told him that the straps had been cut by a thief, thus the whole pack, or pocket, was gone.

"Fanny pack," the first guard said. Saying it gave him permission to stare at my ass. "Fanny pack."

He let me through without paying.

The air inside was palpably damp, and no surprise given the archives were housed in an old monastery with thick stone walls that weep as a matter of clichéd atmospherics.

I walked past the exhibit halls to the computer terminals, located in a crypt-like annex. I enlisted the help of a clerk wearing a bolo.

"Dominique Varga," I said. "Everything you have."

The clerk disappeared through a turnstile activated by an ID card hung from a chain that dangled to his groin. He was gone for so long I suspected he'd used my request as an excuse to eat his sandwich. A half hour later the turnstile beeped.

He beckoned me to follow him. He placed a binder on a desk; he pulled it gingerly, like evidence of a long-unsolved crime, from its clear plastic bag.

"No films?" I asked him.

"*Madame*," he said, understanding the sort of films I was referring to. "No."

The binder contained chronological photos—of Varga's elementary school class (girls in braids and shin-length jumpers), of Varga in a skiff, of Varga on a park bench framed by plane trees, of Varga at a gallery opening, of Varga at her murder trial, of Varga on the courthouse steps beneath the damp crow slump of an umbrella.

At the back of the binder I found a sealed envelope with my name typed on the front.

I checked to see if the clerk was watching me. He wasn't.

Inside the envelope were photos of the naked protester who'd lain in the courtroom aisle during Varga's trial to exonerate her of the murder charges, the woman who'd appeared in her fake snuff films.

A close-up of her face made my pulse seize.

I passed a hand over the image of my mother lying on the courtroom floor. "Excuse me," I said to the clerk. "Who is this woman?"

The clerk, wary, approached.

"Ah," he said. His face assumed a sly cast.

"She was . . . an actress?" I asked. I wiped my forehead; according to the blue light cast by the overheads, I was sweating a clear liquid the color of antifreeze.

"She was her muse," he said.

"Her muse?" I said.

I recalled Irenke and her apologies. *She used me and then she dumped me, pretended I'd never existed. I had to make her suffer for what she did.*

This voice-over loop accompanied an image I retained from my first visit to the Parisian hotel lobby, the day of Irenke's audition—Madame Ackermann stepping blithely off the elevator while the women around her wept.

This image hiccuped, rewound itself. Madame Ackermann stepped off the elevator again. And again. Finally the film rolled forward. Madame Ackermann strode toward the front door. Her hand grazed my cheek, flicking the exact spot I'd burned during my Dr. Papp balloon exercise, the spot that had darkened despite the ointments I'd applied, becoming an indelible shadow.

And I knew.

That woman was not Madame Ackermann; that woman was my mother, fresh from her audition. She'd avoided Irenke. I witnessed her moment of no longer needing Irenke's help, of "dumping" her. She'd won the role, she was the muse. Did that explain why she hadn't stopped to talk to me? Because I was sitting near the last person she wanted to confront?

She must have known I was there. She must have known. How could she not have known? A funny thought occurred to me—funny because it was temporally impossible, also funny because it was so banal, it was such a predictable and self-centered daughterly gripe—*she chose her career over me.*

I turned over the photograph.

152 West 53rd Street, Room 13, on October 24, 1984, Borka had written. *We have our deal.*

The stone walls bulbed outward like overfull sponges. I could see the pores. They leaked, and I could hear them leaking, but the sound wasn't of plain water, it was the hiss produced by acid, a cold wetness that is also a burn.

I had to get out of here.

"You don't look so good," the clerk said.

He offered to escort me to the exit. En route we passed a woman in a headscarf.

"Hey," I said, grabbing the sleeve of Borka's coat.

But when the overhead fluorescents illuminated her face, I saw it wasn't her.

I walked more quickly, the hallways contracting and lengthening and making it seem as though I were moving backward on a conveyor belt.

Just beyond the stinking lavatories, the clerk and I passed an exhibit room. A black-and-white banner inside caught my attention.

"Wait," I said.

The clerk followed me into the room.

"What is this?" I asked him.

"It is a traveling show," he said. "It translates to 'Unexplained Tchotchkes.'"

The exhibit resembled the others I'd passed on the way to the computer room—random objects in vitrines.

These particular cases were filled with bits of paper pinned to cork. I recognized a few: A parking ticket from Provincetown (expired meter). A receipt from the Norma Kamali store in Manhattan (two maillots and a turban).

I pressed a hand to the wet glass. I left a beaded print.

"I worked on this exhibit," I said. "It must have traveled from Scotland."

"Mmmm," said the clerk.

"This woman's parents were Viennese," I said, as though trying to explain to myself what the hell this exhibit was doing in Vienna.

The clerk didn't respond.

"It's called ParaPhernalia," I said.

I put a hand to my face. My fingers could feel the cheek but the cheek couldn't feel back, as though the nerve endings had retracted into my spinal column, leaving my face to die.

"That's the word in English," I said, leaning on the clerk's shoulder.

The clerk hustled me to the exit. I was fast maturing into a problem.

The guard stationed near the front desk waved and smiled.

"Fanny pack!" he called after me.

Once outside I hailed a cabdriver, then realized I had no money with which to pay him.

———⊷———

I spent the next four days in the hotel my cabdriver recommended, one that accepted Alwyn's credit card. I lay on my bed, I gripped Borka's key, I tried to regress. Borka had lied; she had known my mother. Apparently she intended to toy with me until I gave her the information she wanted.

For obvious reasons, I did not think too much or too vividly about the implications of the photo I'd seen in the archives, because to do so required a leap my brain could not, given my special brand of inexperience, make. Dead mothers don't have sex because dead mothers don't have bodies, they do not kiss fathers or partners, they do not nurse children, they are not touched and fondled and invaded and reviled, they have never provided a confusing source of comfort, disgust, shame, delight. I had not grown up with a mother, true, but more specifically I had not grown up with a mother's body. I had not understood this body, from the time of my first awareness, as a body used with and by the bodies of others.

To contemplate her as a sexual being placed me in the strangely inverted position of a mother contemplating her daughter as a sexual being—what never was suddenly *is*. An innocence is lost. Arguably that innocence was mine. I saw things in my head that I tried very hard not to see, and only on occasion succeeded in not seeing them.

Instead I lay on my bed and held Borka's key, but the trail had gone cold. The key rested in my palm and refused to lead me anywhere. I blamed my days at Breganz-Belken. My talents had been stifled by that bunker. I also blamed the woman I was trying to find, the reticent owner of Borka's key. She did not want me to visit.

After four days, I gave up. I hadn't eaten; I'd barely slept. This could not go on. I'd die trying to make this key talk. I required something more—an object. A portal. I required an open wound.

I knew what met this criterion. The film still the old snapper owned of Borka after she'd been catapulted through the windshield of a car. What crucial details Borka would not disclose to me, I would force her old face to admit.

For the first time in four days, I left my room.

As I was about to climb the steps to the old snapper's building, his front door opened. I ducked behind a newel post. Familiar voices said "many thanks" and "best of luck with your research."

Colophon, it seemed, was no longer in Paris.

He looked awful, his cheeks erratically whiskered like those

Wooly Willy games where you drag the metal filings with a magnet-tipped pencil and deposit them in clumps on Wooly Willy's smiling face. The notable difference being: Colophon was not smiling.

I tracked him to a café. From across the street I watched him order and, right when his coffee arrived, dash to the bathroom.

By the time he returned, I was sitting at his table.

"Hello," I said.

He was not happy to see me.

"Alwyn told me that you'd gone back to New York," he said.

"I can just imagine what she's told you," I said. "She wasn't doing the work we thought she was doing, was she?"

His shoulders tensed.

"You knew?" he said.

"That she was using me to do her own 'research'? Yes. I knew."

He dipped a sugar cube into his coffee, watched as the brown stain soaked upward.

"You're taking it better than I did," he said. "It appears we were just a means to an end."

I wasn't sure which end he was referring to in his case; but nor did I need to understand. I knew why and how she'd used me. That was all I required.

He gave me a bleary once-over.

"You seem well," he said.

"You don't," I said. He really did look like shit, like Virginia Woolf after she'd been dredged from the river bottom.

"How did you find me?" he asked.

"Were you trying not to be found?" I asked.

He withdrew his cigarettes. He gestured at a nearby busboy for an ashtray.

"I know where you've been," I said. "At the old snapper's flat. I saw you there."

"What's an old snapper?" he asked.

"A paparazzi," I said. "But not a young one."

"Oh," he said. "Jonas."

I was ashamed to admit that I'd never learned the old snapper's name. An apparent trend. I interrogated people but failed to ask them the most basic questions.

Colophon handed me an envelope.

"I planned to mail this to you," he said.

I opened the envelope. Inside was a sizable check, payable to me.

"But I didn't find Varga," I said.

"I've put you through a lot," he said, "and for nothing, as it turns out."

"What do you mean?" I asked. "Varga's dead?"

I didn't want her to be dead; I needed for once to talk to a living person. Relying on the dead to help me understand the dead—it was not panning out for me.

"In a matter of speaking," he said.

"In whose manner of speaking?" I pressed.

Colophon studied me, as if trying to decide whether or not I was worthy of knowing what he knew.

"I thought Alwyn might have told you," he said.

"Told me what?" I said.

"She isn't dead," he said.

"And you—or she—discovered this how?" I said. *Wait*, I thought. *Alwyn* knew?

He didn't answer. Instead he reached into his briefcase for a pair of folders, one of which I recognized as belonging to the old snapper.

He handed this file to me. The other he pinned beneath his elbow.

I flipped through the familiar Varga film stills. Possibly, I thought, the old snapper had sold Colophon the still of Borka's post-car-accident face.

He hadn't.

I shut the folder. I handed it back to him.

"Where is she?" I asked.

He stalled for time, lit another cigarette.

"She's currently involved in a distasteful art piece," he said.

"How unlike her," I said.

Colophon cross-hatched the utensils of the two unused place settings. He lay the knives perpendicular to the forks. He made me think of a man stranded on an island, creating a pictogrammic SOS of branches in the hopes he might be rescued from above.

"She had a baby, as you already discovered," he said. "A daughter that she gave up for adoption. Later, when the daughter was an adult, she tracked Varga down."

From the folder beneath his elbow he withdrew a photograph of Irenke in a familiar hotel lobby. Whoever had snapped the photo had been sitting in the chair I'd sat in when I'd visited her there.

The photographer might even have been me.

"That's her," I confirmed dully. "That's Irenke."

"It's possible Varga had no idea Irenke was her daughter until after Irenke was dead."

"Oh," I said. Was he still making excuses for Varga? "When did she die?"

"She died in 1984," he said. "She killed herself, you know."

"She killed herself?"

All along I'd understood Irenke to be dead. Why was this information any more unsettling? Yet it was. I was blind to the secret mental sufferings of the people right in front of me. Alwyn, Irenke. I might have intentions to kill myself about which I was unaware.

I knew, as Borka had claimed, so much nothing.

Though it was the last thing a person like Colophon could handle, I couldn't help it. I was so tired, I was so very, very tired.

I started to cry.

"That was the assumption," Colophon said. He busied his hands with a napkin so that he had an excuse for not soothing me with them. "She didn't leave a note, exactly, but . . . there were indications."

"What about Cortez?" I asked, not able to learn anything more about Irenke.

Colophon reconfigured his fork-knife pictogram.

"There was never anything between Cortez and Varga. Somehow Cortez ended up with Varga's film reel. For all we know she gave it to him on purpose, to mock and derail the careers of future scholars like me."

"I'm sorry," I said. I knew how much he'd banked on the Cortez-Varga connection. She could have been an aesthetic double agent, her moral lapses redeemed. Now she was just a dictator's former propaganda minister whose acts could not be ideologically salvaged and repackaged, not even by an academic.

"You really do look well," he insisted, despite all immediate evidence to the contrary. "I'm glad, at least, that something good has come of this. You've recovered your health, I mean."

We sat without talking. Colophon smoked his cigarette to the nub.

Since he did not intend to offer them to me, I pressed him for the details. Where and how he'd found Varga.

Colophon flagged the waiter; this time he ordered a whiskey.

"I should lie to you," he said. "But I don't know you well enough."

"Well, hooray, I guess."

He patted the second folder. "Look in here if you're curious," he said. "However, I don't recommend that you do."

He excused himself to the restroom.

I held my wrist over the folder. The veins contracted, cautioning me to go no further.

I disregarded these warnings. Besides, I knew what Colophon didn't want me to find. My mother had acted in porn films. He, like my father, didn't want to be the one responsible for my knowing this.

The file contained newspaper and wire clippings about the surgical impersonation case, some of which I'd read before, some of which I hadn't. In particular I had not read the classified Interpol reports, which described in greater detail the sightings and, in a few cases, the arrests. When questioned, the impersonators claimed to be working for a leader whose name they could not disclose because they did not know it, they communicated with this leader via a website that, once traced by authorities, was proven to belong to an artist who'd assumed the identity of a Hungarian cosmetics heiress named Borka Erdos.

I experienced a brain disorientation so intense it was like an upheaval of tectonic plates. I did not need to be told who this artist was.

But this was hardly the worst of it. Included in the file was Dominique Varga's mission statement for her current performance art piece, *Memorial*.

We are against forgetting the dead. We are against recovery and healing. To "heal" is to entomb, forever, the sickness. To that end we are bringing the dead back, not to haunt, but to remind us that we are always in the presence of their absence. Because when are we most aware of missing someone—when they are not with us, or when they are?

I experienced her words like the over-and-over falling of a dull ax against the exterior of my mundane egg. At first my shell resisted, but soon a powdery indentation appeared that deepened into a crevice and then, as the ax-head penetrated, I felt my eggshell explode into a million crystallized pieces, like a windshield after a body's been catapulted through it.

Which is to say: I knew what I was going to find before I flipped to the final page, and not because I was psychic, but because I was no longer blind to what had been right in front of my own eyes.

On the folder's inside back cover, someone had taped a grainy telephoto head shot of Borka—I mean, Dominique Varga. She wore a scarf over her head but it did not disguise her so thoroughly that I couldn't discern, from within its shadows, the beginnings of my mother's face.

The Goergen appeared to have aged a decade during my absence; a slab of facade, the shape reminiscent of Munch's *Scream* figure, had crumbled off the south wall, exposing a rusted capillary system of rebar.

I couldn't say what I was doing here, but I knew that it involved a surgical intervention, it involved blood. I would confront Borka— or rather Varga—and tell her that this was *not* our deal, we were no longer helping each other, and I'd urge her to take a knife to my mother's face and slice it off, and if she didn't, I would do it for her.

And then what would I do? What would I do? Keep it? Bury it? Drape it over my own? It was her, even if it wasn't her. I imagined folding that face up tiny and swallowing it like a pill, I imagined that it could make me better, or it could make me sicker, but regardless I was the chosen receptacle, I was the urn, I was a functional neutrality, I no longer mattered.

These were the kind of deranged thoughts I was thinking.

I also thought about Irenke, Varga's daughter, who'd killed herself without a note. This, apparently, was where the hotel room key was meant to lead me. *How does it feel?* I wanted to ask Varga. *How does it feel not to know why? But is it any mystery? I can tell you without ever visiting that room. She did it because of you. I'd kill myself too if you were my mother.*

Gutenberg Square was oddly empty of both snappers and nodders. On the pavers someone had traced with yellow paint the shape of a fallen body, its arms raised overhead as though slain in the act of making a snow angel.

I shivered. I hated this square, which wasn't even a square; it was a circle, or more of an oval, and it had tricked me to underworlds I had no further need to explore.

Before I could cross the street, a white van pulled up. Two suited men walked inside; seconds later they escorted Varga from the Goergen, head shrouded beneath an overcoat.

The van drove away. No sirens, no pomp. It might have been the very casual kidnapping of a person nobody would miss.

This was exactly what it was.

The van turned the corner and I experienced the same stretching and snapping sensation as when the wolf had retreated into the woods.

But this was different. I did not turn around to search for her, and I did not experience an emptiness when she was gone. I experienced a release, a blessed absence of pressure, as though a tumor that had been pushing on my diaphragm had been removed.

I never, never wanted to see that woman again.

Also—I was done. I experienced this conviction as a measurable drop in blood pressure; this certainty I could have physiologically recorded, if I'd had the tools. I was going home. Wherever that was. I would begin my search by a process of elimination. Home was not here.

I was leaving.

As I readied myself to walk back to my hotel, pack my bags, take a taxi to the airport, fly as far away from this place as possible, a limousine stopped in front of the Goergen. This struck me as odd; most guests did not travel by limousine because a limousine was a snapper magnet. The driver discharged his passenger, a woman. She turned in my direction and gave the square a quick once-over. I hit the pavers; I felt her gaze move above me like the slow-motion trajectory of bullets, a murderous optical sweep of the area.

Madame Ackermann.

I panicked. *She found me.* But then I remembered, with a brief, bitter chuckle, that she'd been tracking Varga, too; she'd discovered, as Colophon had discovered, that Varga was at the Goergen.

She was not here for me.

Unfortunately for her, I was all she'd find.

So sorry, Madame Ackermann, I imagined saying to her. *You* just *missed her.*

I fantasized our confrontation scene, one that might take place in the dining hall over liver tea. I imagined telling her what a shitty psychic she was, slower even than an undistinguished academic when it came to locating her research prey. But nor was that her most notable failure. In her capacity as a psychic attacker, she'd really been outdone. She thought she could haunt me with a stupid e-mail attachment of my "mother"; did it ever occur to her to bring her back to life?

Compared to Dominique Varga, I imagined saying to her, you're an unimaginative bully.

I remained on the pavers, hands in a push-up position, ready to launch if I heard her approach. A pointless plan; what good had running away ever done? I'd run a quarter of the way around the world, and here she was, and here I was, and here we were, and somehow, even though she sucked at psychic attacks, she remained to blame for my life's every crappy turn. Fair or not, I fingered her as the reason it had become a black hole, where nothing proved tangential, where everything, to a cruelly comical degree, mattered.

As I raised myself off the cobbles, I noticed that I'd been lying face down inside the expired person outline. This seemed less creepy than apt. As far as Madame Ackermann was concerned, I was about to rise from the dead.

⸺⸺

The concierge was not pleased to see me.

"I don't suppose you've returned to settle your bill," he said.

"My bill was covered," I said.

He handed me an invoice. "The Internet costs extra," he said. "Also your friend left you something. We charge a storage fee."

He handed me a manila envelope marked by Borka's handwriting.

I refused to take it from him.

He rattled it impatiently.

I took it. Inside was something small, something hard; maybe, I thought, it was her fucking heart.

"I need to talk to her," I whispered.

"Regrettably, 'Borka' is no longer with us," the concierge said.

"Not Borka," I said. No, no, *not* her. I was unmoored, a balloon adrift and about to burst into flames. Who did I need to talk to? What was I doing here?

"The woman from the limousine," I said.

"I'm not at liberty to talk about our guests," he repeated.

"She's no *guest*," I said. "She's my attacker. Call security and tell them the Goergen's been compromised."

He rang a tiny bell. A pair of bellhops, or maybe they were orderlies, stepped from behind a pillar.

"This woman is no longer with us," he said to them. "Please escort her to the outside."

"What?" I said.

The head-bandaged women in the lobby held their playing cards higher in order to more invisibly observe me.

I appealed to their sense of paranoia and elitism.

"The woman who's been attacking me is here," I informed them. "She's posing as a guest. This is an unacceptable security breach."

A woman in a sequined turban approached. I recognized her. She was some Hungarian variety of countess.

"Is it true what she's saying?" she asked the concierge.

"There is no knowing the truth from this person," he said.

"It's the truth," I said.

The countess spoke German to the orderlies, who retreated into the shadows.

"Let's get you some tea," she said.

She gestured me toward a club chair. "You are Borka's friend," she said. "Or whatever her name is."

I wasn't sure how to respond to this.

"Of course I suspected she was not Borka all along," the countess said. "I knew the real Borka when we were girls. We called her Potato. The real Borka was always struggling with her waistline."

"Do you know where she went?" I asked.

"I'm sure she's just dead," the countess said. "She was not a very original girl."

"I meant the woman who was pretending to be Borka," I said.

"The police took her away," the countess said. "And what about all that money? She inherited millions. I wonder what will happen to it now."

I thought, but didn't say, that she probably didn't have much money left after bankrolling all of those surgeries.

"And what she was doing to her own face," the countess said. "Some people have no taste."

"Yeah," I said. "It's pretty tasteless to want to look like some-body's dead mother."

"Why choose to be a person so ugly?" the countess asked.

I started to correct her—Borka didn't look anything like my mother, some varieties of ugly are innate to the host, you cannot excise them with a scalpel—but I did not bother. Who knew what varieties of ugly were innate to my mother? Maybe Borka's new face was unflinchingly apt.

The countess peered around for a new conversation to join, as though we'd been chatting at a cocktail party and tapped our single vein of common interest.

"Excuse me," said a voice behind me, "but is this chair free?"

I froze.

Her voice was both unmistakable and unrecognizable. The girl-ish rasp had hoarsened, her voice box clogged with wet lint. Also it had none of the sonorousness I remembered; instead it was flat, toneless, generic, like a voicemail's mechanical beep.

I turned to confirm that it was her. It was. And yet—it wasn't.

Madame Ackermann lowered herself into the club chair. She set a teacup and saucer on a nearby side table, the porcelain rattling, the acoustics of the lobby seizing upon the noise and amplifying it to the decibel level of an alarm.

"So sorry," Madame Ackermann whispered to her more imme-diate neighbors.

She removed a pair of foam plugs from her robe pocket and screwed them into her ear canals.

Afflictions, many of them, had befallen her. The limp, the robotic voice, the sound sensitivity, yes, but her aura, too, pulsed a damaged Morse. Her face had lost its youthful puff and sunk into dusky channels, her eyes obscured beneath lids so thick they looked blistered.

For a moment I forgot that this woman was attacking me. That this woman was responsible for ruining a year and a half of my life, that she was petty and jealous and deserved to have every ounce of marrow sucked from her bones by a hummingbird.

Even so, a violent wave of *need* surged through me. A need to hit her. A need to pull her hair, tear her face to pieces with my teeth. A need to kiss her.

I stood. To present myself to her, to deliver my accusations, to proclaim to her, as if it needed proclaiming: *you lost.* But as I did so, the envelope fell from my lap. In Varga's understandable haste, she hadn't sealed it; the short drop to the tile floor jogged the contents loose.

It was an engagement ring. I knew in an instant whose. The setting was blandly traditional and the diamond minuscule, a blink-and-you'd-miss-it shard of carbon, the most lavish thing my father, then an assistant adjunct professor in geology, could afford with his negligible savings.

It was pretty, demure, nothing my mother would ever wear, and hadn't.

Inside the envelope was a note from Varga.

I was trying to help.

I fisted the note into a sharp star. I threw it under my chair and retrieved the ring, I cupped it in my palm and waited to receive from it a transmission, bell clear, turquoise in color, a cool swim of talking. But it told me nothing. As an object it was not so much hostile as expired.

But I tried. I did try. *I am not*, I imagined saying to Varga, *too scared to try*. I gripped the ring, that indifferent loop, that metal homage to an eternal, round nothingness. The vise-contraction of my fists shot my blood against the current, reversed it up my arm, backwashed it into my heart.

It was pointless. It was as pointless as trying to force a confession from a corpse.

Then the Goergen's walls made a move on me. The ceiling descended, as did the perversity, the absurd and fucked-up *illness* of my situation. I turned to Madame Ackermann, obliviously mouth-reading a pamphlet.

Inside, something broke. Because the truth was this: I was so, so happy to see her.

Our sick irony, or maybe it was our marvelous one: no one cared about me more than she did. If she was my mother substitute, fine. Better her than Borka. Or rather Varga. Better to be hated by her than to be loved by a monster. I wanted more than anything to hide my head in Madame Ackermann's lap and sob for days. I would beg her to forgive my pettiness, my hubris, my disrespect. She could even keep attacking me for all I cared.

I wanted, more than anything right now, not to be alone.

"Madame Ackermann," I said. "Madame Ackerman. It's Julia." She couldn't hear me through her earplugs.

"*Madame Ackermann*," I yelled, probably crying now. "Please. It's Julia."

From the corner of my eye I noticed two orderlies and a doctor. They held the edges of what appeared to be a white matador's cape.

The concierge smiled at me, quite pleased with what he took to be the imminent resolution, in his favor, of the situation.

"Julia," said the doctor, his concerned tone telegraphing his secret take: mentally, I'd gone rogue.

"How have you been feeling?" he asked. "I hear you're out of sorts."

"If she would talk to me," I said, pointing to Madame Ackermann, "I wouldn't be out of sorts. I'd be in full command of my sorts, if she would talk to me."

He sighed.

"I've made a terrible mistake," I said. I couldn't quite put my finger on what I'd done wrong; but I knew in my bones that I'd done it.

"So I understand," he said.

"I'm glad you understand," I said, "because then maybe you can make me understand."

The orderlies grabbed me. I stared at the countess shuffling cards in her lap.

She'd drugged my tea, that witch. She'd drugged my tea and then she'd faked an interest in me so that the drug would have time to take effect.

The orderlies fastened the straitjacket around my torso. They handled me roughly, so roughly that one of them knocked my mother's ring from my hand. It landed on the floor with a glassy clink (*The dead bell, The dead bell, Somebody's done for*) and slid toward a drain I had never noticed in the lobby floor, a drain identical to the drain I remembered from my dream, one that created in the tiled plane a gentle depression, like a nascent sinkhole tugging on the earth.

The ring tipped over the edge, its vanishing soundless.

I couldn't help myself.

I laughed. And laughed and laughed, until it sounded as though I was yelling at someone. Maybe I was.

My commotion must have achieved a frequency that even earplugs couldn't impede. Madame Ackermann turned her head. She stared at me. She trembled as though hypothermic.

"*You*," she said to me. She pointed a shaking finger. She clutched her stomach and made helpless, wheezing noises.

The doctor attempted to help Madame Ackermann into her chair, but Madame Ackermann stiffened and refused to sit.

"No," she said. She struggled back to standing. Doing so required that she grasp the doctor around the neck and press her cheek against his breastbone.

"Take deep, slow breaths," the doctor said.

"That woman," Madame Ackermann whispered. She refused to say my name. "That woman is attacking me."

"What?" I attempted to say. "No. That's not true."

It wasn't true. It wasn't true.

"This sort of stimulation isn't recommended," the doctor said. "We'll soon have this situation under control. In the meantime, I've sent for a massage therapist."

"A massage therapist," Madame Ackermann said. The bitterness of her tone made the doctor recoil. "You think I need a massage therapist? What I need is a gun."

"It's important to remember," the doctor said, "that those who commit murder are not making smart choices."

She spat at him, a weak ejection of stringy droplets.

"*Murder*," Madame Ackermann said, mouth skinny and wet, a mouth I could never imagine wanting to kiss. "As if I'd waste my energy killing her."

She attacked her face with her fists. She swung like a girl, all her effort channeled into her flailing neck and head so that it appeared as though she were dodging her own blows.

Then Madame Ackermann wet herself. The urine trickled down her leg and over her fleece slipper, pooling on the tiles. The bandaged women vacated the lobby, all mean whispers. Madame Ackermann's feminine hold over the doctor and the orderlies, such as it was, evaporated.

The puddle broke toward me like a slow-motion current

traveling from a flipped switch to an electric chair. *Somebody's done for.*

The orderlies fumbled nervously with the belts near my face.

"Are you worried I'm going to bite you?" I said. Although I think my words were no longer clear.

"I am my mother's daughter," I warned, as they cinched me in. "You should be worried. You should be very, very worried. I am a bad person, you see."

I heard the rasping sobs of Madame Ackermann as she, too, was stuffed into a straitjacket.

I continued to track the urine's progress, now less than a foot away and closing in.

In my head I began a mantra that I hoped Madame Ackermann could hear. *Stop*, I begged. *Please please please stop.* Soon this simplified to *Please.*

I repeated it over and over until I didn't recognize the word anymore.

Please please please please.

I thought the word so loudly I could hear it.

I peered up from the rivulet long enough to catch a glimpse of Madame Ackermann, hair curtaining her face in snotty ropes, the two of us a pair of ruined, straitjacketed twins.

Please please please continued the mantra, uttered by a voice so pathetic and stripped of dignity I was ashamed that it belonged to me.

And it didn't.

"Please, stop," Madame Ackermann begged as the orderlies dragged her past me. "Please," she said beseechingly, as though I were a person capable of saving anyone.

part Six

We decided it would be in poor taste for me to rent Madame Ackermann's vacant A-frame.

"We don't want people to talk any more than they're already going to," said Professor Yuen.

Plus the A-frame was on the market, had been on the market for months. "You wouldn't want them to sell it out from under you," said Professor Yuen, though we both knew it was unlikely that the A-frame would sell, given what had happened to Madame Ackermann. Too many people in East Warwick were sensitive to bad psychic residue, especially in matters of real estate.

Instead I subleased a small apartment on East Warwick's three-block-long stretch of student-oriented commerce. Located above a store that specialized in flannel nightgowns and henna kits, the apartment belonged to Professor Blake, now on semi-permanent sabbatical at a drying-out facility in Kansas. Sparsely furnished with a feeble kitchen but featuring a well-equipped bar conveyed, for no additional fee, to the subsequent tenant, the place proved great for parties, even though the bathroom was a literal closet, privatized by an accordioned rubber curtain that slid back and forth on stuttering runners.

I arrived in East Warwick with very few belongings. What

clothes I had filled two of the five drawers in Professor Blake's dresser. I online-shopped for basics in neutral shades like *groat* and *topsoil*. I purchased a lamb's-wool coat at a vintage store. Winter in New Hampshire was always coming.

While it was never explained to me why I'd been offered a three-year lectureship at the Workshop, compared to the other mysteries of the world, this one didn't haunt me much. The letter from Professor Yuen, by the time it reached me at my father's house in New Hampshire, had been forwarded three times. "We have an opening for a three-year renewable lectureship," her letter read. "I think you'd be perfect for the position."

The letter confirmed that the rumor of my psychically attacking Madame Ackermann had not remained limited to the staff at the Cincinnati headquarters of TK Ltd.

"You're *the* Julia," my TK Ltd. counselor said when he accepted the paperwork I'd filled out to officially unvanish myself.

WOULD YOU LIKE YOUR VANISHING FILM TO REMAIN AVAILABLE FOR VIEWERS?

I checked the NO box.

WOULD YOU LIKE TO MAKE A COMPANION FILM EXPLAINING YOUR REASONS FOR UNVANISHING?

I checked the NO box.

"I'm *a* Julia," I replied, accepting the safety deposit box. Inside was my driver's license, a set of keys to my New York apartment, three silver sticks of gum that had dissolved, coating the drawer with a membranous goo.

"You messed that Madame Ackermann person up," he said. "You should watch her vanishing film."

En route to the bursar's office, I was stopped by a man wearing a pair of elbow-length leather gloves. He introduced himself as Timothy Kincaid. He shook my hand overzealously.

I flinched.

"Bah," Kincaid said. "You can stop with the delicate act. But you sure had me fooled. Any chance you'll authorize me to screen your film for training purposes? We need to be able to spot sleepers like you."

I denied him authorization.

"I'd like to take my original with me," I said.

Kincaid shook his head.

"Not possible," he said. "You signed a contract stating that the original belongs to TK Ltd. But you can stipulate when it can and cannot be seen, of course. We're not total monsters."

From Cincinnati I flew to Boston; my father met me at the airport to drive me back to Monmouth, where I planned to spend the spring and probably, too, the summer.

We didn't talk about my vanishing or my unvanishing. Mostly we talked about quartzite, and I asked him what he knew about an electrobiologist named Dr. Kluge, because it was one of those moments, so rare in our relationship, when my paranormal life intersected with his scientific one. He lectured while I fiddled with the radio. This was a familiar configuration for us, one that had always worked—him driving, me in the passenger seat. We'd always had our best conversations in the car because it allowed us to be in close physical proximity without his ever needing to look at me.

After seeing the photo of Varga's half-finished surgery, I better understood the daily haunting I enacted on my father with my face.

A few weeks after arriving in Monmouth, I received an e-mail from Maurice, my former Workshop colleague who'd not once, while I'd been sick, bothered to contact me. The breezy tone of his e-mail tipped me off. The font twanged on my screen with envy and curiosity.

Got the yen to reconnect, Maurice wrote. *Wondering what you've been up to.*

A day or so later I received an e-mail from Maurice's Workshop confidante Rebecca, never a friend.

Glad to hear your health has improved, she wrote. *Need your address so I can invite you to my wedding.*

She was orchestrating a viewing for my old classmates, I thought. Their idolatry of Madame Ackermann didn't trump their need to inspect the person who'd proven to be the most powerful psychic of all, if the rumors of my destroying our mentor were to be believed. How did she do it?

For all of these people, I constructed a fake auto-response message.

If you're receiving this message, I wrote, *it means that the person you're trying to contact is no longer at this address. Of course there's always the possibility that the person you're trying to contact remains at this address, but does not wish to be in contact with you. Additionally, it's possible that this address has been compromised, and in the amount of time required for you to read to this point, a virus has been downloaded to your computer. Among other forms of havoc, this virus will send all the flame mails you've saved in your "drafts" file, the ones you wisely thought better of sending but couldn't bring yourself to delete, because the anger is still so real.*

In August, the letter arrived from Professor Yuen offering me a job.

Over dinner that night (grilled andouille and grilled bread and grilled radicchio—my father and Blanche prided themselves on never once, during the summer months, turning on their stove), I told them I was returning to the Workshop.

"To take a job," I said.

"A job," said my father. The fact that the Workshop would hire me confirmed its unceasing commitment to charlatanism.

"It's a three-year lectureship," I said. "Renewable."

"Why?" Blanche asked.

"Because if I do a good job, they'd like the option of keeping me."

"No," said Blanche.

"What she means is," my father said, "why did they hire you?"

"Because you don't even have a terminal degree," Blanche added. Blanche was bothered by incomplete degrees and any other endeavor embarked upon and abandoned. She always finished the movies she checked out of the library, even if she hated them. Experiences needed to be sealed up by credit sequences, commencement speeches, death. Closure was her thing, though she viewed it less as a vehicle for acceptance and recovery than as a matter of hygiene.

My father sawed at his radicchio.

"I would think that your health problems would make it difficult for you to commit to a three-year position," Blanche said.

My father cut his radicchio into smaller and smaller pieces until he'd reduced it to a purpled mush.

He pushed his plate away.

Blanche hadn't put scare quotes around "health problems," nor did she need to.

"Sometimes one can resolve the unresolvable by accepting it as unresolvable," I said.

"Hmmm," Blanche said.

"Meaning it only registers to the brain as unresolvable if your brain is trying to resolve it," I clarified.

"So you're not looking to get better," my father said.

"I am better," I said.

Since leaving the Goergen, I told them, I'd been asymptomatic. This was true.

Dinner wound up in the usual manner. My father smoked a pipe on the rattan chair with the giant circular back that rose behind his head like a woven-reed thought bubble. Blanche and I did the dishes and listened to a radio show, on which a curvy actress was interviewed about how it felt to be fat, at least compared to other actresses.

We said good night. We went to bed.

Before I drifted into sleep—sleeping was no longer a problem—I allowed myself to consider the unthinkable: that Madame Ackermann had never been attacking me. But this possibility I let seep into my mind for just a second or two. To release Madame from the blame I'd assigned to her only put me at the mercy of a greater and scarier unknown. What had made me sick?

Maybe Madame Ackermann was innocent, I thought, as sleep closed in. Maybe she was. But of one thing I was fairly certain: I had never intended to attack her.

—∞—

"This will be your office," Professor Yuen said. The walls stank of paint. Without Madame Ackermann's posters—of the chairs from the Vitra Design Museum, of Henry Fuseli's *The Nightmare* (which featured a woman splayed on a fainting couch, a troll-like incubus hunched on her chest)—the room reminded me of an operating room, all brightness and anti-bacterial smells. "We'd prefer if you didn't tack things to the walls," Professor Yuen said. "Certain previous occupants were very disobedient when it came to this rule."

Professor Yuen excused herself to a meeting; she'd be back in an hour, she said, to pick me up for lunch. She was itching to bring me to a new Japanese restaurant, located in a renovated mill that hung over the banks of a river.

"Rural sushi," she said, without a flicker of humor, "is no longer an oxymoron."

I closed my office door. The paint stink, bell-jarred, intensified. From my window I watched Professor Yuen exit the building and hurry down the walkway to her pumpkin-colored Saab. We'd become friends of a sort. Buddies who respected an implied boss–employee hierarchy (she took pains to remind me) as we did banal domestic errands together. She'd driven me to the nearby bigger town, the one with the strip mall, and helped me pick fabric for curtains I'd never sew, and new bedding for Professor Penry's futon at an overstock store that sold discounted sheets, cashews, and pool noodles. She'd requested that I sit by her during the first faculty meeting—because, she implied, the faculty needed to see that she supported me as a new hire, despite my controversial situation. She was assuming the valiant role as my protector. For this, she made clear, I owed her. But soon this gambit revealed itself as a sham, a cover-up of her real motives, as well as a distortion of her actual understanding of the constellated relationship between me, her, the faculty. By befriending me she was taking a stance against Madame Ackermann, thereby challenging those who might seek to defend her, or argue that she should, upon her release from whatever secret asylum she'd been committed to, return. She was locating herself on the side, or so she believed, of true power. I was the muscle. I was the one not to be messed with.

Because look at what I had done.

I did try once to tell Professor Yuen that she might be mistaken. Over a meal of lame dim sum, I'd tried to hammer a dent in her certainty.

"Funny that I don't have any memory or knowledge of attacking Madame Ackermann," I'd said.

Professor Yuen's eyes hardened like those of a person hearing that a loved one has died in a plane crash, then liquefied again when she remembered, *But no, he changed his plans at the last minute, he took the train.*

"The most virulent psychic attacks issue from the unconscious," she said. "Whether 'you' intended it or not is immaterial. We are helpless before our lower power. And isn't it kind of fun," she said chummily, "to think you're living a parallel life about which you're unaware?"

She offered to bring some book by my apartment later that night; she needed me to be as convinced of my covert ruthlessness as she was.

I wasn't. At least I was pretty sure that I wasn't. However, the more I attempted to deny my involvement with Madame Ackermann's misfortune, the more passionately Professor Yuen believed I'd masterminded it all.

So I stopped denying it. Living the lie seemed less aggressively mendacious than failing, by trying, to set the record straight.

Living the lie was not such a bad way to live—especially given the respect I was afforded by those who, in the past, had afforded me so little. When my hire was announced in a Workshop alumni newsletter, I received congratulatory e-mails from Maurice and from Rebecca (*so sorry you missed the wedding*). Professor Janklow invited me to headline a psychic attack conference in Berlin. Professor Hales forgave me for failing to accept his submission to *Mundane Egg*.

Their attentions made me feel good, but not easy. Each morning I awoke and conducted an examination. Head: no migraine. Torso: no rash. Anus: not fiery. Finally I'd get out of bed—cautiously, in case gravity should prove, as it did in the past, my undoing—and run through a checklist of possible failures.

No.

No.

No.

No.

Then I would get dressed.

At the same time, I was regressing like a champ. Gone were the days of patchy psychic activity, impossible to harness. Simply lying down on my new Florence Knoll bench was all it took to send me off to specific destinations, and for hours. Professor Yuen assigned me a stenographer, a young girl named Sheila, soon forced, due to my prolixity, to wear a brace on her writing wrist. She came to my office every morning smelling of men's sporty deodorant, an annoying trait I vowed never to comment upon. Save for the basics, we never spoke.

Despite these successes, the key that Varga had given to me still proved psychically useless. It did, however, unlock the actual door to the actual room where Irenke had committed suicide in 1984; I knew because I'd visited 152 West 53rd Street over a long weekend to collect my few possessions from a storage unit. I'd been unsurprised to discover, at that address, the Regnor Hotel. An interview with a gossipy lifer janitor, a man who functioned for the Regnor as its memory morgue, revealed the grimmer specifics of what I'd known to be the facts—that Irenke had checked into the Regnor Hotel on October 24, 1984; that she'd swallowed a lethal combination of whiskey and diazepam; that her belongings, including a heavy pendant necklace, had been shipped, per the instructions detailed in the note she left behind, to her mother in Paris.

So I'd checked into Room 13, I'd taken a nap on the bed. Contrary to what many believe, rooms in which people have killed themselves are often the quietest rooms, unrattled by restless electrons. My mother's bedroom was a neutral space, a psychic beigeness. I left Room 13 having experienced the same peaceful vacancy. Why Irenke had killed herself remained unknown to me, and just as well. Reasons were for the survivors. They did Irenke no good.

But after my trip to Room 13, Irenke began to let me visit her again in Paris, and pretty soon we'd developed a routine. Every morning we hung out for an hour, like friends meeting for coffee at a local East Warwick café, though Irenke preferred to drink whiskey sours, a bad habit she'd earned the right to enjoy. We had one of those relationships that was organic and easy because we didn't discuss the unpleasant things, and the refusal to do so was not viewed by either of us as an act of cowardice, nor did we view it as an indication that we were incapable of real intimacy.

Because I'd decided—this kind of hating, this kind of faultfinding, this kind of symbolic matricide, it had to stop. If I'd formed an allegiance with Irenke, it was because I'd decided that to befriend Irenke was to ensure that my mother's death did not perpetuate more pointless, self-defeating rivalries among women who, in the end, were only killing themselves.

Besides, we had a lot in common, Irenke and I. We were sisters of a sort.

At the Workshop, meanwhile, my classes were a hit. I dated a variety of blue-collar, off-campus men. I even reconnected with my first boyfriend, James, which is to say that I started sleeping with him again, and we thought, for a week or two, that we were doomed to be a couple. But he was a bit of an emotional mess, his own mother having recently died of something prolonged and horrible, the length of which had enabled him to have too many wrenching conversations with her about how she missed both what hadn't happened to her yet and what had happened to her already with equal vividness. Her dying, she said, made her miss James's childhood and the childhood of his unborn children in the exact same moment, with the exact same nostalgic intensity, which had rendered her life both timeless and collapsed, an immortality in which she existed forever or a grave into which her past, present, and future disappeared. This sort of talking had undone James, and it also, even when related to me secondhand, for reasons I couldn't pinpoint, undid me. We decided to part ways before we overrode our old good memories of one another with new bad ones.

But my illness, even in its absence, made it hard for me to enjoy life. Good health means being unaware of one's health. I was not yet unaware. I visited a number of physicians in the area, all of whom pronounced me *fit as a fiddle*. If it had been difficult to convince my former doctors of the medical validity of an illness comprised of many contradictory symptoms, it was even harder to convince these doctors of an illness whose only symptom was a complete absence of symptoms.

I consulted Professor Yuen, who was sympathetic.

"It's not easy to do what you do," Professor Yuen said. As far as she was concerned, I was still attacking Madame Ackermann.

She recommended that I visit Patricia Ward.

Patricia Ward lived in a winterized cottage, part of a twenties vacation development called the Occum that included a pond, a shingled club house used for staid second weddings, and a five-hole golf course.

"Patricia Ward," she said, giving my hand a hard, efficient shake.

Patricia Ward was too tall for her own house, her hyperbolic blond hair near-skimming the rafters as she walked me to her office, a small room off the kitchen that looked out, through multipaned windows, at a tangle of burdock. She wore severe black glasses, jeans, and a shrug made of linen and tie-dyed in a muted way that whispered, "pricey tribal."

My resistance to Patricia Ward intensified when she led me into her study.

Two black Barcelona chairs faced off over a glass coffee table.

"Sit," she said, gesturing to one of the Barcelona chairs. The leather cricked when my bottom hit it. I winced.

"Are you comfortable?" she asked.

"Very," I said.

She smiled.

I smiled.

I noticed the video recorder on a tripod.

"Is that on?" I asked.

"It can be," she said.

"But it's not currently on," I said. I wanted no more recordings of me that I could not control.

"Not currently," she said. She turned it on to demonstrate. She turned it off.

"See?" she said. "I do, however, prefer to videotape my clients. It's a process thing with me. Also a legal thing."

"Maybe we can work up to it," I said.

She flipped through my Workshop medical file, sent to her by Professor Yuen.

"Do you mind if I ask what you do?" I said.

"Do?" she said. "Didn't Karen tell you?"

Professor Yuen had not.

She handed me a business card that read PATRICIA WARD, SPIRITUAL MIDWIFERY.

"I'm not pregnant," I said, trying to return the card. Patricia did not accept it.

"I'm a *spiritual* midwife," she said. "Primarily I birth stillborn emotions, the fetal remnants of bad pasts. But sometimes I help people birth their true self from within. Sometimes the person you are now is the mother to the future you."

A tiny mobile device rang on her side table. She picked it up, glanced at the screen.

"Excuse me for a moment," she said. She texted with her thumbnails.

"Thank you for your time," I said. "I don't think spiritual midwifery is for me."

Extricating myself from the Barcelona chair required me to roll to my right side, lift my ass in the air, push to a standing position. Among the countless hostile design elements of the Barcelona chair, it featured no armrests. *These fucking chairs.*

I straightened my legs. A wave of nausea knocked me back down.

(I tried not to get too excited about this; a stomach flu had been making the rounds.)

Patricia replaced her phone on her desk.

"There!" she said. "Do you need some water? You're green."

"No water," I said. "I just need to go home."

"You know what Robert Frost wrote," she said, opening a door to a half bath. " 'Home is where, when you go there, they have to let you in.' "

Water battered a tiny basin.

"The cheap platitudes of art," she said. "Home is the oven where you stick your scared little head."

She reappeared with a Dixie cup.

"Then again," she said, waving my file, "when the home teems with emotional vermin, sometimes it's best to return and hire an exterminator."

"That would be you?" I asked.

She flipped her glasses into her hair.

"Your mother," she said.

"My mother is the exterminator?"

"No," Patricia said. "Your mother is the gift. Your stillborn gift. Death is a gift to some people. Death was a gift to your mother. But is death a gift to you? It might be, if you can't give birth to this dead baby mother. But my point: you have options."

The urge to vomit tsunami-rushed my esophagus. I tamped it back.

She flicked on the video camera.

"Tell me about her," she said.

I stared into the camera's eye, determined to give it nothing.

"She's dead," I said.

"But not really," Patricia said.

"Yes, really," I said.

"She lives in you," Patricia said. "Decomposing in you. Poisoning you. Attacking you."

I flashed to that rainy afternoon in the Carpathians, and my encounter with the wolf that had peripherally revealed a dark-haired woman.

"Attacking you," Patricia repeated. "And yet you blame innocent people for your illness. Why? Because she's your mother. She would never do anything to hurt you. She doesn't even know you. A person so uninterested in you couldn't be the cause of your sickness. In order to want to hurt you, a person has to care."

"Fuck you," I said.

"Consider it," she said. "Consider how you've brought this on yourself."

"I'm leaving," I said.

"The sick are never blameless," Patricia called after me. "Remember that when you stick the pistol in your mouth."

I stumbled toward the front door. Why would my mother attack me? Neglect was one thing, but targeted hostility? Then I heard in my head—*you're the hostile one*. And maybe I was. Maybe what I'd interpreted as her inattention, she'd interpreted as mine. And wasn't it true? My search for her had never been a search for her; I'd been searching to feel what I knew I should, by biological rights, feel, but couldn't. Grief, basically, or a variety of grief—one that didn't involve missing a person, one that was far more self-involved. A grief over a grief.

I made it as far as the road before vomiting. I did so discreetly, behind a tree. Afterward I covered the vomit with dirt. Because I was polite even when incapacitated, I thought. Because I was such a decent person that I didn't want to inconvenience anyone, not even Patricia Ward. But as I scuffed the dirt over my vomit, my patch of shame, I felt less like a highly evolved human than a dying animal, covering its tracks so that it could expire with dignity under a rock, alone.

∞∞∞

Toward the end of September, I received an e-mail from Colophon. He'd landed at a university in Lyon, a yearlong scholar-in-residence position at their film studies department, a sinecure he seemed to find beneath him.

He included a link at the bottom of his message. No explanation.

I didn't follow the link, and soon forgot about it. I had a faculty meeting that day. That night I was hosting a student party at my apartment and I'd been tasked to find eclectic bitters for my volunteer mixologist, a scholarly alcoholic named Klaus.

The following day, I was busy being hungover, a state of self-induced illness I'd been experimenting with more and more. My father and Blanche arrived that afternoon for a weekend visit, the two of them in a throbbing marital huff. That night we ate dinner at a French inn-restaurant. After the wine arrived, my father handed me a skinny box.

"What's this?" I asked.

"I found it," he said.

"He didn't find it," Blanche said.

My father glanced at her stonily.

"What?" Blanche said. "You didn't find it."

"It was mailed to me," he said.

"By whom?" I asked.

"It arrived in the mail after you moved back to East Warwick," Blanche said. "No return address."

I opened the box.

Inside was the pendant made by my mother, purchased by Varga, stolen by Irenke, returned to Varga. The surfaces had a molten rumple to them, like metal just pulled from the forge.

"Your mother made it," Blanche announced. "See? Ugly."

Each sinew furled to a menacing point. I pushed against one with my fingertip. Hard. I didn't break the skin. But I could have.

It was as hostile an object as I'd ever touched, and yet I experienced with it an instant kinship. Despite the long line of tragic women who'd owned it, it seemed to have always belonged to no one but me.

I slipped my head through the chain. The pendant hung to my navel, and was so heavy it pulled on my shoulders, dragging me downward. I closed my eyes and imagined: this is what it felt like to be her, or to be around her, or both.

"Was she always unhappy?" I asked.

"Depression ran in her family," Blanche assured me.

"I could never tell if she was happy or unhappy," my father said. "I suppose that says something not very flattering about me."

My father stared into his wineglass.

"She was emotionally remote and impossible to read," Blanche, the old dog, said.

My father made a wall of his hand; he showed it to Blanche.

"I'm sorry," he said to me. "I can't ever seem to tell you what you want to hear."

"You shouldn't worry about what I want to hear," I said. "You should just tell me what you want me to know."

I placed my palm against his, the one he'd erected as a Blanche silencer, and our hands hovered there, supported by our elbows on the table. We might have been arm wrestling except we neither of us pushed against the other. We held our own weight.

My request, I understood, was complicated; what you want a person to know is often the last thing you want a person to know. For example, I wanted him to know about the terrible war waging in my brain. For months I'd lived in terror of seeing Varga's face again, because even that single glance, via a grainy photograph, had initiated a scary variety of override. I could no longer conjure my mother's face without seeing Varga's half-baked rendition, as though the two had been combined by a lenticular lens, resulting in a stereoscopic 3-D effect in which, depending on the angle from which I viewed them, my mother became Varga and Varga became my mother, a rapid alternation that risked a dangerous blurring, even an extinction.

If I'd spoken to anyone about it, I would have spoken about it to him. But I never did. I'd made certain he never knew a thing about Dominique Varga. Given his general incuriosity about the aboveground world, and the fact that most of the press about Varga was in Europe anyway, it hadn't been difficult to shield him from her.

"I've always assumed that you could know whatever you wanted to know about your mother," my father said. "Thus I never had to make the decision about what *I* wanted you to know. Or what she would have wanted you to know. I'm embarrassed to say—that you didn't require me to do this for you, I found it to be a great relief."

"It's OK," I said. "I understand."

"There's so much I can't tell you," he said. "No matter how much I might want to do so."

Then he did what he could bring himself to do so rarely—he looked me in the face. I saw there, surging to the surface of his pupils, an oily flash of shame so repugnant I had to force myself not to look away, to receive this confession he'd chosen, maybe involuntarily, to unloose. He was relieved she was gone. Maybe not immediately, but very soon after she'd died he'd realized— he'd been spared. In their marriage the bad had long outweighed the good, but she would never leave him, at least not by half measures. By dying she'd released him from a life of vicarious, and then increasingly not, misery. She'd been toxic, a chore. Then she died, and he'd never forgiven himself for getting so lucky. He'd been spared her worst, but allowed to keep her best in the form of me.

I understood why he couldn't share this with anyone. I doubt he'd ever shared it with himself.

"In America today," I said, smiling, because I knew when I smiled that I chased her resemblance away, "people overestimate the value of expression."

I meant it. If he was incapable of telling me that we'd been better off on our own, I was just as incapable of telling him that there was a woman living (last I heard) in Paris with my mother's face.

I stored the necklace in its box in the top drawer of Professor Blake's wet bar, alongside his monogrammed muddler. For the obvious reasons, I never touched it. I came to view it as an unusual pet I had to keep in a cage, a small snake or lizard. One night I decided to wear it out.

The party was being thrown by and for Professor Hales, whose manuscript had won a prestigious English prize, the occult equivalent of the Man Booker.

I'd planned to drive with Professor Yuen, who came up to my apartment for a pre-party old-fashioned. She critiqued my outfit as

I muddled the maraschino and the sugar in the bottom of her high ball.

"A little *meh*," she said. "Do you have a colorful scarf?"

I didn't do scarves. Scarves were risky for psychics to wear unless you were Madame Ackermann, the equivalent of accessorizing with a crystal ball and a shoulder crow.

"How about a statement necklace?" Professor Yuen asked.

Since I was, at that moment, replacing the muddler in the drawer beside my mother's necklace, to claim I didn't own such an item would be too much of a bald-faced lie.

"Perfect," Professor Yuen said, eyeing the pendant. "Is that some kind of a dog?"

"Dog?" I said.

She pointed to the pendant.

"It's abstract," I said. "It's nothing."

"That's the eye," Professor Yuen said, pointing to the red stone. "And the snout. A wolf, maybe."

I squinted. It had only ever resembled a mean alphabet to me.

"I'm not seeing it," I said.

The night was clear and cold. I smelled woodsmoke as I walked to Professor Yuen's Saab, parked in a handicapped space in front of the vegan pizza parlor. The full moon shone with arctic intensity over East Warwick, reflecting off the tin roofs of Main Street, glaciating the landscape. We drove past the Workshop buildings, glowing in the woods, and took the scenic route along the river, sinuous as mercury between its banks. The night assumed a déjà vu creepiness that intensified when Professor Yuen turned off the river road and started to climb up the hill that led to Madame Ackermann's A-frame.

"Where does Professor Hales live?" I asked.

"Top of this ridge," Professor Yuen replied.

We passed Madame Ackermann's driveway with its hinged For Sale sign. Through the woods it appeared as though the house was brightly inhabited, but really it was just the moon's reflection in the windows.

The party was like every other Workshop party. Martinis and oven-warmed hors d'oeuvres, high-pitched congratulatory chitter-chatter ballasted by sotto voce bitching. Professor Hales gave a toast to himself—"there's no one better qualified to tout my many virtues"—and a cake the size of a dollhouse was served. I'd drunk too much Prosecco and decided to take a breather in Professor Hales's study, one wall of which was glass, affording a helicopter's-eye view over the White Mountains. I pulled a chair close to the window and stared out at the mostly wilderness. Here and there signs of civilization blinked—windows, a cell tower, the sweep of car headlights on an unlit road—but primarily the scene promoted emptiness and loneliness, an ocean void of lifeboats.

I massaged my neck and between my shoulder blades, which had begun to ache. I lifted the pendant in my other hand, reliev-ing myself of its weight. I was buzzed and trying to relax. Maybe I honestly did fall asleep, and maybe I only dreamed that I stood at the threshold of my parents' old bedroom, the door in front of me a square outlined in light like an e-mail attachment I could click open by touching my hand to the knob. I waited. I heard wind. I touched the door. It opened. The interior was obscured by clockwise-swirling fog.

I entered.

A shadow at the back of the room took on volume and shape. My mother. She lay on the bed. I said nothing, not wanting to dis-turb her, not knowing if I was welcome—nor if I wanted to be. I took a step closer. Then another. She watched me approach; she did not, like some uncertain bird, flee.

Why now? I wanted to ask her. Why now, after all of these

years? But I didn't dare talk. Words had no place in this foggy cocoon. We were, for the first time, meeting. We were only bodies.

But as I drew alongside her bed, she died. Before I could grab her hand and expect it to grab mine back. She closed her eyes and she died. Her body vanished. On the bed there was no trace of her, not even a fossilized rumple of sheets.

This was astonishing. Stunning. Then a boiling, obliterating rage burst from my mouth. The words ricocheted like bullets shot by a person sealed inside a shipping container. Trapped velocity. These words could hurt no one but me. This did not stop me from saying them. Couldn't she have waited until I reached her bed to fucking die? Was that too much to ask? I was sorry that she'd been so miserable. But I did not accept this as an excuse. She'd had a duty to be interested in me; that alone should have kept her alive, at least until my first Christmas, or until my first day of school, or until my first heartbreak, or until my first bad haircut, or until the first time I had a stomach bug and needed someone to hold my head out of the toilet. I had never blamed her for this failure. Not once. Nor did I blame her for possibly sickening me for over a year, or for my entire life. If I had never properly grieved, was that my fault? I couldn't miss her because there was no one to miss. Which made me confused, it scrambled my emotional compass, this magnetic craving toward norths that didn't exist. It was like missing a missing. So the least she could do was wait until I'd reached her bed to die. The least she could do was give me one experience, one, so that I could grieve her—not her absence, *her*—every single day of my life.

The necklace choked me. It was a drag, an unhealthy attachment. I freed my head from its noose. I threw.

Professor Hales genially chalked my misbehavior up to drunkenness, and asked that I pay for the cost of replacing the giant window, which would run me $2,000. Professor Yuen confiscated the necklace from me as though it were a mace I might use to brain an innocent party guest.

"Keep it," I said.

"I'll keep it for you," she said.

"You can sell it on eBay," I said. "You can throw it in the fucking river."

"I think there's been enough throwing for one evening," Professor Yuen responded curtly.

That night I went home and put a block on my e-mail account. aconcernedfriend was not and had never been Madame Ackermann. aconcernedfriend was my mother. And I rejected her variety of concern. I did not need her fucking concern. Concern was a bullshit way of caring for a person you couldn't or wouldn't love.

I figured my breakdown at Professor Hales's would mandate a tarnishing of my status in Workshop circles—I was a lunatic—but instead the shattering of Professor Hales's window was read as further proof of my fiery unpredictability and reinforced my reputation as a person who caused interesting harm.

I was the not-to-be-messed-with genius.

I was the new Madame Ackermann.

This was my victory. This was fate—to become the bad person I apparently, despite the extreme measures taken to prevent my contamination, could not help but become.

In the short term, taking Madame Ackermann's place was my way of graciously permitting the mistake that had been made, for the time being, in my favor. This lie I cultivated because I preferred it to people knowing that I experienced every day as a solitary hell. If I had come to miss my pain, it was not because I was a masochist or a martyr, but because to be free of pain was to be, in the most soul-vacant way, alone. The reason I preferred pain was nothing that a poetic if inaccurate application of the first law of thermodynamics couldn't explain. If matter cannot be destroyed, neither can the lack of matter be destroyed, because the lack, over time, becomes matter, it becomes the equivalent of the plaster cast of the interior of an empty room.

———

A year later, I scrolled through my e-mail inbox—somehow I'd accumulated 3,689 unread messages since I'd returned to East Warwick—and noticed the e-mail from Colophon to which I'd never responded. His yearlong position at the university in Lyon had terminated in the interim, and he hadn't bothered to send me an update on his whereabouts.

Again I saw the link he'd included. This time I followed it.

IS FAILURE TO GRIEVE A CRIME AGAINST THE DEAD? read the headline of an article published in a London art journal. I examined the accompanying photo of Alwyn and Dominique Varga.

A severe bob fit Alwyn's skull like a downhill ski-racing helmet. She sat on the arm of Varga's wingchair, Varga's hand stilled in the act of smoothing Alwyn's head, a gesture so familiar it made me— as though I were the one being touched—recoil.

Varga's face, fortunately, was obscured by shadow.

The article detailed what I'd deduced to be true about Alwyn's involvement with Varga. Varga had contacted Alwyn after she'd seen Alwyn's film homages to her own work. Alwyn, as coincidence would have it, was by then assisting a scholar named Colophon Martin who was writing a book about Varga. Varga'd quite liked Colophon's theories that she'd been "exploiting an ideology," and so hired Alwyn in order to manipulate the story being written about her from within.

"We decided, however," Alwyn was quoted as saying, "that the truth would be more fruitfully misleading than yet another lie."

Alwyn spoke about her undergraduate dissertation—scheduled,

with updates, to be published as a book—that promised to show
how Varga's portrayal of female exploitation and passivity (deemed
"masochistic" and "viciously retrograde pornography" and "satire
without the satire" by her critics) could be construed as an anti-
feminist message that was, in fact, urgently feminist. Feminists,
Alwyn said, had been "killing the mother" or "killing the daughter"
for decades in the name of advancement.

"We are the feminists who know," Alwyn said, "that self-
exploitation is the only safe expression of empowerment and
love."

Finally, the article delved into the financial and legal disputes
surrounding Varga's latest project, *Memorial*. (There was no mention of a woman named Elizabeth Severn. All three of us, apparently, were quite happy to forget about her.) The families of the
impersonated had filed a case against the volunteers who'd had
their faces reconstructed, demanding that these volunteers be
legally required to have their surgeries reversed.

Varga, meanwhile, had, with Alwyn's help, secured the support
of an anonymous patron and hired a criminal attorney to clear her
of the death of Borka Erdos—who had, according to Varga's testi-
mony, died in a car accident "of her own design" on Ibiza in 1980.
Now this same attorney had, on Varga's behalf, filed a countersuit
against the families of the impersonated.

Varga, the article claimed, intended to sue them for murdering
the dead.

───

I left my office. It was October again, the leaves bronze again,
wood-smoke tannins in the air again. Walking to my apartment, I
passed the office of East Warwick's one real estate agency, Slaven

and Slaven, the window papered with listings that obscured the interior from view, as if the office were undergoing a top-secret renovation and would soon be unveiled as a Pilates studio, the first definitive sign: East Warwick was turning into a smugly enlightened yippie hell. The real estate prices seemed to bank on exactly this variety of invader. There was a stone house in the Occum for sale, one that promised a backyard view of an active beaver dam. A contemporary Colonial boasted a stereo mudroom. A dingy ranch on a private mountain awaited its manor rebirth.

None of these houses spoke to me; their prices were beyond my relatively modest income, unless I did as Professor Yuen had suggested I do, namely to sign up with a speaking agent who could, Professor Yuen guaranteed, book me university gigs that would double my annual salary.

You're in demand, Professor Yuen assured me.

Maybe it would be worth it. I imagined spending my nights in university Sheratons, brewing single-serve coffee and amassing a collection of tiny mouthwashes because I liked the turquoise color, pay-per-viewing rom-coms until dawn, suffering the rapidly alternating traveler states of ravenous hunger and, after enjoying a free Continental breakfast of precut melon cubes and shrink-wrapped Danishes, queasy disgust. On the plus side, I would look forward to returning home, even if I still lived in Professor Blake's sublet with the closet-shower and the smell of old cat litter that wafted, on mysterious occasion, from the floorboards near the kitchen sink. My windowless lofted bedroom, the dark alcove furnished by a small desk and a poster of Dürer's woodcut, *Melencolia I*, would seem—in comparison to my hypothetical Sheraton room, papered the bronze of a bad tie—the pinnacle of tastefulness and airiness and light. I would enjoy East Warwick more if I were forced to leave it. And I could make enough money, perhaps, to sublet Professor Blake's apartment back to the undiscerning student population from which it had been wrested, and buy myself a proper house.

Three-year lectureship. Renewable. Workshop code for: unless you molest an initiate (and even if you do), you're a lifer.

I decided to embrace it, my lifer life.

Inside, Mrs. Slaven greeted me. I knew her in the same limited way that I knew most of the locals—a familiar face enhanced by a gossip brushstroke, the equivalent of a photo caption or a gravestone epigraph. Mrs. Slaven was a woman of inscrutable peerage, her Hepburnesque bearing suggesting blood relation to the minor robber barons who'd built country houses in the area at the beginning of the last century, and whose children and grandchildren and great-grandchildren, with the dwindling familial spoils, settled around East Warwick to eke out a year-round life of parsimonious leisure.

But complicating this read was her accent, a local New Hampshire variant with hot-potato vowels and barely hit consonants, diaphragm spasms that sounded like the grunts of a person being punched. It wouldn't be paranoid to suspect that the locals intensified their accents when speaking to us, such that they ever did, underscoring the fact that we did not share so much as a common language. That we were the locals' source of income did not increase their desire to make us feel welcome in their town or in their stores. For this failure to sweeten their demeanors for the sake of money, we heartily respected them. For this respect they respected us. It was a tenuous social means of constructing a town, but it worked.

As per the East Warwick codes governing such interactions, Mrs. Slaven treated me, when I entered her office, as an intruder whom she refused to acknowledge. She busied herself with the unhurried completion of an envelope-stuffing, addressing and stamping task.

After five minutes, she took grudging note of me.

"It's my lunch hour," she said.

"I can come back," I said.

She ignored my offer. She gestured toward a black-lacquered university chair of the physically punishing sort my father owned in triplicate, each with a different gold seal on the narrow backrest, one for every school attended. The seat was slippery and the butt indentation too deep and wide for most butts; plus the seat was canted so that the sitter slid backward until her vertebrae rolled against the spindles and the seat's sharp edge dug uncomfortably into the tendons of her popliteal folds. If there was a chair more hostile than the Barcelona chair, it was the university chair.

I sat.

Mrs. Slaven clicked around on her computer. In a back room, a printer exhaled.

She disappeared and returned with a pile of listings.

"You won't like this place," she said, handing me the topmost listing, for a modestly priced cape. "Built as a summer house, you'll never be able to heat it."

"OK," I said, setting it aside.

"This place might kill you," she said, handing me a log cabin contemporary. "There's a mold problem that will cost thousands of dollars to eradicate."

She showed me a few other places that, she announced before handing me the listing, I wouldn't like.

"Well." She glared at me as though I were the hard-to-please one. "Why don't you tell me what you *do* want."

I stared at her blankly. I wondered how she could ask me this question. I wanted what everybody who walked through her doors wanted. I wanted a home.

Above her computer she'd tacked a calendar, the one given

for free by the heating oil company to its customers, the one once magneted to Madame Ackermann's fridge. They used the same photos every year, switching out the numbered grids below. I experienced for the October photo—of the pond papered shut by red leaves—the muted fondness I felt for a childhood cup, lost for decades in the back of a cupboard. As I stared at the leaves they broke apart and shifted like ice floes. Through those peepholes I could spy the pond beneath, filled not with water but a familiar swirling whiteness.

I saw her. My mother floated in that foggy ether, suspended in a netherworld that was as safe for her as it was empty. I realized: I'd missed her e-mails. She'd sent me that attachment, again and again and again she'd sent it to me, not as an explanation, not as her version of a vanishing film, not because she wanted me to understand why, when she'd been at that crossroads between living and not, she'd opted for not. She wasn't making excuses. She wanted me to be with her at that darkest moment in her life. She wanted not to be alone.

I waved to her as the leaves notched back together, sealing her under the red. Connected by blood, divided by blood. She was my blood. She was my mother. I'd missed her. She'd tried to keep me safe from the pain of her, she'd tried but she had failed. I'd been, from the day I was born, contaminated. She was, even if she wasn't, entirely to blame for me. I was her bodily fault. But I bet, if pressed to choose, she wouldn't have wanted our relationship, insomuch as it existed, to be any other way. Not because she was a bad person. Because she was a person. Because who doesn't want to be blamed by the people she loves, or might have loved? Blame is the cord you can never sever, the viscous umbilical you can swipe at with your hands, but there it will always ghostily hover, connecting you to monsters exactly as pitiful and needy and flawed as yourself. People can vanish or even die, but the blame keeps them present and alive. To be forgiven is to be released into the ether, untethered and alone.

I vowed: I would never forgive her.

I hauled myself out of the university chair. I lay on Mrs. Slaven's couch. I instructed her to take notes.

I described to her what I wanted. A seventies-era A-frame home drastically reduced in price and uninhabited for over a year, formerly owned by a beautiful, sexually promiscuous woman and filled with the residue of a once-fantastic life such as might provide a sort of psychic compost for the next owner, namely me, a person who'd lived in pasts that didn't belong to her and forfeited to feminist pornographer filmmaker performance artists the one that did, a person whose soul was so encrypted by pain that she had come to miss it with an intensity that had mutated into pain (this absence of pain registering as pain), and maybe it was the spirit of her dead mother sickening her, or maybe it was her inability to grieve a person she should, by biological rights, have grieved, but as with so many diagnoses it is, in the end, the symptoms that matter, not the cause, because this is what being alive means, this is what being a person means, to be sickened by an illness known as you.

Also I wanted, while in the study, to be able to hear the baying of coyotes that could be mistaken for wolves. And a Faraday cage in the basement. And a crappy Internet connection so that I could watch, in evocatively slow motion, e-mail video attachments of my mother in the fog. And Barcelona chairs that conveyed, so that I could maybe, on occasion, keep her company there.

Mrs. Slaven finished writing. She capped her pen. She read back to me everything I'd said to her.

She told me she had just the place.

Acknowledgments

All books are collaborations, but this one in particular owes its completion to a team of adult caregivers.

I would like to thank Vendela Vida for her savvy parts replacement help with an early Franken-draft. Ceridwen Morris turned her keen "why do I care" eye on those places where the caring was a little thin, and sent me important fashion links I always cared about. Telica Connelly held our family together when its founders became preoccupied. My *Believer* colleagues Andrew Leland, Ed Park, Vendela Vida, Dave Eggers, Andi Mudd, Sheila Heti, Ross Simonini, Karolina Waclawiak, Meehan Crist, Daniel Levin Becker, and Max Fenton picked up the slack when I was lagging, and made me feel that I was part of something exciting, even when I was by myself. I wasted far too much time writing e-mails to Cath Le Couteur, but in return she always made me laugh, so I guess it was worth it. Binnie Kirshenbaum and all of my students gave me a reason to wear the nice clothes in my closet, and graciously led me to believe that I was making a difference.

The gifted Henry Dunow intuited when I needed confidence

transfusions and when I required tougher talk, but regardless he never bullshits me, and for that I am forever grateful. The team at Doubleday is comprised of the kindest, smartest, and most accommodating people—Melissa Danaczko, Emily Mahon, Alison Rich, Nora Reichard, thank you for humoring my ideas and thirteenth-hour fiddles.

The inspiration for this book came from another book—*Psychic Self-Defense* by Dion Fortune. I hope she won't attack me for using, without her permission, an incident from her life as my springboard.

Bill Thomas cannot be "thanked" under the usual thanking rubric. Genuflection is the more appropriate acknowledgment of his editing wizardry. In his calm-stern way, he drove me to do way better and to push way harder, past my usual exhaustion point; he saw what I envisioned but could not execute. I am a different writer because of him.

Delia and Solly took me on essential daily head vacations. My parents allowed me to take essential vacations from Delia and Solly.

The Guggenheim Foundation and the MacDowell Colony contributed precious space, time, and validation.

Ben Marcus remains the best thing that ever happened to me.

"Entertaining, devastating and as slippery as a strand of its
anti-heroine's lank hair."
—*Los Angeles Times Book Review*

THE USES OF ENCHANTMENT

One Autumn day in 1985, sixteen-year-old Mary Veal vanishes from her Massachusetts prep school. A few weeks
later she reappears unharmed and with little memory of
what happened to her—or at least little that she is willing to
share. Was Mary abducted, or did she fake her disappearance? This question haunts Mary's family, her psychologist,
even Mary herself. Weaving together three narratives, *The
Uses of Enchantment* conjures a spell in which the halluci-
natory power of a young woman's sexuality, and her desire
to wield it, has devastating consequences for all involved.

Fiction/Literature

ANCHOR BOOKS
Available wherever books are sold.
www.randomhouse.com

Meet with Interesting People
Enjoy Stimulating Conversation
Discover Wonderful Books